PARIS
BECKONS

SUSANNA SOLOMON

ALSO BY SUSANNA SOLOMON

Point Reyes Sheriff's Calls
More Point Reyes Sheriff's Calls
Montana Rhapsody

"Evocative and personal, heart-wrenching and illuminating, Susanna Solomon's *Paris Beckons* showcases 34 stories revealing what lies beneath our deepest fears and memories. Poignant and for those with pasts that refuse to remain buried."

—Cara Black, author of the award-winning
Aimée LeDuc Mystery Series

"Often heart-rending, sometimes surreal, but always intriguing, Solomon's *Paris Beckons* transports the reader to amazing places in and around Paris and in and around the human heart."

—JT Morrow, artist, author

"Susanna Solomon's fantastical musings reveal a clandestine Paris of temptation, imagination, and unease—ghostly "Shakespeare & Company," time-bending "The Clock," *Twilight-Zone-esque* "The Teddy Bear," and Oscar-Wilde-reminiscent "Hello, Human." Other tales derail the mind's comfort zones—risky soul-searching in "Among My Own Kind," braving Parisian streets as a first-time motorcyclist in "Julia," and communing with a Musée D'Orsay sculpture that thinks outside the box in "The Dancer." Deft, whimsical, with the hovering shadow of a domineering father, these stories rank among Solomon's best.

—J. Macon King, *Mill Valley Literary Review,* author of
Circus of the Sun and *Drinking with a Dead Cat.*

A Lucky Bat Book

Paris Beckons

Copyright © 2022 by Susanna Solomon

All rights reserved

ISBN: 978-1-943588-99-2

Cover Artist: Tabitha Lahr

Cover photo by the author's father, 1957.

Published by Lucky Bat Books

10 9 8 7 6 5 4 3 2 1

Categories: 1. Fiction - Literary, 2. Fiction - Contemporary Women, 3. Fiction - General

Discover more from this author at susannasolomon.com

This book is dedicated to my mother, Jean Blanchard Roth Solomon; to my brother, Christopher Tonkin Solomon; and to my children, Chris and Alissa Van Leuven

Contents

PARIS BECKONS

My mother was not privy to flights of fancy. She was practical, down to earth, and no-nonsense. She was ordinary but beautiful, elegant but unhappy, resilient but opinionated, hurt, forceful, and she had a fury that scared me. Her rage, coupled with my father's, would make me cringe. I was not allowed to cry.

Now, fifty years later, I ease my hands over her last letters to me, the four-cent stamps, her unique handwriting, a life then full of secrets from her children. Not much news there, except for one thing. She wrote:

"Your father is going to Paris by himself for a few weeks to be alone." He had told me the same thing. But that had not really been the case. He had gone there to meet his lover, an event that would change our lives forever.

Now that he was gone, I wanted to go to that same place and feel the ground that he had walked on to find answers to the questions that have haunted me all my life.

Café Deux Magots

Could this be where he took her?

I am standing across Boulevard St. Germain, looking at Café Deux Magots. Chairs and tables spill out onto the sidewalk. Tourists swarm around the café and in the crosswalks, pecking at their cell-phones, milling about on corners, waiting for traffic lights to change.

My father, fifty-four years ago, likely had sat at one of these very same tables, staring at a woman and holding her hands. The café had been quiet then. Radiance filled his face. The woman, a model, was looking back at him with passion in her eyes. She wasn't my mother. Mom had been at home, writing to us kids while we were at camp, wondering when her husband would return. Wondering what her life had become.

My father's feet had touched the same sidewalk that my feet touch now.

He had no idea how his actions would affect him, his wife, and his children.

Now, standing here in Paris, it all plays out again under my feet. Paris I can feel in my bones. I watch the Seine roll by, my family history swirling and gathering and disappearing into the current. The dreams we had. The truth I tried to cling to. The lies my father told.

It was an interlude, he said. "Things with your mother were hard, so I went to Europe for a few weeks. Alone. To be alone to think."

And I believed him. I'd just turned fourteen. I'd been away at camp for the summer.

"A week later, I was back home from Paris," he had said, "and I reached over for your mother in our bed, but she was gone. I got up and walked through the house, calling her name. From the kitchen, I heard a motor running. In the barn, I found your mother, asphyxiated, in the car. The cops came. I can't tell you any more than that."

A few days later, he came to my camp to tell me the news. I remember the smell of horses, the breeze across the Vermont hills, the sound of gravel crunching under our feet. And I remember him telling me to tell my friends she had died of a heart attack. Which I never did.

Years later, I look at the café and imagine him here.

My father had smiled, placed some francs on the table, and helped the woman on with her coat. They walked away from the café under a moonlit night full of stars.

Within a year, he brought her home, starting a new life built on lies. He never told me he knew her before my mother died. She sat where my mother used to sit, her back against the same yellow cushion in the kitchen. I didn't know who she was at first and was confused. When my best friend told me that everyone knew they'd been having an affair for years before my mother died, I felt both sick and stupid. Eventually, he married her. I couldn't look my stepmother in the eye and refused to be a part of "our" family dinners anymore. My father yelled at me. I found solace in restaurants and stayed away as much as I could.

If years can heal, then we want years, but they never erase the pain of betrayal. As a motherless fourteen-year-old, I had to make the decision to close my mind and harden my heart. I had to keep people at bay. I stopped feeling, focused on just surviving. I went to school, did my homework, and kept my thoughts to myself. Told I was being sullen, I was sent to a psychiatrist. Life is hard, my father said. He threw away my mother's family history book that went back at least a hundred years. Then he threw away most of her photos. He wouldn't let me have even one. It took more than fifty years for me to get a few back. When people say you never get over it, I say they're right.

Now Paris gleams under twilight. The lights along the Seine come on. Traffic flows by, green lights, red lights, amber lights. People, visitors and locals, cross or stand or gather or wonder about their own family histories, stuck in time and place, while lovers, holding hands, wander off into the moonlight and disappear.

Paris breathes into me as I walk along her quais. I remembered so well, being here with my mother, with my brothers. I follow wherever my feet take me, down narrow streets, across cobblestones, into alleys, museums, and the Métro. And always I hear my father's voice, my mother's voice, and occasionally I feel her beside me, holding my hand—or being so unhappy she could break glass.

Place des Vosges

1962, Paris

We were having a picnic. My mother was sitting on the grass. My teenaged brothers, Mark and Chris, their long legs folded underneath them, were looking at girls. And my father, his hair dark, black glasses framing his face, was talking about art and museums and where we were going for the afternoon. My mother handed me a baguette—a slice of cheese, some bologna, and fruit. After lunch, with my hands sticky from the juice of a pear, a Handi-Wipe made its way to me. Fifth in line (after my father, mother, and two brothers used it), I got it last, when there was no longer any moisture and most of the cloth was gray. "We're saving money this way," my father said, adjusted his glasses, and pulled out a copy of the *International Herald Tribune*.

July 2019

Now, in the same place, at Place des Vosges, parents hover over their children, pleading with them to stay close, to not throw coins, sweaters, sneakers, or themselves into the two-tiered fountains. Three-story tan and red-brick buildings with arches surround this oasis in the Marais and above them, steeply pitched roofs of blue slate reach for the sky.

A toddler in pigtails and a smocked dress wobbles on her year-old legs. Her parents steady her. She grabs their sweaters, shoulders, hands as she pulls herself up, staggers from one to the other, and tries to run after her older brothers.

Was I this young when I still felt happy and safe with my parents? Of course. So was I older, like the six-year-old trying to catch a ball, mostly missing and laughing while the red rubber ball came rolling by my sixty-seven-year-old feet? No, the six-year-old is too young to know any different. How about that ten-year-old in braids, laughing and giggling with her girlfriends, at an age when I still loved coming home to a roaring fire and cinnamon toast and tea my mother made for me? No again.

It was when I was eleven when I started to fear coming home to my parents yelling at each other in our cavernous house. Their strident voices rang down the empty halls.

Now I look across the park, at a father and mother resting on a bench where, at the other end, a sullen twelve-year-old sits and stares at her hands. She's wearing jeans, sneakers, and a sweater. Her parents do not hold hands. I see my young self in her.

She's familiar. Her mother barks at her to stop sulking. Her father moves away from the bench, turns to face the mother, says something sharp.

The girl sits quietly and watches the water flow in the fountain.

That was the age when I knew everything was wrong.

Paris, 1962

That was when we'd made our sixth trip to Europe, the year I didn't want to go anymore. All my parents did was fight. For days on end, I argued with my brothers, all three of us stuck in the back seat of our father's car, sweaty, carsick, and bored. We whined and fought until my father's—and sometimes my mother's—hand came flying into the back to slap us on our faces, one, two, three. That would shut us up.

Even though our picnic in the park was a respite from being in the car, I still felt miserable.

My brother Mark, standing about twenty feet away, juggled a small red rubber ball he'd found and gestured to me. My other brother Chris was waving at a blonde with a too-short skirt and oblivious to our game.

"Come on! Play catch, Nina!"

With a glance at our parents, I ran after him. My catching wasn't so bad, but I "threw like a girl," which made my brother laugh as my throws went wild. We took off across the park running, Mark nimble over the low metal fences that reached to the middle of his calves. I took off after one of his throws—dodging families on blankets, tiny dogs in bags, babies in strollers—vaulting over the low black fences, feeling fine sand between my toes, then grass again. I had one eye on the ball in the air and another watching where I was going, and with the ball coming down, coming down, I put out my hands, tripped over a toy train, rolled over the round lip of the fountain, and with my back arched, caught the ball with my right hand, then fell backward into the fountain.

"Nina!" my mother yelled across the park.

"I got the ball, Mark!" I said, shaking off the water from the side of my head, shoulder, and arm.

"Get over here!" my mother demanded.

Making my way over, I tossed the ball to Mark, then stood face to face with my mother, her hand ready to strike my cheek. Though I stood firm I was ready to flinch—I'd learned—but it was worse not to come to attention. I had to stand there and take it. Her slaps hurt.

She glanced at the other parents in the park who were looking our way.

"You know better. You're a wicked, wicked girl."

That word "wicked" pierced me like a poison dart. Nothing could be worse. I was worthless and she knew it.

Her beautiful face was twisted in a grimace of disapproval. My wet shoulder and arm made me shiver, though not from cold. Today, tomorrow, in our hotel room or in the car, I'd receive my punishment. And for what? Catching a ball?

Maybe this time, her slap wouldn't be as hard as last time, when I flew backward across the room. I was used to the red sting on my cheek, but the humiliation was the worst part.

"I wish I'd never be born," I said.

"Speak to your mother in a respectful tone," my father said, joining the fray.

I looked at her, then at my feet. Grains of sand stuck between my bare toes. Across the park, someone was laughing.

I felt defeated, useless, a disgusting excuse for a human being; tears came to my eyes. I looked at my mother's fierce frown, her displeasure and anger easy to see, and whispered words that spilled from the depths of hurt and anger welling up from my belly.

"I wish you were dead."

"What did you say?" my father snarled.

"Nothing," I replied and turned away.

Mark, sullen and withdrawn at the end of the black bench, sat looking at the ball. I was hoping he would give me a wink, but he would not look my way. Chris, however, did give me a glance before looking away. The middle child and the recipient of most of our parents' anger, he knew more than anyone how I felt.

July 2019

Now, fifty-seven years later, I walk around the Place des Vosges, step gingerly over the low black railings, and feel the fine gravel under my feet. I stroll to the fountain. The water makes the same tinkling sound it did when I was here as a kid. Children still play nearby, catch balls, and run through the grass. I remembered my words to my mother clear as the blue sky overhead, the buildings standing sentry, shadows across the arches, and grass cool under my toes.

She would love this park today. She would love the tinkling of the water in the fountains, the arches, the matching buildings, the wind blowing wisps of hair over her eyes.

Home, 1962

At home, in Cambridge, her last summer, I failed her for the final time. I hadn't meant anything. I loved her—sure, always, more than the mountains and the sea—but it was hard, as angry as I'd been those years, to watch my father slowly destroy her. I wanted to protect her, but I was too young, too naïve, too desperate to avoid both her and my father's anger. Later, much later, I realized he had tried to do the same thing to me. Even though I moved three thousand miles away from him, his infrequent phone calls would make me feel useless for a week or more.

As a kid, though, I was confused. I remembered well when he called her crazy in front of us children, and we had laughed, out of nervousness or fear I can't recall. I had felt so bad for her that day. All she'd done was change her hair. One winter afternoon while my father was away, she told me he'd told her she was too stupid to go to college.

My father traveled all the time, and she knew he was up to something, so when he came home, they got into horrible shouting matches, and I wanted to disappear. Once he left for an overseas trip, she came to tuck me in and say goodnight as she usually did.

She sat on the edge of my bed, unusual for her. She told me that my father didn't love her anymore, and that her children didn't either. Something terrible was happening. I wouldn't, couldn't, lie about my dad and say that he did indeed love her, but I could tell her the truth about me and my brothers. I said, over and over, "But I love you, Mom, I do, I do, I really do, I love you, Mom," until she got up and walked out the door.

I was sure it was my fault when we lost her that summer. If only I hadn't said those hateful things in the park, if only I'd lied to her that night, if only I'd convinced her, if only I'd run after her, she'd be with us still. Finding out that my father had been unfaithful for years did not alter my opinion in the least. My words had power and had come true. She was, indeed, right; I was a worthless human being.

And since I wasn't worth much, I didn't deserve much. *Everyone* knew I was a horrible person, which is why I didn't seem to have any friends. If I grew close to someone, I reasoned, it was only a matter of time until they learned about the true me and the horrible thing I'd done. For years, I kept my distance. No one could know my terrible secret. I kept it in my core.

It took more than twenty years before I was convinced otherwise. I was with a friend, floating on a small boat in a pond, and I guess I was feeling relaxed or open or safe or something and hadn't been thinking about the shame I felt, when I told her about my mother that night and she looked at me with a soft smile and said, "What a burden she put on you," and something happened that I can barely explain. She was the first person I'd ever told.

"What a terrible thing to tell a child," she said. "You were much too young to do anything about it. You don't need to carry that burden anymore."

And I felt better, as if a spell had broken.

July 2019

This year, I've come to Paris to push myself, to let myself know that I can be on my own, that I can be safe and enjoy a foreign country and not get lost or scared or any of that.

What I haven't expected is to feel my mother's presence everywhere I walk. She's beside me still, in this park, by the fountain, as we stroll by a little girl, about two, with multicolored ribbons decorating her three pigtails, sitting in her mother's lap, holding a cloth doll, and I'm beside mine. We laugh together, as adults, as, across the park, a six-year-old girl plays with her sisters, and in the distance, a twelve-year-old girl, wearing jeans, sneakers, and a sweater, reaches for a red rubber ball.

My father loved museums. Actually, he loved certain art in particular museums, one piece or two, and he would march us into museums in Paris, my mother and brothers in tow, through gallery after gallery, and go as fast as his long legs could carry him, while we would run to keep up. If it was an attempt for us to like the same works, it failed. If it was an attempt to teach us anything about art, that also failed. If it was an attempt for us to learn to dislike him, it worked great.

Now I go back to these same museums to try to understand him.

The Dancer

It was late afternoon by the time I arrived at the museum. A line snaked across a concrete courtyard where tourists without tickets or a pass shifted their feet and glared at me as I sauntered by with my Pass Musée. Only half of them would make it inside before the museum closed at five-thirty. A light rain fell outside huge plate-glass windows. A brief pause at security and I was in.

The guidebooks were right about a few things, for sure. Musée D'Orsay had been built inside an abandoned train station, and the museum pass was not only an easy way to get in, but a cinch to buy at the airport. I followed a group walking through the lobby and stepped onto an escalator. Overhead, huge trusses held up an open ceiling of metal and glass. A huge interior space, it had an enormous clock at one end.

Built in 1898-1900, the building was converted from a train station into a museum in 1986, twenty years after my parents had dragged me around Europe for the last time when I was twelve. In other places in Paris, memories of my parents flooded through me—in museums, near the Seine, along city streets, amid the din of autos and motorcycles, at the cathedrals and the booksellers on the quais. But not here.

Still, when I walked into the galleries and saw paintings by Monet, Seurat, and Pissaro, works of art that had once been housed in another museum—the Jeu de Paume, where I'd been many times with my parents, I felt my father's presence just as much as I felt the breeze from the air conditioners and heard the slap of leather on wood floors from a thousand tourists. The paintings were like old familiar friends. As if guided by my father, my feet rushed me past the paintings, through gallery after gallery, in a hurry like my father always was, on a mission to find his favorite sculpture, Degas' Little Dancer.

When I found her, encased in Plexiglas, I stopped and felt him beside me, studying her, breathing hard from his excitement to see her.

Her hands were clasped behind her back as she looked disdainfully at the world.

"Doesn't she have the loveliest expression?" my father used to say. "And her ribbon. They always replace it when it gets ragged."

I could also picture my mother, in her shirtdress, adjusting the alligator purse on her arm and sighing. "Yes, Arthur, she's lovely. From now on, could you go a little slower, please?"

He would have none of that. Instead, he stayed silent, shushing us if we made any noise at all, as he examined the fourteen-year-old girl, sighed, and adjusted his glasses. Twenty minutes later, he'd march us out of the museum.

Now, decades later, I lingered, wanting to understand both him and the young dancer better.

People filled the gallery. They kept pushing on my shoulder bag and I couldn't get near enough. I took the opportunity to disappear for a moment and went down two flights of stairs, but, finding long lines for the WC, I returned upstairs to be with her until the museum closed.

The second time, the gallery was almost empty. A romantic couple in the corner was holding hands and then they left, urged on by the guard.

Now the dancer and I had the whole place to ourselves. Far from a lovely expression, I found it insolent. I wondered what was behind it. Never too young for a broken heart? Or standing up to her father?

As I was looking at her toes in the ballet slippers, I swore I saw one of them move. I blinked, stood up straight, took a deep breath, and looked again.

"Get me out of here!" It was a young voice, a girl's voice. I thought no one was in the gallery. I turned, expecting to see a guard admonish me for lingering. It wasn't five-thirty, not yet, anyway, and I wasn't bugging anyone or anything.

But the guard was a heavyset man and he wasn't looking at me. He was looking at one of the paintings. Unless he was a great mimic, the voice didn't come from him.

I scratched an itch on the back of my neck.

I looked at the sculpture again. I could see what my father loved in her—imperious, haughty as hell, and grumpy-looking.

Not the way I'd ever been as a child. I had always been a good girl, eager to please, and punished whenever I grew angry. So I smiled all the time no matter what. Hiding in my room, no one could tell me I was wrong when I wrote my feelings down on paper and hid it in my desk.

How could my father have loved this young girl, this bronze haughty dancer, for being more human than I was ever allowed to be? I stared at her, but she didn't look at me. I heard the whine of the air conditioner, the closing of doors downstairs, a cough from the guard.

This young girl, obviously, had never had a father like mine. If I'd ever made that same face at home, he'd have slapped me across the room or to the back of the seat in the car where there was no place to hide.

&

"It's hot in this box," the girl's voice said.

Was it my phone? I thought I turned it off.

Maybe he loved her because she was a dancer, or she was prettier than me.

Maybe it was time to return to the hotel and get my senses back.

Smaller than me, sure, but she had a temper, I could tell, with her I-take-no-prisoners look.

Did she want to come home? With me?

I could take her out of the box. Easy. Surprise him!

Would he love her still? If he could see her every day?

Would he love me more? I mean, if I brought her home? Would he hug me, and tell me I was a good girl, and put this sculpture, this beautiful girl, next to his other Degas sculpture in the hallway? Would he finally be happy?

I've always wanted a sister.

My brothers would know I was the preferred child and treat me way better.

☙

I ran my hand through my purse, came across a plastic disk about the size of a quarter with a retractable blade, and wondered for the thousandth time why no TSA agent had ever confiscated the dangerous weapon that had cost twenty cents. I thumbed past it on my way to my cell phone. It was off. Thought so. I'd been careful to save my batteries ever since I'd arrived in Paris.

I glanced up at the girl. Her little bronze feet were now turned the other way. Maybe I shouldn't have had that beer at lunch.

"It's so hard to stand like this all the time."

Did someone leave a listening device near the sculpture? I'd seen people carrying these small black boxes as they wandered through the gallery, tuning in the recorded descriptions. I walked around Degas' sculpture but didn't see any earbuds on the floor.

I was hearing things. And I feel fine.

Was she talking to me? Was she alive? I mean, she was moving and all.

Like my stomach. Gurgling and tight with tension.

BUT MY FATHER WOULD STILL LOVE her more than he loved me, my brothers, my mother. He'd come home from the lab, make a drink, pull up a chair, close the door, and tell her his secrets: why he loved other women, why his family disappointed him, why no one loved him.

She'd murmur to him, her eyes soft and understanding. And with her nose in the air have nothing to do with the rest of us.

FROM THE OTHER END OF THE room, a clock struck five. I started walking around the statue and almost tripped myself on a loose shoelace. I bent over to tie it and, standing up too quickly, felt a little light-headed. If I brought her home, he would love me, if only a little, wouldn't he?

It would be easy to take this young girl home. Cut her loose from her box, throw her over my shoulder. Be a princess for the day! Have my father say, "Nina, you understand me, you love me, you've brought her home! How I love you!"

But just for the moment. Maybe he'd cover me with kisses, but then he'd take her from my arms and disappear.

She had stooped too. I swear. When I brought my head up, she straightened her back, let her hands return to their resting position behind her, raised her head, and turned to face me.

"You'd be stiff too, if you had to hold this position for a hundred and thirty-five years, *madame*."

I took off my glasses, rubbed my eyes, and looked again. Had her face softened a little? We were alone. I heard the rat-a-tat-tat of rain on the roof, the footsteps of the guard pacing the gallery next door.

"Tell them my hair needs a new ribbon. This one's in tatters. I can't dance like this."

I stood back a little, then came forward and walked around the statue a second time.

"Are you listening?" she demanded. "It's me! I've been here forever. I hate it here. Being stared at. Get me a new ribbon and tutu. These are torn. No, don't shop. Take me with you. Please. Surprise your father!"

An undigested bit of lunch could be going to my head. My stomach was still growling. Time to eat. It was always time to eat. I stood in stunned silence.

"Cat got your tongue?" she asked. "Listen. Galleries Lafayette. You know the place?"

"Of course," I said. I'd been there with my mom.

"Would she like it if you were wearing tattered clothing?"

"Umm, no," I said, seeing that the guard was now watching me through the dancer's glass box. I bent down on the other side of the sculpture. My laces were still tight, but I redid them anyway. The guard couldn't see me if I stayed low.

"Even if I could get you out of the box," I whispered, "how would I get you outside?"

"Carry me out under your raincoat."

"You're three feet tall," I said.

"Who cares? Use your imagination. You have an imagination, don't you? You *are* talking to me."

She had a point.

"You can do that. You can do anything. You're real, aren't you?"

"Real as rain," I croaked, whispering so that the guard wouldn't think I was crazy.

"Slip an edge of that blade under the glass."

"How do you know what's in my purse?"

"Do you think I was born yesterday?"

I fumbled for the plastic disk. If I didn't open it properly, it would cut me.

"It's too puny," I said. "I'll get caught and go to jail."

"And you'll be in a box instead of me," she crowed. She stopped talking, looked at the guard. "Now, girlfriend, get to work and set me free." She whispered, "Think of your father's face when you walk in the door."

I slipped the blade out of the disk all it would go, one quarter of an inch. My brother always said to carry the disk with me—a quarter inch can do a lot of damage. And it did. I drove it between the caulk at the separation between the glass and the wooden box and it slipped in like butter.

One side was clear. I heard a distant chime. Closing time? I wasn't ready.

I walked around the sculpture and, with my back to the guard, made another cut on the opposite side, slicing the caulk just below the glass. I could hear the guard's footsteps coming closer. What was I supposed to do now? Stop? The girl was looking haughty again, staring into the mid-distance.

"What are you doing?" the guard asked. He was suddenly beside me. I hid the disk inside my palm.

"Wiping off some dust," I answered. "Isn't she beautiful?"

"We are closing, madame."

"Could you give me a minute or two?" I asked. "My father—he loved this sculpture. And . . ." I'm not very good at lying. "We lost him at the beginning of the summer." He would kill me for lying. He'd been gone fifteen years. What was I to do? I could sense the girl squirming in her box.

"Two minutes, madame, *c'est tout*."

Ah. With two minutes, I could do anything.

I stood at the back of the box and slid the blade through the caulk. Now, only one side was still connected. I had saved the front view for last.

When I came around the front, her toes were wiggling. There was a tremble in her knees, down her slumping stockings, and she looked down at me, saw my hand trembling a little, and smiled.

How can I explain? I had to have her.

It would be nothing now, to collect her, put her over my shoulder, fly her to Boston, drive to Cambridge with her in the passenger seat while I talked to her about the sights, and she'd be by my shoulder when I walked up the front stairs of my father's house and rang the bell.

Noticing someone moving in the kitchen, I'd stay very still with my *very big surprise!*

My father, even if he were alive, wouldn't come to the door. He'd be in the back of the house, pecking away at his manual Olivetti typewriter, writing scientific papers and not wanting to be disturbed.

My stepmother, who spent her days in the kitchen, would see me through the window.

I would wave.

Hold up the sculpture.

And mouth hello, hello, hello—while she used the phone to call the police.

THE GUARD LOOKED AT ME FUNNY. I felt the blade in the palm of my hand. I removed my hands from the Plexiglass so he would know I hadn't done anything wrong.

"You would like me to call the gendarmes, madame? Open your hand."

I looked from the guard to the sculpture, at the entrance to the gallery, at my shoe. And uncurled my thumb.

The red plastic disk was there, blade extended. A pool of blood on my palm.

I was in big trouble.

⚮

THE POLICE WOULD TAKE ME TO the Cambridge substation, for sure, or to Mount Auburn hospital for observation.

The nurses would take my blood pressure. The blond one would look at my hand. Wrap it in gauze.

"I was only trying to get my father to love me," I'd say.

They'd mutter and shake their heads.

"Honey," one of them would say, "your father died years ago."

"Not to me!" I'd say. "They never told me."

They would confer.

⚮

WHEN I OPENED MY EYES, I was lying on my back on the oak floor of the gallery. The guard was kneeling down next to me. A white-haired man whom I thought might be the director of the museum was accompanied by a blond woman in a white shirt.

"Did she hit her head?" the blonde asked.

"I don't think so," the guard said. "She was talking to the sculpture, Director Sulpice, when she took a spin and drifted to the floor. I think she fainted."

"Madame," Director Sulpice spoke. His face came into focus. Glasses. A stern look. "Are you okay, madame? We are all worried about you. Are you all right?"

I muttered, "No more red-eye flights for me, that's for sure." But I was thinking, *is my father going to follow me everywhere?*

As I wandered around Paris, some places seemed to jump out at me with their beauty. I remembered them in a vague sort of way, being there as if I was still a child of five, or six, or ten, holding my mother's hand, standing in line with my brothers, waiting to go inside. One of these places was the Chapel of Sainte Chappelle. The stained-glass windows held secrets I wanted to know.

SAINTE CHAPPELLE

"I've been here before; it's well worth the wait," I said to the man in front of me while we waited in line for entrance into Saint Chapelle, the thirteenth-century chapel full of stained glass in Paris. In his midforties, he was struggling to make his three tow-headed children behave, the same way my parents had with my brothers and me more than fifty years earlier. Even then, as a kid of twelve, I had been awed by the stained glass. Perhaps his children would also discover the magic I'd found here.

"I hope so," his wife said. She had the same tired look my mother had had.

The line was shorter than I thought, and, within a minute and using my Pass Musée, we were inside. The family stopped to look at a sign while I kept going.

The chapel smelled musty. Now, alone in a space made for angels, I walked through the nave and looked up into a forest of wooden gothic arches. There weren't many tourists here. I glanced back at the entrance; to the left and right were narrow doorways leading to spiral stairs. I entered one, and, remembering all the worn-down, polished stone steps I'd climbed with my father, chastising me for being too loud or moving too fast, I took my time, held onto the railing, and kept quiet.

When I reached the chapel, the light was astounding. A multitude of fifty-foot-tall windows soared overhead, filled with hundreds of stained-glass panels that told the story of the Old and New Testaments. Brilliant blues and reds spilled into the space above me. I couldn't move at first. Rich and dark and wonderful, the ceiling was so tall, it looked like the sky held up the glass. Behind me, on the fourth wall, was the incredibly beautiful Rose Window, full of panels, easily fifty feet across, extolling glory in the Lord.

Other pilgrims came up and had the same reaction, stunned silence at first, faces raised to the heavens. Then they slowly drifted over to plastic-covered notebook pages, on stands, in many languages, that described the work above. I opened one of the notebooks. The chapel, built over a period of seven years, was commissioned by Louis IX to house Passion relics, among them the Crown of Thorns. I turned the well-worn plastic page, crackling with age and thousands of hands.

I was in a cathedral of light. I stood closer to a window and peered into one of the story panels. Then, looking closely at the notebook in front of me, I scanned the windows above and, finding one full of horses, I checked the notebook for the explanation. But what I saw on the page was nothing like what I saw in the glass. In the binder, the colors were flat, and the horses looked tired and gray, while in the glass windows, they galloped with the wind. Sunlight poured down as I once again studied the notebook.

In one panel, three men on horses were making a charge. In another, a man on horseback, two following on foot. It was evening. They were following a star. The Magi? Perhaps.

Everyone and everything around me disappeared as I studied the scene.

The face of the man on horseback was lined. Touching his shoulder, I felt the shudder of something underneath me, a shifting, a moving of earth. I spread out my hands and felt horsehair and him come alive under my hands.

I stroked the horse's back. The master looked over my shoulder. "Edouard, please, be careful."

"Yes, master," I said. The edges of the glass were sharp. Scars covered my fingers; callouses had thickened my palms, so I didn't feel the new cuts as much. My fingers traced the horses, the riders. My ears picked up their voices, pleading with me to tell their stories.

"Pay attention. Do not dawdle. We have to finish this panel today."

My job was to draw the scenes first, cut the glass to fit the scene I'd drawn, then join the pieces together using lead canes. Then I painted the panel and affixed the stabilizing metal frame. I had to be infinitely patient. I'd grown up a peasant used to riding horses, mucking stalls, and chasing pigs, but I'd had to learn to slow down since I'd joined the guild six years earlier. I took a breath before I picked up the diamond cutter, took another when I held the cutter in position, and held it when I made the cut. I was lucky to create a panel a month.

In a studio with six others—Anton, Gaspard, Pierre, Jean-Louis, Georges, and Christian the underboss—I knew them all. I'd come up with them, apprenticing at twelve, carrying coal from the basement and shoving it into the furious ovens, helping the masters create. I slept on a pallet in the back of the studio with the other boys. I'd been one of the lucky ones. Taken off the street, I'd made a good impression on our teacher/mentor Master Bertrand, and I'd made the grade when so many other boys had failed. Still, my hands sometimes didn't behave, and the master watched over me carefully.

Now my hands moved with precision over the brittle glass. Carefully, I raised the cutter, but I touched the sharp end on what would become one of the soldier's shields and tapped. A touch too far.

"Edouard!" My master's face fell. "You've cut off his hand! Can't you do anything right? Start over!"

I started again with a new piece and eventually got it right.

Each scene took hours.

There were ten guilds, each with six men. All of us huddled over well-worn wooden tables that filled a large room with the stove at the far end. Despite the heat from the stove, two of us at the back of the studio were too far away to feel any of it. Our backs tingled with cold as snow curled through the slats in the wooden walls behind us and settled on bare skin. The sweater my mother had knitted for me was full of holes and the sleeves were tattered and torn. Still, Maman had made it, and if it weren't for the sweater, I'd probably freeze like poor Thom, whom we buried last week.

Six days a week, we rose before dawn and toiled well into the dark beside oil lamps, our pencils slowly tracing lines and our cutters not far behind. After assembly with the canes, we once again pulled out our pens and brushes and colored in detail, our artists painting faces on the glass, a whole army of craftspeople poring over the creation of one of God's houses. There were thousands of scenes, and we had to fill all the backgrounds with decorative flourishes.

Before Thom died, he called for his mother in the middle of the night. I comforted him the best I could as he coughed and spit up blood. Not wanting to suffer the same fate, I wrote to my own mother, telling her that I missed her. I'd left so very long ago. I couldn't take off to see her, but perhaps she could come see me?

Once, as a hungry young teen, I'd stolen potatoes from our neighbor, but refused to share them with my sisters. Mother banished me from the house in disgust, but I was too proud to go back and beg forgiveness. So, in the middle of the night, I tied a few things with a cloth and headed off for Paris to try my hand at the trades, hoping to find one that would teach me a living. The chapel, of course.

To this day, I regretted every bite of potato, and even now, when I crunched what was supposed to be its sweet flavor, I tasted dirt. I sent her money over the years, coins tucked inside leather satchels full of letters, but I couldn't be sure any reached her. My sisters should be in their teens now. With Thom's face haunting my dreams, I didn't sleep well.

Mail was handed down from person to person and took weeks to cross the country. I prayed that my letter arrived at our shack in Alsace-Lorraine, where I hoped Maman still lived. I'd given up wishing that my latest letter reached her when I was sitting at a nearby bar and a traveler had heard of an older woman making her way alone to Paris from Alsace-Lorraine. Could it be her? I raised my glass of beer to the stranger and watched him disappear into a snowstorm raging just outside.

Back at work the next day, I adjusted my leather apron. Was it her? Would she cry? Would she even recognize me, a man of nineteen? Would she come close enough for me to kiss her cheek? I collected potatoes from every meal, filling my pockets, tucking them under my coat, until I had a bushel. I kept them away from the other boys and woke when I heard the sound of rats crawling over the dirt floor toward my basket.

Now I was an old hand at cutting glass. I'd forgotten what Mother looked like, so I'd come to adore the mother I saw every day, Mother Mary.

She'd always be with me. But I longed for my own.

The master hadn't yet allowed me to work on any of her scenes, but I looked with wonder at Gaspard, bending over the panel, a fine paintbrush in his hand, as he worked on her face, a thing of beauty and solace and love.

After Gaspard, Christian worked the lead—setting the glass a piece at a time into the form, using canes to give shape to each color, then soldering. His face was lined, concentration furrowing his brow as he took a metal prong in one gloved hand, a sliver of solder in the other, and melted pieces of lead together, the bright spark at the end of his tool brighter than the sun, brighter than the star that led the wise men to Jerusalem.

Christian looked around, while his prong heated in the oven, and caught me staring at him. His eyes were tired, but his gaze narrow and piercing. "Don't think I'll ever teach you."

"But Christian . . ."

"Twenty years your senior and you think you can paint Mother Mary? A mere boy?"

"But you learned."

"And so?" he asked, his hard eyes narrowing even further.

"I would like to draw her."

"Some other time," he said.

For weeks I watched Christian, kept an eye on my potatoes, and had my ear to the ground. Then one day, Gaspard patted me on the shoulder. "There's someone here to see you."

And there she was, my maman, stooped and standing at the door.

She'd aged. Gray had colored her hair and her hands had grown knobby knuckles, but her face was the same, full of light.

"Mother!" I cried.

I'd missed her so much. Were my sisters alive? Had they starved? How had she walked to Paris, in the middle of winter? Had she received any of my money I'd sent? Questions ran through my mind as my legs moved slower than I wanted. I longed to run to her.

I was about to call her, to bend on one knee to ask forgiveness, when a voice came out of the back of the studio.

"Edouard!"

It was Christian.

"You want to learn or not? Get over here!"

"Mother!" I saw her eyes, saw the cane she carried and the sad look on her face.

"Now or never, Edouard!"

I couldn't move.

I would have covered her face with kisses. I would have asked about my siblings, filled her hands and pockets with coins, brought her my bushel of potatoes, made sure she had a hot meal and a warm drink and a companion for the long journey back home.

But I walked toward the workbench, to Christian.

When I looked back her eyes were full of tears when she turned and walked away for what we both knew would be the last time.

Under my hands, I felt the horsehair turn brittle and hard. I lifted my hand from the plastic notebook in front of me and looked up at the man on horseback.

I'd done the same thing. Fifty years ago. Turned away during my mother's hour of need. I was thirteen when my mother came to me at bedtime to give me a kiss and uncharacteristically sat on the side of my bed.

"Your father doesn't love me," she said.

That I knew was true. He traveled all the time, arguing with her when he was home, calling her crazy, belittling her in front of me and my brothers. I could not disagree.

"Your brothers don't love me either."

"They're teenagers, Mom. You know they do. They love you lots."

"And you?"

Something terrible was happening.

"You know I love you, Mom," I said. "I do, and the boys do."

She got up, walked to the door.

"I love you; you know I do," I said over and over. Pleading with her to listen, trying to save her, knowing at the time I had failed.

A year later, just after my fourteenth birthday, she committed suicide.

For more than twenty years, I lived with the shame that it was my fault. If only I'd lied to her about my father.

I looked at the window above me at the three men on horseback, then at the notebook. My eyes filled with tears.

The crowd was pressing forward, eager for a closer look. I backed away from the notebooks, from the windows, and feeling lost, wandered back to the stairs. The sky changed, dark clouds overtook the sun, and the scenes, in their brilliant colors, disappeared into gray.

A vision of my mother was still with me as I took a last glance before stepping out into the Paris drizzle. I remembered her look of wonder as she herself had stared into the same brilliant stained-glass scenes, more than fifty years ago, the same windows Edouard had created as he thought fondly of his own mother, now portrayed in glass, over my head.

As a kid, for a while, I had hated to read. But my father forced me to. I had to read an hour a day and, despite my best intentions, I fell in love with reading. We had a deal. I could go to the local bookshop, The Coop, and put one book on his charge account, account number 989, as long as I'd finished reading the last one.

So it only seemed right that I check out Shakespeare and Company, the well-known English-language bookstore on the Left Bank.

The cramped and tiny bookstore, like many places in Paris, had a surprise in store. And this time, it had nothing to do with my parents.

SHAKESPEARE
AND COMPANY

"No, it's true. I used to live here," he said with a grin. "Upstairs."

"You lived in this bookstore?" I asked.

"Name's Tom," the man said, extending his hand. A sweet smile and half my age. After a week alone, it was wonderful to talk with someone.

"Can you think of better company?" He grinned. "Ever since the store opened in 1951, they've always provided places to stay for inspiring writers. We're called tumbleweeds."

The tiny bookshop was a warren of little rooms where people happily jostled for space. Overflowing bookshelves rose from floor to ceiling. Outside, a small crowd gathered and waited their turn, while a security guard let one person in at a time. I had had to wait five minutes myself. Now I was in—breathing history, standing with the greats, cheek by jowl with other tourists; no one seemed to mind the small quarters or the packed conditions.

I ran my hands along the spines of the books in the mystery section tucked under a staircase at the back of Shakespeare and

Company. I'd been in Paris for a week, and it was my second visit to the bookstore. The giants of literature had been here and the collection of books in English was unsurpassed: Camus, Sartre, Hemingway (of course), Faulkner, and today's history, philosophy, biography, everything. And in a corner, tucked under the stairs, the mystery section.

"They have bedrooms upstairs?" I asked. "An apartment? A studio?"

"Of sorts," Tom laughed. "Sleeps three. Two single beds and a fold-out Murphy. People stay up there for years."

"Windows?" I asked. I don't like small spaces and was already feeling a little too tucked in at the back of the shop under the stairs.

"A view of the Seine," he said. "And Notre Dame."

"Good lord," I answered and sat down on a stool.

"You have to ask gently, and not be aggressive in any way. It's like anything—you don't want to make yourself a pest. There's a fine line. I wanted, I asked, I got in. But it took two years."

"And now?" I asked, thinking of the comfort of my hotel room with the en suite bath.

"All I have to do is stack shelves for two hours a day and read a book a week," Tom answered, making space on a shelf for two paperbacks he held in his left hand. "But there are . . . stories."

"Ghost stories?" Sleeping above a bookstore anywhere in the world would be fun. But Paris! "Like Scott Fitzgerald, or James Baldwin, or Hemingway? James Joyce?"

"Hardly," Tom laughed. "A thin ten-year-old in a white night-dress holding a candle."

"You're pulling my leg."

"You've seen her?" asked an American girl to my left. Too many braces, too much hair color, but she certainly had a healthy literary appetite and that was good. Her hands were full of books.

"Two years ago. After the shop closed. At midnight. Fernando, the Murphy bed guy, was out in the Marais, and the other resident," Tom pronounced the word res-i-dent, "had just moved out. So it was just me. Mostly. I was holding a cup of espresso."

"You drink coffee that late?" I asked, scanning the owner's picks. "Must've kept you up all night."

"I could drink it twenty-four hours a day. Coffee doesn't do a thing for me. Only doobies do." He sighed. "But I hadn't even struck a match when I saw her. No, I wasn't high. Are you?"

"Hell no," I answered.

"Stone-cold sober and I hadn't smoked a thing. She was there, I swear."

"Floating by the door, I suppose?"

"If you're going to make fun of me, go on, leave. There are lots of other pretty girls in the store I can talk to," Tom said.

"Oh, sorry," I said, feeling kind of bad. He thought I was pretty?

"She was on my bed, actually." He thought a sec. "Not quite under the covers. Standing over it, like apparitions are supposed to do."

"A character from a novel you just read?" I asked. "Madame Bovary?"

"When she was twelve, miss . . . ?"

"Nina."

"Nina. It wasn't Madame Bovary when she was twelve. No one knows what she looked like then."

"Show me. Show me now," I asked. "Upstairs. Just up there. Would the owners mind?" I gestured to the front of the store. He towered over me, but still, there were possibilities . . . .

"If you buy at least three books," Tom answered.

"Now?" I asked. I wasn't really ready to choose a book, much less three. I steered the conversation back. "So, tell me, the ghost—"

"The apparition. Cammi's her name."

I nodded, my palms sweaty.

"She was crying, sobbing quietly. I asked her why."

"What did she say?" I nudged closer.

"'If you'd been stuck in an attic a hundred years, you'd be crying too, buster,' she said."

"That's kind of modern language."

"Maybe she reads too," Tom replied.

"I wouldn't know," I said dryly. "I mean, how can a ghost read a book, much less hold one?"

He didn't take the bait. "She leaned toward me. I was trying to back up to the stairs—those stairs just above my head. Then she stopped, held out her hand, and spoke again. 'Get me out of here, Tom.' Hearing her speak my name, I practically fell down the stairs. They're steeper than you think."

"Tell me everything," I said.

"'I won't hurt you,' Cammi said. She was wearing a bright white bow in her hair, like those photos of Victorian girls you've seen. 'I couldn't find a brush,' she said. 'Pardon my somewhat disheveled appearance, but there are no beauty supplies here, as you can see.' She ran her hand through the air and sparks flew out of the ends of her fingers. 'Only guy stuff,' she said. 'No good for me. Don't you guys ever bathe?'

"How could I tell her?" Tom went on, almost in a trance, ignoring my attempts to participate in the conversation. "There's a sink downstairs, at the back of the store, and a shower at the Youth Hostel down the street, but . . . But. She scowled, wagged one finger at me, sending sparks. 'You're afraid I'll be seen if I go out on the quai?' I wasn't sure what to say, so I sat down on the bed."

"Were you afraid, Tom?" the girl in braces asked.

"She sat beside me. About four-ten, her feet in her blue shoes stuck out as her legs were too short to set on the floor."

"Did you try to touch her?" I asked. "Did she feel like fog? Or water? Or maybe jello?"

I watched as Tom returned to the present. He seemed surprised that a few more people had arrived and were now leaning in doorways, listening.

"You have some kind of wild imagination, Nina," he said, remembering, apparently, who I was and that he was talking to me.

"And?" I asked.

"Mist, yes, that's right. She felt like mist. Cool. Young. Beautiful."

"And sad," I added.

"How did you know?" he asked. "She had reddened, watery eyes."

"From living a few hundred years too long?"

"No. From people asking stupid questions."

Oh, that shut me up fast. Stung, I caught my breath. "You're the one who started it."

He went back to ignoring me. "We spent some hours together. She told me a little about her home in the sixth arrondissement. The walk she took on her way past St. Sulpice, down the alley, the strong hands that grabbed her. She hadn't planned on being out after dark, but she'd been playing with Sophie—and had lost track of time."

"One of the Twentieth-Century Murders," said one of the onlookers. His face was lined, his body thin and wiry. He put one hand on the banister going upstairs. "I'll protect her."

"No!" Tom cried, pulling up his long form and pivoting so he was at the stairs, his one hand on the stranger's arm. "She doesn't handle visitors well."

Just then an ear-splitting scream came from the front of the store. We all ran in that direction. Several of us found our way out the door.

"*Ce n'est rien.* It's nothing. A pickpocket. He was caught," a security guard said. I saw the commotion, people running about, and thought about the ghost upstairs. She could have used some security that night.

While everyone was milling inside and outside the door, I snuck back to the stairs and started to climb.

"Cammi?" I called gently, hoping no one would hear the creak of steps. Two, three, four steps. "Cammi?" I pushed open the door, expecting an apparition, a girl who had never had a chance.

"Can I help you?" answered a voice, a man's voice, a real man with a fashionable two-day stubble and a gravelly voice. "Customers aren't allowed up here, miss."

I blinked my eyes. "Tom . . . He was telling me about . . . about . . ." I felt so strange, couldn't get air.

"Ah. *Oui.* Thomas. Again," the man said. "The ghost."

I nodded. "You've seen her?" I asked.

"Only through Tom's eyes," he said, walking toward me. He was very tall and looked down on my face, then took my hand. His hand was dry and warm, suddenly holding mine.

"We are in a shrine, a sanctum, of storytelling, miss. A monument to the greats. A place where dreams are made. Did Tom give you a dream? That you believed?"

I turned my face. I couldn't look at him.

"Would you expect anything else at Shakespeare and Company? In Paris?" He grinned. "Can I offer you some kir royale? Or absinthe, perhaps? Come take a look from here. You are not the first and you won't be the last, but you are the prettiest."

How could I resist? I was in a haunted attic above one of the world's most famous bookstores, standing by the window, while the sun cast its last rays on the spires of Notre Dame.

"I'm Christophe," he said.

I was about to tell him my name when his lips closed on mine.

The sidewalks along the quai seemed to glisten as I meandered my way around tourists. Someone had kissed me! As a woman of a certain age, I never expected that to happen. Despite the fact that Paris spelled romance, I'd become accustomed to the feeling of being a nobody as women passed me by with their flirty walks, men strode by whispering and waving at them, while older people—mothers, fathers, and grandparents like me—disappeared into the crowd.

ALPHONSE

"*PUIS-JE VOUS AIDER?*" THE BALD MAN behind the counter held his hand above the handle of the espresso machine. "Espresse? Café crème?"

I shook my head. "*Thé, avec lait et sucre, s'il vous plâit.*"

He roared with laughter, brought me my tea with milk and sugar, and I sat down just inside the open doors. I would've sat outside, but cigarette smoke filled the air. Inside was not much better, just enough.

Most French cafés are on corners and this one was a doozy, with four busy roads radiating from out in front. And cars, motorcycles, people everywhere.

There was too much energy out there on the streets for me.

Electronic music blared from a speaker over my head. A good thumping beat—did I know the song? Of course not. As a Baby Boomer, the music I know is from the Sixties.

"Alphonse!" A skinny man with tight blue jeans and a white shirt flew in from a side door, leaned over the counter, and hugged the bald man. Two false kisses, two cheeks embracing. Yes, I was in France, where life was good.

A moment later, after the man in the white T-shirt disappeared with a cup in his hand, I studied Alphonse more carefully. In his early forties, and though he didn't have a hair on his head, he was fit as hell. Camouflage green T-shirt, tight against his biceps. It was ten in the morning, but anytime was okay for me to look at guys. Slowly at first, then without a pause, he started to dance behind the bar, moving to the beat of the music. He had easy brown eyes and flirted with a couple of women customers who came and went.

He didn't pay any attention to me, not at first, anyway. But I sure hoped he would.

A few more customers entered. Alphonse kissed them on the cheek, wiped down the bar with a flourish, and went back to moving and shaking. The beat was repetitive and catching. Pulling an espresso, he gave me a long look. I thrilled at the thought.

Most of the time, I'm invisible. A woman in her sixties, well past child-bearing age and with a body to prove it, I'd come to accept that romance and I were distant friends. And we weren't going to pass this way again. I rested my chin on my hands and, feeling safe and comfortable, kept one eye on Alphonse and one on the beautiful women walking around outside. Surely, he'd been looking at one of them, not me.

Some people say you have to be in an unhappy marriage to look at men, but I say phooey. I was alone in Paris. That says everything. And as for the other people who say you have to be in an unhappy marriage to travel alone, I say, again, phooey. I was having a wonderful time.

I've been coming to Europe since I was six. It felt like home and Alphonse, good lord, he was making my skin tingle. And my husband, at home, was taking care of our three dogs and happy as could be. What he didn't know wasn't going to affect him.

Alphonse gave me another look. Jesus, did everyone in the café know how red my cheeks were? I looked out the window, hoping to disappear.

Coming to my senses, I went up to the counter to ask for the restroom. I saw that just to Alphonse's right, there was a rectangular hole in the floor and a ladder going down into the basement. Not even a steep staircase. A ladder. His feet were right on the edge. Couldn't he move over a little?

Five minutes later, I found my way back to my table and, finishing my dessert, watched Alphonse dance around, hoping he wouldn't fall through the floor. Me, I wouldn't go close to something like that hole. I didn't have the courage, but I had the courage to watch Alphonse. God, he was beautiful.

He was looking at me! Again! Embarrassed, I looked out the window, focusing on one of the three-wheeled motorcycles just outside. That, perhaps, I could ride. When I pulled my gaze back from the window, he was helping another customer.

I've never really gone for the bald look, but something about him pulled me in. His big brown eyes, his tight-ass T-shirt coating his biceps, his flourish with a rag, the way he moved around the room, graceful, like a dancer, and hot too, as he gyrated his hips to the music that blasted my ears.

How different our lives were. He, a Parisian, a smoker, probably, spoke French as fast as humanly possible, and kissed all the customers on their way in. Me, a sixty-something American tourist whose awkward French eluded me every time I wanted to speak. A woman past her prime. Yet Alphonse looked at me, looked through my doubts, my fears, and smiled.

I melted.

I could go with him, follow him to a garret, make love under the eaves, the Eiffel Tower just outside the window, his caresses like sparks on my lonely body.

Heavens, it was hot in the café.

The door opened and a woman in a skin-tight white dress strolled in. Alphonse watched her move.

Of course he didn't want me, he wanted that full-figured woman who just bounded into the café and embraced him. His lover, his paramour, his beloved—in the low-cut dress that showed, basically, everything.

Even then, Alphonse looked at me over her shoulder, paid attention to me. And winked.

I stared into my tea.

In a moment, I looked up. He was still staring at me.

Was he making fun of me? I finished my tea, eager to go, to hide. I shoved some euros onto the table and hoped to disappear. He made his way around the woman in white, who whispered something in his ear and glided out the door.

Then he stood by my table, his waist even with my face, stared at the few euros on the table.

"Not enough?" I asked, fishing in my wallet for more.

"No, madame, no bill today," he said in French.

Obviously, my translation skills were on the fritz. I stood up, reached for my purse.

"Madame, please, sit," he said, and graced my shoulder with the touch of his index finger. "May I?" he asked and sat down as I did, then gestured to the other waiter to take over. "Been to Paris before?"

My body grew hot like it was in front of a fire. I'd already removed my sweater. If I took off anything else, I'd be arrested.

"Yes, of course," I said, wanting to tell him how many times I'd come to Paris over how many years, but it was difficult in French. I struggled to find the words for "since," "a long time ago," and "love." No, no, no, not that kind of love, just how I loved Paris, but now I was confused.

He grinned. "Can I get you something good?" his voice like honey over my bruised and broken heart.

Oh, I'd had my share of lovers and marriages over my lifetime, though, lately, my love life had become kind of predictable. But

Alphonse, he held promise. The heat came off that man like a warm croissant, delicious and buttery with each bite, while wave upon wave of lust surged through my heart. Would he mock me after we kissed? Stab me after making love? Throw me into the Seine? All these thoughts came through my mind, along with the lust for love, the hope of being admired, an eagerness for physical contact I didn't know I had or needed.

He stared at my face.

"You are so lovely," he said, finally, placing both hands on the table. "What's your name?"

"Nina," I said, trying not to sputter. Trying not to cry.

"Lots of women come through my door," he said, his tenor voice reverberating through my nervous system. "A hundred, two hundred a day, and yet, and yet . . ." he paused. I was his all right, ready to follow him anywhere.

I stared into my empty coffee cup, unable to say a word.

"Nina, I'm an admirer of women who've . . ."

Been around? I thought, the dirty dog, which loosened my tongue. "Not much for the young set, are you?" I asked, feeling bolder. Maybe I had entered another universe; maybe I had lost my mind.

He laughed. "Miss Nina," he took my hand. "I love all women."

Was it possible for him to take me on the small table by the window? I was game, rustling around in our clothes for the important parts, the people inside and outside the café oblivious to our passion.

"Young, old, all women?" I croaked.

"Of course. But I prefer, what do you say in English, a seasoned woman. A woman like you." He covered my hand with his other. A trickle of sweat ran down my back. Surely, he would release me and I'd be normal again. Surely, he was a player, about to add another to his long list of conquests.

"Dear, dear Nina," he stood, and brought me to my feet.

"You deserve a special kiss," he said, and embraced my mouth, devouring my last strands of resistance. "Gotta go back to work now."

My knees buckled beneath me. My mouth was eager for more. Loud music blared from the speakers over my head. Cigarette smoke from customers outside filled my lungs. I didn't care about any of it. I looked to the bar, to Alphonse, but he was focused on the door. I looked to see the woman in white coming through it again. When I looked back, Alphonse had dropped down the hole beside the bar into the basement.

When he came back up, he was carrying a bottle of champagne and two glasses. He looked at me and headed to my table. I straightened my spine, eager. This was my chance, my chance at love in Paris, a petite adventure come true; I was worthy of love.

I watched him work the foil on the top of the champagne bottle. Eager for the fizz, I gripped the table as he approached and said, "*Une minute*, Nina," and slipped by me. He sashayed over to the woman in white, moving his hips to the beat, and held two champagne glasses high over the other patrons as he moved by. She gave him a quick glance, then looked out the window.

Alphonse pulled out a chair and was about to sit down when the woman in white waved to a man standing across the street. "*Merci*, Alphonse."

He abruptly readjusted the chair, placed the bottle and two glasses on her table, and spun away.

He looked deflated. No beat. No dancing. For a tall man, all of a sudden he seemed kind of small, with droopy shoulders and a hang-dog look. He meandered back inside the bar and dropped out of sight.

He was crestfallen.

That made two of us. He didn't want me and she didn't want him. I wondered if he had thought about her for days, or for hours, or just minutes like he'd thought about me.

I pulled myself together. I'd had my fun in the sun, my little fantasy, the idea of some Parisian guy thinking I was hot. Best feeling ever. I couldn't remember the last time a man had flirted with me. The guy trying to pick me up in the Celtic Cowboy Café in Great Falls, Montana, last year didn't count. He'd been drunk. And Alphonse was not only sober; he was French.

My chances for a do-over were slim to never. I'd meander back to my hotel room, alone. But Alphonse, he'd get lucky. He'd have a new squeeze by nightfall. No one could resist the way that man moved.

I left the euros on the table and, in the warm light of a Paris afternoon, stepped outside and waited for the walk signal to turn green. The cobblestones were uneven under my feet. Cigarette smoke wafted into the air. If I didn't pay enough attention to the street signs, I'd get lost again. Streets in this area of the Marais go every which way.

I was about to step off the curb when a motorcycle came by too fast, scaring me, and I jumped back. I would've fallen over if a broad shoulder hadn't saved me. It was Alphonse, standing behind me, whispering in my ear. "I would like to show you something special," he said, but he didn't need to say anything. I had been his the moment I'd walked into the café.

I had no problem finding my hotel room later that afternoon, but it was so bright, I had to shield my eyes from the sun when I walked out of Alphonse's courtyard. Four blocks away, I could still smell him on my skin. Maybe I'd never take a shower. Maybe I'd never wash my clothes. Maybe I'd never go home.

Maybe I'd come to my senses. But not today.

THE NEXT MORNING, I SWUNG BY the café again. But Alphonse was gone, on vacation with his girlfriend, they said.

I stared at the new guy behind the bar, but he was kind of boring, so I headed to the Métro. I had only a few more days in Paris to go and lots to see before I headed home.

My daughter taught me not to be afraid. Oh, I'm afraid of all types of things. I don't like heights for sure, or small spaces—both phobias from my mother's side of things—and I'd always been afraid of public speaking and making a spectacle of myself. But one day while my daughter and I were searching the Internet for things to do in Paris, she said, "Go for it, Mom. You only live once. The worst thing they can say to you is say no." So I said yes.

Among My Own Kind

I WAS READY, BUT I WAS a little nervous, which is how people usually feel before they go on stage. I had a little over an hour before making my appearance. I knew my routines, I had my music and costume, and I'd stretched this morning. My stilettos were the challenge, though I could still move like a professional dancer—well, almost. But I still couldn't shake the butterflies. This was, after all, the Moulin Rouge. Huh!

Thirty minutes before I was due at the club, I was nursing my second cup of coffee near the Sacre-Coeur Chapel in Montmartre. I hadn't come for the church, but I did step inside for a few minutes and spoke to Him, and He said, fine, go ahead and dance. I'd even given five euros to the beggars outside, just for luck.

At the table next to me, some girls were chatting in English. I pretended not to listen. "It's him. I know it's him," the girl said, gesturing at a short man with a beard and a cane. She was in her twenties, blond, and smoking a cigarette.

"Lautrec died a long time ago, Denise," her friend said.

Denise stared into her coffee. "Guess I should get out more, eh?"

Across the narrow cobblestone street, a sign painted in gold letters on a wall caught my eye. Aimer, Manger, Boire, Chanter—Love, Eat, Drink, Sing. Lautrec would love the saying, but he wasn't, to be sure, wandering around here reading it. He'd be painting the picture that was in my father's house for years. It's in a museum now. Would Lautrec, paint spattered and muttering, have ever imagined a thing like that?

Hordes of tourists thronged the narrow streets. There were no sidewalks, and between the beeping of cars and scooters and the honks of trucks and buses, I could hear, as well as see, the tough competition for space. I turned down a narrower road, glad to get out of the busyness.

Lautrec, indeed. Didn't he die over a hundred years ago? He would probably have hated to see what had happened to his old stomping grounds. Poor Montmartre, once cheap and sleazy, was now a tourist attraction, at least during the day. At night, the roads got dark, the lights sputtered, and some strange people came out for a stroll.

I should know; I was one of them. I'd been to the sights, walked the stairs up the Arc de Triomphe and down from the Eiffel Tower. Fine monuments, sure, but sexy? Never. Place Pigalle and Montmartre, on the other hand, had been sexy ever since Lautrec went to the Moulin Rouge to see the dancers, then went back to his studio and painted whores on canvas.

I walked down the hill alongside the tram. It was getting dark and when the streetlights came on suddenly, the mist gave the city a dreamy and spooky feel. At the bottom of the hill, I turned right, then right again, and was soon on Boulevard Rochechouart right in front of the Place Pigalle. Whatever I was wearing wasn't nearly interesting enough. The women around me sported fishnet stockings, impossibly tall heels, and lipstick that could start a fire. In my backpack, I had stuff like that.

My daughter Lucie in Milwaukee had helped me pack my things. Over the course of six weeks of watching *So You Think You*

Can Dance, I had painstakingly sewn sequins to my bustier, which was a little longer than the ones that the gals wore on the show. But hell, if they were grandmothers like me, they'd want longer bustiers too. I'd studied every dance and even taken notes, in my illegible scrawl.

I picked up my pace, with only fifteen minutes until I was due at the club. I needed time to review my notes once more before going on.

Following in Lautrec's footsteps, I saw the neon lights of the Moulin Rouge across the street. At home, Lucie and I had read on the Net that the famous cabaret was putting on a contest for amateur dancers. "Anyone can dance and compete for prizes," the posting had said. The graphics were full of women in flowery dresses and tight bodices, whispering to the camera. "Come dance with us. One day only. September 12." Back in May, had Lucie suggested I try it, then signed me up. That Lucie. At first, I felt like a fool, but now, after two whole months of lessons, I felt like a pro.

I crossed the street. Lucie was a Nervous Nelly when I'd told her I'd go alone, but once I said I'd be near a Métro station and was just fooling around, (who hires a woman of a certain age to be a dancer for the Moulin Rouge anyway?), she got it.

Outside, the bouncer, a bald man of about six-foot-five and pushing two hundred fifty pounds, grunted when I showed him my invitation and opened the door for me. Pulsing music enveloped me as I walked down a dark hallway. Beyond, red lights flashed on a wall where a smaller man checked my invitation, muttered something in French I didn't quite understand, and said, "Go to the bar, ask for Marc. *Vite!*" That I understood. I was a bit late.

Marc, the master of ceremonies, had a Van Dyke beard and was even smaller than the second man. He glanced at me up and down and frowned. My blue jeans and baggy sweater didn't impress, but the invitation sealed the deal. He waved me through the back of the bar to the women's dressing room.

Inside, women in all stages of undress lounged in front of well-lighted mirrors. Jars of lotions, brushes, lipstick cases, and ashtrays covered every surface. Smoke spiraled in front of half-made-up faces. I grinned and said hello as the professional girls—and what beauties!—motioned me down to the end of the counter where the amateurs were.

There, I was among my own kind. Large Indian women with enormous breasts giggled as they pulled out their Spanx, super-sized. I wasn't so far off. God and age had given me an additional thirty pounds, and I had Spanx of my own. We shared a laugh.

A seat in front of a mirror was reserved for me. I'd never been backstage anywhere before, but as Lucie had said, "Go on now, Mom. Just try. Take some photos backstage, have some fun, and come back home safe." I didn't have time for photos. There was too much to do!

I unpacked my three bags, lined up my makeup, and started searching for my dance notes. I found them in the bottom of my purse, all crinkled up and torn, and had a hard time reading them, as I'd forgotten my reading glasses and was too embarrassed to ask anyone if they had a spare pair of 2.5s.

In preparing for this moment, I'd taken lessons in pole dancing and jazz, and hip hop, which I loved. My flabby muscles had groaned at first—all those extra pounds—but now I felt pretty good. Some of the extra flab I'd carried had turned into muscle. Off went my tennis shoes, socks, and jeans. On went my Spanx and fishnet stockings. They kind of irritated my butt as I sat on the chair. But anything for beauty, right, Lucie? She'd get a kick out of this.

To my right, an Asian woman whose name placard read Pi-Wen applied lipstick. She was wearing a spangly bra and panties. A short girl, she giggled when she got a glop of mascara on her cheek.

"Ten minutes 'til showtime, girls." The voice over a loudspeaker made me jump. I carefully squeezed my ample bust into a tiny bra. I thought I looked pretty good for a woman way beyond child-bearing age and with wrinkles to boot. For those I had makeup. A ton.

Pi-Wen and I checked ourselves in the mirror, then looked at each other and burst out laughing. We quickly pulled up photos on our cell phones, hers of her grandchildren from California, mine of Lucie.

"Five minutes until curtain call. Get your numbers from Marc. Places, please." The loudspeaker crackled like the intercom on the New York subway.

Pi-Wen put on a hat with a tiny hummingbird on it. I went for the garden look—flowers in my hair, on my hips, and on my shoes. Four-inch heels, no platforms, and room for my bunions. I was set.

We stood, stretched, air-kissed each other. I tried not to stumble as we meandered backstage. I passed a man holding the ropes and he gave me a long look.

Ahead, I watched Pi-Wen walk into a brilliant light. Her music came on and she approached the pole with a bit of a hesitation, then turned her back to the pole, lifted her arms over her head, tucked her feet behind her, and climbed. From the top, she gave the audience a come-hither look as they applauded, then dropped into a death dive. She missed her landing, though, and as soon as she was backstage, she held her arm in pain. The house lights went dark, and it was my turn before she could say, "Break a leg."

The pole was warm in my hands. The music had a thumpy beat, a different song than the one I'd requested. Now what? Improvise, girl! I turned, spun, slid my body up and down the pole. Was it a four-four beat? I wasn't sure. Three-four? Six-eight?

The men in the audience groaned.

I bent my head back, slipped a little, but caught myself just before I fell onto the sticky wooden floor.

They cheered!

Gathering my feet under me again, I flicked fallen flowers from my forehead and climbed up the pole again and spun. This was way more fun than at home in Milwaukee.

They started throwing stuff. I couldn't see what. Flowers? Stuffed animals like they do for ice dancers? The music was too loud. The lights were so bright, at one point I forgot to smile.

I painted one on real quick.

I would've climbed up the pole higher, but I figured it wasn't so attractive for the guys in the front row to see my almost-naked rear end, so I turned my back and gyrated my hips to the beat of boogie-woogie, great dance music. "Blueberry Hill"! Fats Domino!

More flowers. But I heard a clink. Someone out there was having a great time.

If only my Lucie could see me now. I grabbed the pole with my right arm and right ankle and spun. It felt like flying. I was grateful, until I forgot my last move and had to improvise; my pause lasted just a little too long. They tell me in show business that pauses are a good thing, but in dancing, it didn't feel right.

The music reached a crescendo as I did, and I returned to the ground glowing. More clinks! They sure liked their bottled beer in this place.

With two more turns around the pole, I gathered myself and stared out at the audience, all warm and sweaty. I had to kick stuff out of the way of my shoes when I finally stood up. Wow! I was way more popular than Pi-Wen! They hadn't thrown anything on the stage for her.

I was about to climb the pole once more when the music stopped. I couldn't move. Was it too early for a curtain call? I held the pole in a sexy pose and heard my name called from off stage. Someone was gesturing at me. I waved back.

Then I heard pops and groans and catcalls, and the next dancer came out on stage. I took a bow and was off.

For some reason, the manager frowned when I came off stage. What was the matter with him? Didn't he know good dancing when he saw it? Or had he had bad oysters for lunch?

The professional dancers were waiting to go on. They gave me a little wave and a smile. My God, they were beautiful in their dresses and bustiers.

"It's okay, honey," one of them said. "Maybe next year." They floated to the stage.

"Did you get your flowers? Your empty bottles of beer?" one of the stage managers snickered. I didn't understand what he was talking about, but I gave him my best death stare. I hadn't seen *him* dance.

I wobbled back to the dressing room, where Pi-Wen was trying to wrap a bandage around her arm. I helped her. Skinny little thing.

"I'm so sorry," she said.

"About what?" I asked. "I didn't break my arm."

"Well, you know . . ." she trailed off, then hunted in her purse for lipstick.

"Know what?" I asked. Pi-Wen looked a little pale.

"Your . . . um," she muttered.

For a pretty clever girl, she just couldn't seem to speak. "Go on, then, Pi-Wen, spit it out." I peeled off one of my false eyelashes.

"Maybe next year," she said.

"Next year, what?" I didn't like the way this conversation was heading.

"Your . . . routine." She coughed into her hand.

"My routine? They loved me! They threw stuff!!"

"But why did they throw all that crap on the stage?" Her face was clouded. "Bottles and shit."

"They were drunk?"

"Probably."

"Disorderly?"

"More like pissed."

"Oh, that's just another word for drunk."

"More like pissed *off*. I'm sorry, Nina. They just didn't like you."

"Now, wait a moment . . ." I said, but I was the one sputtering.

"Get a grip, Nina. You're not made for this."

I looked down at my spare tire, the one that had been growing since I'd turned forty. "Doesn't look so bad to me."

"They threw bottles at you, Nina."

Oh, God. I buried my face in my hands, getting makeup on my palms. They felt greasy, my stomach felt upset, and I felt like a fool. "At home . . . we, I mean, Lucie and me . . . we thought . . ." I stuttered through sobs. I felt like a whore, just like my father had seemed to imply all through my teenage years. A whore and stupid, and fat, and ugly. The sobs came faster now, threatening to choke me. The Indian dancers, the amateurs, came over and put their arms around me.

"There there, now, dear, it's not so bad." They were round and squishy and warm and wonderful.

But I kept on sobbing. The tears wouldn't stop. Someone handed me a box of tissues. I thought I was going to burn through them all. The stupid stage manager came to the door, but the girls hustled him out. Eventually, I stopped crying.

"I'm so sorry, Nina," Pi-Wen said. "I didn't mean to hurt you."

I sniffled back tears. My face was a mess, but I was sitting in the middle of a bunch of women who were hugging me and saying sweet things, and I loved them for it. Loved them all. It was worth it, for the hugs.

The Indian women went on stage, but I didn't have the heart to go with Pi-Wen and watch them. Alone in the dressing room for the moment, I slipped back into my old blue jeans, tennies, and oversized sweater. I placed my dancing clothes in a canvas bag, along with the makeup I hadn't donated to the professional dancers.

I went down the darkened hallway to the stage door, red lights still flashing. The big bouncer pushed the door open for me—just as the loudspeaker came on. "Nina Johnson, Pi-Wen Chang, please come to the stage."

I wasn't going to be humiliated again and started walking out the door. But when the bouncer heard the announcer, he gently pulled the door shut, and said, "Aren't you Nina Johnson?"

"Hell no!" I said and tried to push by him.

"Just put your things down here. I'll watch them for you."

"I'm not going back there . . ." I grabbed his arm. "*Go* away!"

"Mam'selle." His voice was kind. "Please. If I let you go, I will lose my job."

I stopped and really looked at him for the first time. Though he was big and strong, he still had sleepless nights and hungry children written all over him.

I raced back out onto the stage to stand side by side with Pi-Wen, in front of the audience again. Fluorescent lights on in the house put us all in a faint bluish tone. And there was no music.

I glared at the manager Marc as he called out girls' names for third and second place; Pi-Wen won honorable mention and stepped forward.

Was he going to give me a consolation prize?

"Nina Johnson."

I stepped forward, my hands in fists behind my back.

"For the courage to improvise to the wrong music. For maintaining composure in the face of a drunk, dishonorable audience. For the ability to smile under pressure and let nothing stop the show. First prize."

The audience cheered and raised their arms.

I blocked my torso from the inevitable glass bottles that were going to come my way.

"Open your eyes, Nina. They're flowers," Pi-Wen said.

Red roses littered the stage. For the second time tonight, I burst into tears. I hugged Marc, who smelled like day-old sweat; Pi-Wen, who smelled like jasmine; and the Indian women, who smelled like lavender. I saluted the audience, bowed, and walked off.

Well, I could say I won first prize now. Lucie would be proud. Now I had plenty of time for photos.

With more hugs all around, a bottle of champagne for me, and Pi-Wen's phone number in my hand, I grabbed my bags from the bouncer and made my way to the Métro. And when I returned to Milwaukee, I'd take more classes. There must be other places I could perform.

The same short man with a beard and a cane, whom the girls at the café and I had seen passing by, was now walking up the Métro stairs. I took a second look. Perhaps that really was Lautrec and he'd be painting me next. I chased after him.

My father collected art, but I collected friends. My first friend, Edna, had a much different father than mine. He built buildings, ran crews, and made things. The day I met Edna, her father fashioned a little man out of silver for me, which I wore around my neck for years. Anyone's father who was handy, to say nothing of inspiring his daughter, made a much better father than the one I had, who talked into his DictaBelt machine for hours, kept jamming the keys on his Olivetti typewriter and told his children at the dinner table to be quiet. This one's for Edna.

The Smell of Money

My name is Edna. I'm a heavy equipment operator. Back hoes, excavators, graders, bulldozers, Cats, loaders—I drive them all. Good money? You bet.

It was tough in the beginning. When my dad was teaching me how to drive his '57 Chevy pickup, he yelled at me, slammed his foot down on the passenger-seat floorboard, and pleaded with me to slow down. Hell no! I liked speed then and I like it now. Trying to teach me how to drive was way harder than teaching my mother, he said. At least *she* listened, but if you ask her, she remembers it differently. On the last day, she told him she was filing for divorce, then ran off to town in his car, with his credit card.

Anyway, I was much more reasonable. He cranked the window all the way down, his brown fedora tipped back from his forehead, rubbed his face, and shouted, "Holy Moly, Edna! The clutch! Please, *please,* don't forget the clutch. Edna!"

Hells bells, I was all of fourteen. I stretched my leg way out in front of me and shoved that big-ass pedal down with all the strength I had. But I learned. When I turned twelve, during summer vacation, I had learned to drive a forklift at my Uncle Dan's farm in Vermont and later ran the tractor. Piece of cake. I haven't looked back since.

When I tell guys who ask what I do for a living, their mouths drop open. But you're such a puny little thing, they say. Ha! Then they come to their senses and say, "Way big-money cool." You don't have to be strong, I tell them, you just have to be careful, and boy am I careful. But while traveling, maybe not so much. Let me tell you about Paris.

It hadn't been my idea to go, but my boyfriend, Larry Mangrove, had a business conference there and I tagged along. Hell, I'm up for a good time, same as the next guy.

Girls' night out? When I told all the wives and girlfriends at the conference what I did for a living and pulled out a photo, me behind the wheel in my Caterpillar D11T dozer, they gasped and moved away. What was their problem? I had makeup on and everything. Mary Ann, of the bleached-blond hair and under-23 set, got a look of horror on her face, pushed away her espresso, and headed into the restroom to cry. What a sissy. What was she so afraid of? I wasn't going to make her drive a dozer or anything.

It's 2016, folks. Get real.

Anyway, Larry was in the conference all day and the girls wouldn't hang around with me, so I headed out. Do I speak French? What, are you out of your mind? They don't push French in northern Vermont. They teach trucks. Learning how to handle a D11 took all the brain cells I have.

Diesel is my perfume of choice.

The head waiter at our hotel suggested that I take the subway and go see the Sewer Museum. What the hell, as long as I don't have to wear a dress, I'm game. He said it wouldn't be crowded.

On the way out, I ran into Mary Ann—yes, *that* Mary Ann. She was twisting and retwisting a red scarf, which made me feel kind of bad. It turned out she was upset that her new husband played poker the night before with the other attendees and lost a bunch (her money, actually: her parents were loaded), and it almost broke my heart to see her like that, so I said, sure Mary Ann, come on, have a big day with me.

At five-one or so she's kind of a runt, but I liked her bubbly personality. Also, it was her first trip to Paris, and I'd been there once before. Mary Ann was kind of cute with her crooked little smile, and probably felt kind of lonely, thinking maybe her marriage was over and all. She marched right on out the door with me and charged down the stairs into the Métro, her red scarf flying out behind her. I could hardly keep up.

She'd never been on the subway before and was scared someone would mug her or push her onto the tracks! When we walked upstairs at our stop and out into a drizzly day, you could have lit up the sky with her smile after having made it out alive. We came out beside Pont de l'Alma. You might or might not remember that this wasn't far from where Princess Diana died in 1997.

What I thought was an emergency exit for the Métro was the entrance to the museum itself, just a tiny kiosk with a small sign that said Sewer Musée and a guy inside, leaning over his little desk.

Mary Ann looked at the guy in the kiosk, then back at me. "Oh, I guess," she said. "It just looks so puny from here."

"It's big inside," the man said in good English. "Trust me."

We bought tickets, went down a flight of stairs, and were in the reception area. Posters lined the walls. Though languages aren't my forté, I can recognize French well enough to understand the word *entrée* and we went through a narrow archway, the beginning of some kind of tunnel. Then it opened up into a room where tunnels led everywhere.

The smell hit me hard. I've worked landfills in my day and hauled dump trucks full of manure, but this odor was so strong, it stopped me in my tracks.

Mary Ann shrugged her shoulders, wrapped her red scarf around her neck, took a deep breath, and grinned. "My dad used to say, it's the smell of money. For twenty years he worked in a wastewater treatment plant. Put me through college. None of the other girls would go on any daddy-daughter trip with us, believe you me."

In a large chamber with grates under our feet with *that* smell wafting through the air, signs, posters, and maps explained the history of how the early Parisians, all of whom lived on Île de La Cité, both drank from and shit in the Seine until they got sick and figured that out. After that, they built open sewers in the middle of the street. Later, they dug tunnels like the ones Mary Ann and I were in, separating clean water from dirty, and everyone seemed to do way better. The city was laced with tunnels. I was studying a map until I realized Mary Ann was no longer with me.

"Mary Ann?" I called out. The only two other people in the chamber looked at me and pointed their fingers down a well-lit tunnel. I followed.

I found her at the end, grinning. "C'mon. Deeper. This way! I love this place!"

"I'm coming," I said weakly, but hell, it looked a long way underground. She took off at a brisk pace.

I followed her down a narrow brick-lined tunnel. Below our feet, open grates exposed Paris's least favorite product. Two tunnels led off from the main chamber, then a third to the left. I saw a flash of red and then she was gone. There was no getting away from the smell, but Mary Ann had gotten away from me. That girl could move! If I could have caught her, I would have.

I set forth down the first tunnel, following where I thought she went, moving as quickly as I could. Shadows splashed the tunnel walls. Yes! Mary Ann's red scarf flitted around a turn. But when I got to the T in the passageway, I had no idea which way she'd gone. The walls were rock, cold and damp to my touch. The smell of sewer was still nearly overpowering, even though I'd left the open channels behind a while ago. I called out, "Mary Ann? Mary

Ann!" My voice echoed off the well-lit rock walls, reverberating in my ears like a friggin' nightmare.

"Where'd you go, Mary Ann?" I asked, more gently this time. I strained my ears to catch the click-clack of her heels on the concrete floor, but I heard nothing.

I headed down the left branch, then sped up, figuring I'd reach the end of the tunnel, turn around, and head down the other fork. I had to find her eventually. Stupid girl, making me sweat like this. At twenty-three, she knew better than to ditch the only friend she had. At thirty-six, I knew better than to wander down unmarked pathways. Well, shit, that girl was gone.

At the far end of the left passage, I came around the corner and saw her red scarf. I yelled, ran up, and turned to face her.

This was no Mary Ann. This was a diminutive woman wearing a red scarf and carrying a large brown shopping bag. What was she doing wearing Mary Ann's scarf?

"Where'd she go?" I asked.

The woman jumped back and yelled at me. "*Quoi?*" Frowning behind huge, owl-like glasses, she pulled her heavy purse back as if to strike me.

"Pardon me!" I said. "Have you seen my friend?"

"*Va-t-en!*" she cried in French.

In any language, "go away" feels the same. I stepped back and studied her for a moment. She looked just like my grandma, who died in the spring of my senior year.

"Sorry," I said. "My name's Edna." I put out my hand.

It hung in the air a minute, unloved and lonely. I put it away.

"My friend, Mary Ann," I said with my best smile, "she had a scarf just like that." I pointed to her neck. The scarf was wrapped around Grandma's neck two times and fell to her waist. "I lost my friend down here. Have you seen her? Short," like you, I was going to say. "Nice eyes, like yours." I said instead, touching the red scarf.

"Hands off!" Her eyes were flinty. "Any closer, miss, and I'll call security."

Well, I didn't know about that. I didn't see any alarm buttons and I always check for them wherever I go. She spoke good English! She looked seriously disturbed, though, vibrating and opening and closing her mouth and stamping her feet and jittery as all get out. Just my luck to give an old lady a heart attack. Especially underground.

"You Americans are so rude," she said and disappeared down a side tunnel. If she saw Mary Ann, maybe I'd hear something. I waited a sec, two, maybe three. Four.

Hearing nothing, I spun on my heels and saw the entrance to another tunnel. Maybe Mary Ann had gone that way. I headed down.

The tunnel became smaller, lower, and narrower. Darker. The lights were fewer and farther between. I headed about a hundred feet or so, but then the lights flickered, dimmed, and went out. Fighting panic, I was relieved when they flickered back on, crackling a bit. "Mary Ann?" I called.

No answer.

"Mary Ann?"

Nothing. The lights went out. And didn't come back on.

"Anyone? Hello? Hello?" Darkness enveloped me. Cold, dark, damp, and smelly.

Which way should I go now? Backward, forward? I felt like a fool.

Grasping my cell phone, I turned it on. Light! Oh God, light. I was straddling the tunnel, my free hand on the slimy wall. Had I turned around? Turned at all?

Way off in the distance, I thought I saw a flicker.

I peered through the blackness. Yes, a light like mine. "Mary Ann?" I called again. My voice echoed down and down the tunnel. "Hello?"

The far-off light flickered and went out. I touched one hand against the damp rock wall as I went, holding out my cell phone's bright light with the other. It stayed bright until I'd walked a hundred yards or more, then it died.

Plunged into darkness, I stifled a scream. Even in the subterranean cold, sweat beaded my temples, the back of my neck, and my hands. Being ever so careful, I opened my purse and slid my phone inside a zippered pocket. No reason to panic and lose everything.

A siren started wailing above, splitting my head open. It was that loud, I swear. Reverberating through my brain, it felt like it would shake my teeth loose.

The sound echoed and echoed until it finally diminished and faded out. A rush of cold air sped through me. Had I gone into a wrong tunnel? Where was Mary Ann?

Forty feet underground, the world above weighed heavily over my head. I hadn't moved since the light went out. I pressed my left hand on the wall. Ten inches away, maybe, if I was lucky. I pressed my right hand out in the opposite direction, the wall about four inches away. The right side was wet. I centered myself in the tunnel. Gradually and slowly, I extended my hand upward, praying that the ceiling was high, but it was directly over my head, six inches. God! This tunnel wasn't for people, it was for water.

I've never been anywhere where it had been so dark. I didn't dare move and I didn't dare stay still. Sooner or later, wastewater would come charging down the tunnel, soaking my shoes, then my knees, my thighs, waist—oh God.

It would be fast if the water came.

I tested for the ceiling. Closer.

I imagined my dad, in his fedora, yelling at me. *Edna! What are you doing? Edna!*

Should I step forward or back?

The bottom of the tunnel sloped down. Then I heard something walking in the darkness. An alligator? A rat? A person?

"Hello?" Gravel beneath my feet.

No sound this time.

I stepped forward again. This was stupid. I should go back. I turned, walked ten feet. The bottom of the tunnel rose and fell, like waves. I hadn't remembered any waves. Had I gone down a different tunnel?

I turned again, one hundred eighty degrees, stepped forward ten feet. No gravel. Wasn't there gravel there before?

What was it Dad said? If you get lost, trace your steps.

What steps, Dad? Which way? Which way, Dad?

I stifled the urge to scream. I was going to die down here. "Dad! What do I do now? Dad? Come find me! Someone! Anyone?"

I stayed very silent. And I listened.

And heard those footsteps, small footsteps, again.

Someone coming after me? Someone coming to save me?

"Hello?" My voice echoed off the cold damp stone walls.

No, these were very small footsteps. Too small for a person. A dog, perhaps?

No, the sound was too small for a dog.

Rats! Tiny toes scrabbled over my feet and I screamed, the echo bouncing between the walls and my ears.

For ten minutes, I stood very very still. The only movement was my trembling all over, afraid that no one would ever save me. I'd be down here forever—unless they found my bones twenty years from now.

You know what to do, Edna, when you're scared? Just tell yourself you're going to be okay. My father's words ran through my head. What had I been—five, ten, twelve? I'd never been this scared. Except that one time. When I was three and he'd taken my hand away from the stove, where I'd burned my finger. He wrapped my hand in cold cloths and told me to use common sense and be more careful.

This was cold, not hot, but the meaning was the same. Common sense told me to turn around, slowly, and with my left hand on the rock wall, feel my way along. When I came to the waves under my feet this time I kept going. If no one was going to find me, I would find them. Dad would say, keep going, Edna! Don't cry, Edna! Stay strong, Edna! Think!

As if. I was terrified. Just an inkling of hope to hang onto.

I reached my left hand forward. Was there was a change in the rock? More pebbly, less rock-like? I extended my other hand and yes, the same. Holding out both of my hands, touching both sides, I stepped forward. The bottom of the tunnel rose. Just a little, but I felt it. Would I walk to daylight?

I duck-walked slowly, my hands trusting the walls. Though I was careful, I stepped on something slippery and fell. The walls closed in, my knees were killing me, and my legs felt shaky when I stood up, the palms of my hands sore where I'd dropped onto all fours. I cursed myself. The top of the tunnel was even lower.

My head swam with the smell of sewage, but I still could hear my dad's voice. Concentrating hard, I held my breath, turned, stepped, and counted. Ceiling? Better or not? Better. I now had twelve inches of clearance. But then panic gripped me again. I can't! I heard my dad say, *Yes, you can!* No, I can't! The walls are closing in! No. Concentrate. Take six more steps. Ceiling now? Rough, I answered. Taller, yes. Edna!

My knees were wobbly, but not bloody under my blue jeans. And not broken either, they worked just fine, just a little stiff. I counted to four. Don't panic. Keep moving. Another six feet. The width of the passageway grew. Don't lose it, don't lose it. Too wide now to touch both sides, I held to the left. Underneath my sandals, the sharp rocks turned into smooth concrete. Warm air rushed in.

I stood up tall. The wall and floor of the tunnel were smooth concrete. The ceiling was too far to reach. And in the distance, a light. I ran the rest of the way.

I found Mary Ann, in the reception area, her face white against her red scarf, her hands shaking.

"I'm fine, I'm fine," I kept telling her, but my voice and hands were so shaky, I knew she didn't believe me.

The attendant came closer. "*Desolée, madame!* So sorry. We were searching for you. Someone left the man gates open. You must have wandered into a restricted area. You were lucky. It must've been terrifying. I am so terribly sorry, madame."

I brushed off his exhortations, sidled up to Mary Ann. We were bathed in light, near the sign saying Sortie. Daylight, above ground, was only steps away.

"You don't look all right, Edna," she said.

I'm not all right at all, I wanted to tell her. I was drenched in sweat. My hands were clammy and my knees were sore. My hand was trembling as I grasped a metal railing, colder than expected, but stable, manmade and steel. Light from upstairs flooded the stairs. Sky? There was sky up there?

"I'll be fine," I croaked.

"We were worried about you," she said as we climbed the stairs. "They were about to send in the gendarmes."

"They didn't need to," I replied. "I found my own way out." Sure. The assistant was right, I'd been lucky. I would've done anything to have had a strong hand in the tunnels showing me the way.

When we walked outside, into the brilliant sunshine, I felt lost. Trees, cars, people rushed around us. Tourists lined up at bus stops. Trucks rumbled down side streets. Everyone looked like they hadn't a care in the world. I longed to hold Mary Ann's hand while we crossed the street like I was three again, holding hands with my dad. The day smelled fresh as rain.

"Did you have breakfast?" Mary Ann asked.

I couldn't remember that far back. I shrugged.

Mary Ann frowned. "Not enough, if any. Let's find a café."

Once we sat down at a tiny table, I shifted my feet and almost knocked over the table.

Mary Ann frowned and stirred her espresso. "I know you don't like coffee, Edna, but you do look a little pale. Tea, then?"

Pale? I was alive, for Chrissake. I didn't care if I was pale. "I had breakfast," I stuttered.

A waiter brought croissants and coffee. I love croissants, but as I broke it in pieces to eat, my stomach didn't agree. On my plate were a hundred little pieces of croissant and not a crumb got to my mouth.

At the adjacent table, a cute little black-and-white dog begged for crumbs.

I pulled myself to my full height, trying to retain my bravado of earlier in the day. But bravado had gone out with the lights.

"How do you like Paris?" I asked Mary Ann, first thing that popped into my mind. I put on my sunglasses and leaned over to pat the dog. She wouldn't mind seeing my tears.

While I was wandering along Boulevard Beaumarchais, looking at all the motorcycles lined up like little soldiers, I thought of Edna and her tractors. She would think driving a motorcycle was a piece of cake. For me, they looked both scary and sexy. But if she could do it, I could do it, couldn't I? Wasn't this trip to Paris an opportunity to try new things, to push myself, to move forward? My daughter would certainly say so, even though my father wouldn't have approved. But we were still here, weren't we? And my father . . . he was long gone.

JULIE

I'D NEVER SEEN SO MUCH POWER on wheels. Fifty or more motorcycles stretched down the sidewalks and along the street, filling every available parking space along Boulevard Beaumarchais. Black and chrome, red and chrome, blue and black, of every kind—two-wheelers, scooters, and three-wheelers with their third wheels in front or back . . . they were sexy as hell and exuded power just being still. I could almost hear the motors roaring with the need for speed. Riders came in and parked, while others headed off in a blur of rumbles and exhaust. Beyond them, bikers on the avenue barely stopped at the light before they blew through, engines at full blast, helmets gleaming under the noonday sun.

I'd never driven a motorcycle, but I'd been on one, my arms around the guy in front, hoping like hell I wouldn't let go, fall off, or be killed. This time, I wanted to be the driver. Actually, "wanted" is too soft a word, I *had* to drive one. It had to be a thrill. Oh my God, I was so excited my knees trembled. I had to feel that engine roar.

For the first time in my life, I felt no fear. My father was no longer around to tell me I couldn't ride a motorcycle or that I couldn't do a thousand other things. I was nervous about the motorcycle shop owner saying no, of course, and I was nervous about learning to shift, and what would I do if it fell over? This was my day to say no to my father.

I'd dressed carefully for the occasion—blue jeans, hot-pink sweater, belly pack, and light jacket. He wouldn't approve of my tight jeans. Ha!

I walked in. It was time to try one of these monsters before it was too late.

I rounded the interior glass door and introduced myself to François, a man with a trim beard, light-blue eyes, curly hair, and leather jacket with a name tag. I asked him kindly if I could rent a bike.

His face clouded. It looked like he was getting ready to call me crazy or stupid or too old, but hey, today I had a direct line to the Almighty. I guess François felt it too; he quickly changed his mind.

"A small bike? A larger one, madame? Day trip or overnight? Need panniers? How many wheels?"

"Two," I said. "They say it's like riding a bicycle."

"Not hardly, madame, but if that's what you wish?"

"It's my first time," I said, rather too loudly.

"Have you ever driven a stick shift?"

"Since I was a teenager," I said. That much was true. "And I still drive one."

With a shrug, he asked for my license and credit card, then led me to a smallish motorcycle. I shook my head and pointed to the largest one on the floor, a 130-horsepower Indian FTR 1200.

"I can't, ma'am. Sorry, but as much as you think you can, I doubt you can handle that big bike. Can you bench press a hundred kilos?"

I tried to calculate that in my head and guessed. "Not more than seventy-five pounds," which was a lie on my best day.

"Most people want to start with the biggest bike, madame. You are not the first one. Perhaps this beauty will work for you. Half the power and half the weight, but it goes. Harley Davidson Iron 1200, comfortable seat. Once you feel this under you, you'll forget about everything else."

That was the plan.

I placed my hand on the handlebar, swung my leg up and over, and could hardly move. My legs were out forever, and I couldn't touch the floor.

François laughed. "It's still a bit big for you."

I didn't think it was funny. This was my big day. I wasn't going to take any of those puny three-wheeled jobs no matter what. I sat back on the seat and stewed.

"We have one more. We call her 'Julie,' very popular with the ladies," he said. "*Un moment.*"

"Not pink!" I shouted after him, insulted with all the pink "lady" electric drills and hammers I'd seen advertised on the Web.

"No pink anywhere, ma'am. And let me tell you . . ."

He disappeared into the back and came back rolling out a beauty—sleek back windshield, blue body and fenders.

"A Yamaha YZF-R3, ma'am, sporty as hell, six speeds. Go ahead, climb aboard."

She fit my body like a lover. I could feel the seat under me, my fingers didn't have to stretch for the handlebars, I could touch the floor, and I smelled leather.

I was in love. My whole body tingled. Oh God.

"Madame, for today, would you like me to accompany you while you learn? I'll get on the back, yell in your ear, instructions, that is. Ça *va?*"

"*Bon,*" I nodded. My mouth felt dry.

François ran through the controls: speedometer, brakes, clutch, lights, signals, starter, and horn, which he punched with force. The blaring bleep made me jump.

"Ignition switch, clutch," he continued. "Now, madame—"

"Nina," I said.

"Get on. Put the key in here. Pull in the clutch lever, turn the key, give it a little gas—"

I did as I was told, felt a thump, and heard a roar. I fairly blew off my seat. What a thrill! Power between my thighs! Power I'd only dreamed about. Forget Paul Newman, forget Marlon Brando, it was going to be me, Nina Cerkonowicz, blowing down the Paris boulevards!

"And this is the shifter then?" I shoved my foot down on the pedal like he'd shown me.

"Madame, not yet!" He turned off the ignition switch.

I deflated like a kid.

"Madame. Helmet, please."

The helmet was tight and confining. Thick padding covered my ears. François had to yell so I could hear him.

He tightened the strap under my chin. "Regulations. And we need you to come back alive, *oui*?"

"*Oui*," I agreed, though I knew I'd be fine. No fear. I wanted that thrum of engine under me again. Power I couldn't believe. The Boulevard ahead was full of cars. And François was going to let me drive in it? I looked at the traffic zooming by on Beaumarchais.

"A side street, perhaps, madame? Rue Amelot?" He climbed on behind me.

With a release of the clutch, my right hand rotated the grip, and we were off—five kilometers an hour, ten, fifteen.

"Madame, stop for the pedestrians, please."

I hadn't seen any. "Whoops!" I slammed on the brakes. A mom steering a stroller gave me a dirty look. Her children grabbed her skirts.

"Desolée, madame," I said.

François nudged me from the back, and we were off.

I felt like I was born to do this—my father and brothers be damned telling me I should never do this—and I screeched to a stop at a red light to turn right. Exhaust from other motorcycles filled the air. How could I have waited so long?

The light turned and I blasted around the corner and down the avenue. One mile, two miles, I worked my way through the clutch and gears, got better at braking, and zoomed a little at Place Republique around the side streets until François said, "Ça *suffit*. Please, madame, drop me off."

I pulled over at a café.

"Not here! At the shop, madame, if you please!"

He directed me back to the store, where I slowed to a stop, felt his weight come off the bike, told him I'd be back in an hour, and punched it.

Whoops! I hadn't meant to burn rubber just then.

I drove by the Métro stops, including my own, Filles De Calvaire, and was through the next square and past the sad Bataclan nightclub and onto another boulevard where there was less traffic. The bike under me felt like a Ferrari, carrying me forward, easy to handle, yet full of guts. She turned like an angel.

At red lights, Julie wanted to buck if I applied the brakes too hard. My thighs had never felt like this. The heat coming off the engine made want to jump the first good-looking man I saw.

Then I accelerated too fast and almost fell off. So I tightened my legs around this clever beast, turned her down a side street, then another, and punched it on the Rue de Rivoli until traffic slowed us all down. It had been a relatively cool day when I had started; now sweat dribbled down the small of my back. I pulled up behind two motorcycles whose drivers were dressed straight out of *Gentlemen's Quarterly*, in natty suits with dress-type white shirts and narrow ties. Didn't they know better than to ride a motorcycle dressed like that? I flashed them my million-dollar smile and left them in the dust.

As the next light turned, I toed the shifter into second gear and blew past a boulangerie. The smell of baking bread made me swoon. Should I stop and eat? Had I eaten today? Couldn't remember. Had I eaten yesterday? Julie just wanted to go. Still, my own appetite got the better of me. I parked in front of the bakery, ordered a croissant and coffee, and took a selfie, or tried to, with crumbs on my mouth and the cell phone battery flashing red, but it worked! I had a photo!

Afterward, I zoomed down a side street but turned down a dead end. All the buildings looked alike, with their balconies, magical doors, and secrets. Stopping for a rest, I realized I was lost. I looked at my cell phone, but now the battery was dead. No GPS, no problem! I stroked Julie by my leg. She knew the way home.

I turned back onto the big boulevard, swerved into a tight U-turn, and headed back, passing the Haussmann buildings, cafés, pedestrians strolling by with dogs, children, lovers, other motorcycle shops, boutiques. I came to the end of the boulevard and ahead was water. It wasn't the Seine. And Julie's fuel gauge was pushing empty.

Motorcycles, scooters, and cars sped by in a swirl of traffic, horns blaring, until I parked Julie, turned her off, and walked into the closest café.

A map of Ethiopia stretched all the way across the back wall. Waitresses in long, beautifully bright dresses meandered around tables. A particularly tall woman, standing behind the cash register, frowned when I asked directions back to the Bastille. She just pointed to the door.

A light rain was falling. I would've walked to the next place, but it was two long blocks away. Giving Julie a forlorn look, I gathered my wits about me and as the rain started coming down harder, I made my way down the street, alongside the canal, and parked Julie, sputtering a bit, in front of another café. The windows were covered with fabric, and I recognized the black, green, and yellow flags as African National Congress. Ordinarily, I wouldn't come within a hundred feet of the place, but today I strode right through the door without hesitation. Inside it was dark. Everyone stared at me and whispered in a language I didn't recognize.

"Excuse me," I said, eyeing a gentleman nursing an espresso at a table, "you speak French?" He bent his head over his paper and waved me away.

Two men behind the bar were wiping the counter down and drying glassware. One was bald, in his thirties, I guessed, while the other had a grand mustache.

"*Centre-Ville?*" I asked them. "*Où se trouve Centre-Ville?*"

They looked at each other and shrugged.

A man sitting at a corner table looked up from his book. "Madame, perhaps I can help you?" he asked in English.

I stepped over to him and smiled. "It's just that . . . my motorcycle . . . out of gas. Centre-Ville." The words flew out of my mouth.

"*Asseyez-vous,*" he said quietly. His face was a spider web of years and experience. A working man in blue shirt, dusty blue jeans, and big motorcycle boots.

"Sit down. Breathe. One word at a time, please. Want some coffee?"

Well, no. I wanted a beer. I wanted a gas station. Dry clothes. My hotel room. I'd take whatever he was offering. "Coffee, yes, please."

"I'm Roman."

"*Enchanté. Je m'appelle Mandy.*" Mandy would work for today.

"I live in this, the Nineteenth arrondissement. And you?" he asked, placing his twisted hands on the table between us.

I'd forgotten which arrondissement my hotel was in. "The Marais, sir."

"A long time ago, Miss Mandy, I lived in the Marais too," Roman said. A cup of coffee arrived on the table for me.

"Then you could tell me the way?" I asked. I sipped the delicious brew.

"I was sixteen, Mandy, when I fell in love. Coming home from school near Place du Temple, that's when I saw Sabina for the first time. I could hear the sound of jackboots from blocks away." He turned toward the window, grabbed a breath. "And everyone disappeared . . . my mother, my sister, how do you say . . . ?"

"He won't tell you anything useful, sweetheart," piped a voice from near a stairwell. "The war, you know."

Roman was lost in his memories, so I looked over at the long-haired man by the stairs. "Do you know the way back to the Marais, sir?"

They laughed. "*Oui, c'est facile, madame.*"

"Then which way?" I asked, pointing outside.

"You must pay first," the white-haired man said.

I opened my wallet.

"Not that way. Madame. You owe Roman. You must listen to him tell one simple story."

I looked from one to the other man. Normally, I'd be out of there like a shot. "Please, go ahead," I said.

Roman pulled out a cigarette, offered me one. "You smoke?"

"Roman is great at this game. Go on, *mon copain*, tell her your story before she disappears."

Roman mumbled, "In 1950, my sister Rose—"

"Since when did you have a sister?" the white-haired man interrupted.

"I've always had a sister," Roman said.

I was getting antsy. "The Marais?" I asked again. "Which way?"

"Stay. Don't break an old man's heart. You're the sweetest sight any of us here has seen all day. Right, boys?"

"Very well." I sat there in front of Roman, hoping my hands would never look like his, listened as he meandered through his life. He spoke with a heavy heart. It was getting later by the minute. Julie was getting soaked. I wondered where I'd find towels, a plastic bag, a way home.

Roman gulped down his whisky. "By then, Rose was sixteen."

Then he stopped talking altogether. I waited a few minutes, feeling bad for him. Finally, he looked up at me and said, "For the Marais, my dear, go two blocks to the traffic light, take a left, continue on the boulevard for a couple of miles. You'll come to Rue Beaubourg, where you take a right. Then you'll know where you are."

If I could remember that much. I sipped my coffee, felt the jitters come on, pulled a five-euro note out of my wallet, and laid it on the table. "*Merci, mon ami.* Thank you for the coffee, story, and directions. Now if you'll excuse me?"

He grabbed my arm.

"Monsieur?" I asked, dry-mouthed. "*S'il vous plaît.*"

His eyes were watery.

"He misses his Rose," the white-haired man said.

"Monsieur Roman?" I asked. "*Je suis desolée.* I must go."

"Rose?" he asked.

"Monsieur, alas, I am not Rose," I said.

His grip tightened.

"Roman!" The white-haired man jumped to his feet. "She died—"

"Don't tell me, please don't tell me," Roman said. "I don't want to hear it."

"Roman, it's okay," the white-haired man said.

"It's never okay. She would be a grandmother by now." Roman covered his face with both hands and sobbed.

I felt bad to leave him like that. I hesitated.

"You better go," the white-haired man said.

I ran back out into the rain. Pressed Julie's starter and prayed. She sputtered and came to life, but I had no time, no time to get lost, no time to waste, no gas to spare. I followed Roman's directions, hoping I was on the right track. Two blocks down, traffic was accumulating at a red light. I took the left, but in a couple of blocks, cars and motorcycles swirled around another monument and then I was free. I kept going in the same direction 'til I finally turned onto a wide boulevard. Cars, trucks, buses, and police cars rushed past me, but I followed, close to the curbs.

Every so often I caught the attention of a pedestrian and yelled, "Le Marais?" and went in the direction they pointed.

I was soaked to the core, but I didn't care. Just as the Métro stop Filles de Calvaire came into view, Julie's gas gauge's red warning light started blinking and she sputtered and died. I pushed her across the broad boulevard, looked up, and saw François pacing in front of the shop. I nudged her up onto the sidewalk.

"Desolée. I'm so very sorry," I said, not through tears, but from unimaginable relief. "I got lost."

"That's what they all say. Just give me the bike."

Julie looked forlorn as I passed her over.

"Why didn't you stop for gas?"

"I didn't see a petrol station."

"You American women. Think you can do anything. But you can't! You just can't!" he shouted and rolled Julie back inside the shop.

What was his problem? I was the one who was freezing. "Get a grip!" I shouted. "The customer comes first."

"Go to hell!" His last words. He closed and locked the glass door and pulled down a metal gate with a clang.

Oh well. I wouldn't be renting a bike from him again, but it didn't matter. I had met Julie! I had done it! Driven a motorcycle! With my head high and my clothes sticking to me everywhere, I walked into the closest bar. I deserved the beer that was soon in my hand.

I WAS A LITTLE LOADED WHEN I inserted my hotel key into the control device on the wall in my hotel room and turned on the lights. Exhausted, thrilled, and eager to relax a little, I had bought a small bottle of whiskey and had another sip. Blech! My father used to drink whisky every night, after a few martinis before dinner and wine at the table. I didn't like whisky then and I sure didn't like it now. But he had taught me to love martinis. I still do. I headed out. Even though he would have never approved of my driving the motorcycle, I can still see a hidden smile above his bright red bow tie.

We don't always get to choose whom we love. I loved my father, sure, but I hated him too. Hated the way he treated me and hated the way he treated my mother more. I chafed under his harsh authority, and I'm sure she felt the same way. If only she had prevailed and left him for good. God knows she tried. Toward the end she had made him move out, but later relented. Then we lost her.

GALERIES LAFAYETTE

WHEN I ENTERED THE GALERIES LAFAYETTE department store, I didn't expect so much sparkle and color. A huge rotunda filled with stained glass and tiers of twinkling lights hanging from each colorful balcony made me feel as if I had walked into magic. I'd planned on spending a modest amount of money; now I wanted to buy everything. I'd just turned sixty-seven, I had a new credit card in my purse, and it was my birthday.

Fifty-plus years earlier, I'd been here with my mother. In a wink, I looked up at her and saw her striding through the store, and just like when we shopped in downtown Boston, the salesladies pulled me aside to tell me how beautiful she was.

I could see her now, my hand in hers as she lingered by the cosmetic counters, re-applying bright red lipstick when it got on her front teeth, the skirt of her shirtdress flowing behind her as she marched the aisles. We came to Europe a lot while I was a kid, and it still feels like home. My father, a scientist, spent most summers giving talks at symposiums, and we tagged along.

On three-inch heels, she stood nearly six feet tall. With her hair in an updo, even then an old-fashioned style wrapped and rolled at the back of her head, she looked regal. Heads turned as we walked in.

But not my father's. To her, she was a nobody.

Now at Galeries Lafayette, older than she would ever be, I wanted some of what she had. Could I become beautiful like her? With my straggly dirty-blond hair, thin lips like my dad, and relatively short stature? I doubted it. But I could dream, couldn't I? Isn't that why people came and shopped, to dream? Upstairs in the couture section, might I try on an Yves St. Laurent dress, black Chanel suit, or flowing Dior dress made of chiffon, or billowy skirt from one of the latest designers? Then with bags in my hands, head downstairs for a makeover? I'd come in for hand soap, but I wanted to leave transformed.

If I bought a fancy gown, I'd dress up for the ballet. Perhaps a sequined dress that hugged my bust and flowed out at my waist or a blue number slit at the thighs? On three-inch stilettos, as I made my way through the lobby at the theater? I might even have my mother's elegance.

All of that seemed too high in the sky for me. But makeup, maybe that I could do. As a teen, whenever I applied even a little lipstick, my father told me I looked like a whore. Fifty years later, his voice still rang in my head.

I perused jars of eye shadow, tubes of lipstick set up like tiny soldiers, color palettes—blue, green, purple, pink—in their tiny black-plastic cases. If only these could work the magic I was seeking. I turned away. Not for me. No, never for me.

"Madame, may I help you?" a woman asked in perfect English. I turned. A lovely middle-aged saleslady in a grand red dress, with just the right amount of lipstick and a slightly unnatural glow to her skin, smiled at me.

"I was just on my way out of the store," I said, feeling like a fool.

"I am Mademoiselle Maxine. Do you wear any makeup at all? Your skin is lovely."

How could I resist? How could I indeed?

"Please have a seat."

She was slight, delicate, and very French. I introduced myself and shook her hand.

She pressed cotton against my cheeks and eyes and asked, "Madame tell me, how do you wash your face? Do you use soap?"

"Only the best, mam'selle." Her fingers on my face felt delicious. With the lightest touch, she covered my cheeks with something cool, then something smooth, using the softest of brushes. She worked her way down to smaller brushes, then started on my eyes. I could tell something was happening.

"Take a look," she said and held up a mirror.

❧

A FAMILIAR FACE PEERED BACK AT me, but it was not my own. It was my mother's. I smiled. It was summer, 1962.

A much younger Mademoiselle Maxine grinned approval. "Do you see, madame? How beautiful you are?"

In the mirror, my long brown hair was wrapped on top of my head, parted on the left and folded just below the crown. The style was dated, but I didn't care. My lipstick, bright red, however, was all the rage, popularized by Marilyn Monroe. I was wearing a drab brown suit and my gloves were folded neatly over my alligator purse. My smile revealed two teeth out of alignment. In our early days, Henry used to say they gave me character, but he hadn't said anything like that in a long time. I used my left hand to move wisps of hair from my forehead.

"*Très belle*, madame," Mademoiselle said.

"I look so different," I said and dug into my purse.

Mademoiselle waved my hand away. "It's difficult to see someone so sad, madame. Had a bad day?"

A bad year. Maybe two, maybe three, maybe forever. I didn't think it showed. "How much do I owe you?"

She just shook her head.

"*Êtes-vous sur?*" I asked and closed my purse.

"*Rien.* Nothing," she replied. "But perhaps you might like to buy some cosmetics? Perhaps," she clucked her tongue, "a dress?"

If only. Henry said I didn't need any new dresses. What I wore was fine with him. Don't change a thing. Starting maybe in year six, maybe seven, and now, after eighteen years of marriage, there was no end to his travels for "business," for "work," for whatever came to mind. He lied constantly about his affairs.

"Madame?" Madame Maxine said. "You deserve it. Go on now."

When I told him I wanted to change my hair, he called me crazy in front of the children and even they had laughed.

"Madame, you are too lovely to wear a plain brown suit."

When I'd wanted a job, he told me that I already had one, taking care of him and the children. When he told me I was too stupid to go to college, I believed him. I'd been sad so long, I couldn't remember ever being happy.

"Go on now, buy a beautiful dress, then come show me how you look," Mam'selle Maxine said.

"*Oui,* yes, *merci bien,*" I said and gave her a kiss on each cheek.

I headed to the stairs to hide my tears.

Halfway there, I realized I was alone in Galeries Lafayette, and, better yet, digging in my purse I found Henry's Diner's Club credit card. He'd given it to me yesterday to settle a bill.

I bought everything Maxine suggested.

When I walked out of Galeries Lafayette that afternoon, I was wearing a light blue suit with a yellow and powder-blue silk blouse. I carried my old suit in a bag, shoved into the bottom, buried, almost, under tissue and my old shoes. Henry would put me first now. Heads turned as I walked outside and climbed into a hansom cab.

I found my husband pacing in the fancy lobby of our hotel on the Quai des Grands Augustins.

"What do you think?" I asked, twirling in front of him.

"You're late. You were supposed to be here an hour ago."

As if I cared. "As you can see, I was busy."

"Put that stuff away. And hurry. Alan is waiting for us."

As Henry paced, I disappeared upstairs. Alan was always in a hurry. Perhaps, this time, wearing my new suit, heels, and pearls, I'd come down the staff elevator and duck out the back. Instead of the lout I married, I'd find myself a movie star who'd stop dead in his tracks when he first saw me, and he'd tell me I was lovely, just lovely, and would I like to go for a ride in his baby-blue 1953 Aston Martin DBZ? We'd travel along the quai, along the river, and have a drink on the Isle St. Louis, and everything I'd say would make him smile and laugh, and we'd make love in his garret, the Paris lights twinkling through the windows, the moon casting shadows on our naked legs, and I'd be so happy, so very happy, and nothing could change that . . . .

The room phone rang. I picked it up.

"Eleanor!" Henry was in a froth by the time I came down. His hands were deep in his pockets, jangling change. The doorman was holding the door, his face impassive, his uniform crisp, a taxi waiting.

I took a glance down a side street. A motorcyclist, wearing a leather jacket, helmet, and chaps, roared away. Not an Aston Martin, but what the hell, I'd go with him just the same. He would work out just fine. Having a sad life at home left me with a crazy-ass imagination. Someday, somehow, someone would tell me he loved me.

We met Alan for a late lunch. Impatience aside, he was really a delightful man and I thought, for a moment, just a moment, that I'd sleep with him, maybe just once, but he kept talking to his dowdy and drab wife, and he snorted not at all quietly and drank too much and had no interest in flirting with me, even with my new Parisian look. Henry kept scowling. I didn't care. I knew how to be a professor's perfect wife, laughing at his tired jokes in front of his colleagues, when nothing about Henry was funny anymore.

Back in the hotel room, he was busy as ever, but found time to be critical, getting under my skin from the minute we walked in the door. I felt like a kid who'd broken curfew.

"You can be more supportive. It's not that hard. Make up for flirting with Alan and come to my lecture tonight. Get a cab. I'll write down the address." He took a sip of his whisky and set it down on a small table.

"I've been to dozens."

"You're my wife, for Christ's sake, you have to come. You can listen to some of the other faculty. Or you could go on the outings they have planned for the other wives."

"Those women are as dull as pigeons." That got me a funny look.

Henry was adjusting his tie. He always looked both cheerful and elegant in his bow ties.

"At least meet us for drinks after the lecture," he suggested.

Like a pig to slaughter, I thought. But I still said yes. I'd better behave. Sooner or later, I'd have to pay for my belligerence.

My life, as he expected it, circled around him. But after all the years and three kids, obedience had lost its appeal. I looked out the window of our hotel window. A slight mist hugged the air.

"See you soon," I said, and he was off.

I grabbed Henry's suit jacket and pants to take them to the concierge and, keeping the hanger on, grabbed my purse and left the hotel room. No more shopping today; I had other plans. I would take a long walk along the Seine and be back in time to grab a cab to his lecture. Halfway down the corridor, I felt the jacket slip. A small piece of paper fluttered to the floor.

It was pink. A receipt from the cleaners? At home, our dry cleaner used pink receipts and as I was a sloppy eater, they sure loved me. I picked up the paper, smelling something sweet. It certainly wasn't me; I didn't wear cheap perfume. I unfolded the paper.

"Tomorrow afternoon, my sweet. V."

I felt sick to my stomach. Another one. I shouldn't have been surprised, but I was. Perhaps because he was being so blatant. He usually was pretty discreet about these kinds of things. And in Paris too! The last time I caught him, he promised. And the time before that. I staggered, put a hand out on the opposite wall to steady myself. This time things would be different.

Where was he now? I swept back into our room and hunted through all of his papers for today's meeting agenda and location. There would be no turning back. I called the States and left a message for my lawyer.

Other women put up with affairs, but I'd had enough of them. While Henry was stationed in London designing radar during the Blitz, he sent me mushy love letters and telegrams, always telling me how much he wanted to be at my side. And now?

I changed out of my new suit and put on an old skirt, low heels, and my favorite blood-red blouse. I couldn't remember why I'd brought it to Paris, as I hardly ever wore it at home. But now, it would be perfect.

I threw his suit onto the floor, grabbed the day's itinerary, and didn't check the address until I was in a cab, heading west.

Henry was lecturing in a dull hotel. He had a bag, the red-and-white L.L. Bean tote I'd given him, beside him and was finishing up his slide show when I slipped in a side door. He acknowledged me with a curt nod and clicked his next slide.

The audience was all men, mostly in their fifties and sixties with gray or white hair. A smattering of students filled the front two rows. I passed row ten, where a man was hunched over, sleeping or dead; it made no difference to me.

When Henry put away his displays and slides, he opened the floor to questions.

I made my way down to the front row, near center, and sat in an empty seat. I pulled out the pink note, unfolded it. My palms were sweaty by the time I was ready to raise my hand. All decorum fell away; this was war.

Henry called on me last with a satisfied smile. "Yes, miss?"

Heads turned all around me. I gave them a little wave.

"Dr. Fishburne," I said, my voice loud. "You've discussed the science behind fifty years of research into ionic transport across red-blood-cell membranes."

My husband nodded.

"Given lectures all over the world—"

I heard whispers behind me.

"Get to the point," said one.

"We're going to miss cocktail hour," said another.

"Who let the girl into the lecture hall?" said a louder voice several rows back.

"Dr. Fishburne." I rose from my seat, holding the pink paper like a hideous disease. "I've attended many of your lectures, but now I can't understand. It should be so simple, but it's quite complex, isn't it?"

I was ten feet away. Henry's face had lost its shine. All eyes—all hundred-plus pairs of eyes—were on me.

I stepped up to the lectern. "I found this, this morning."

"Eleanor, please," Henry said. "We can discuss this at home."

I waved the pink paper at him.

"Colleagues, scientists, postdocs, thank you for your attention," I said.

The hall quieted down as the men leaned forward in their seats.

"Eleanor, this is neither the time nor the place."

"It's never the time or place, is it, Henry?" I drew closer to the microphone. "It's this part that I don't understand. What does this note mean, professor? 'This afternoon, my sweet. V.' Who's V., Henry? And why is your face so red?"

"Call security!" shouted one of the professors in the front row.

"Henry, please. Explain." I looked him in the eyes.

"It's not what you think, Eleanor."

"Ah, gentlemen, my husband is taking me for a fool. Don't you agree?"

At that moment, the double doors on the side exploded open and two large men, one with a white mustache, the other bald, both wearing khaki, came marching into the lecture hall. Right toward me.

I made a beeline for the curtained door at stage left.

Henry, at the lectern, looked askance at me, addressed the audience, and then the security guards. "She's crazy," he said. "Please, this is unnecessary." He held up his hands; the guards stopped short, turned around, and stood their ground.

I'd disappeared behind the curtain and, hearing nothing more, peeked around the black fabric into the hall. My husband was still standing at the lectern, but his audience was heading for the door.

That evening, I packed my bags, put on my new blue suit, hailed a cab, and went to a different hotel, where I booked a morning flight back home to Boston. I called my lawyer again and, having time to spare, found I was two blocks from Galeries Lafayette. I had something to do.

Mademoiselle Maxine was putting on her coat when I came in.

"Madame," she said, "have a good day?"

"Indeed so, *merci*," I said and looked in the mirror.

NOW, FIFTY YEARS LATER, MADAME MAXINE's face is showing her age, despite a light brushing of makeup. My pockets are full of euros and my credit card is in my name. I have all the magic I need. I buy a bar of soap for twenty euros and head to the door. Perhaps, tomorrow, I'll be stunning like my mother. Perhaps, tomorrow, I too will be beautiful.

While I was wandering around Paris, I was charmed by shop windows. Delicate and wondrous, these small worlds held captivating stories I wanted to know. The peddler with his clown shoes and puppets in his window, the chocolate shop with impossibly small musical instruments, sheet music, and a piano, all made from the confection. The shoe stores with the tennis shoes that looked like hamsters and the sexy high heels with pom-pom toes. When I walked down narrow streets and peered into each window with the sun shining over my shoulder, it took no effort at all to disappear into the worlds inside.

Hello, Human

Hemingway liked pastries. So do I. But as you can see by the shape of my belly, I haven't eaten too many. I still need suspenders to hold up my pants.

Hemingway didn't wear suspenders, and that was good. He was a hunter, which isn't good—at least from my perspective. I'm too small and yellow for monsieur to go after. Lucky for me, I'm the opposite of what you Americans call big game.

I have a watch—see? And a marvelous thin mustache like Mr. William Powell in *The Thin Man*. No, madame, as you can plainly see, I'm neither thin, nor a man. What am I? A horse? With this long face? My wife, Angelica, sometimes has a long face, but I'm afraid, my friend, if you called her a horse, she would slap you.

Hello, human.

You might be wondering why I live in a window, in front of a pastry shop, in the Marais. I didn't always live in a window, and I didn't always have suspender straps. No, no, madame, perhaps you misunderstand. I am held up by a string, but I'm not a marionette. Heavens. I can move my arms and legs on my own and take off my pants if I need to.

Six months ago, Angelica, who is as blue as I am yellow, and I were taking a stroll together through the Place du Temple, where we were admiring the lawns and trees and bridges and things. Angelica wept when we went by the sign commemorating the Jewish children who were taken during the Holocaust. Her deep purple tears made a mess of her dress, as I recall.

It had been a quiet morning, that Saturday, and a man and a woman—we don't know their names—strolled by with their dog. He was off leash, dashing around the park, breaking two cardinal rules of Parisian life: off leash and in the park. Mostly black, mostly shaggy, very big. His owners were scolding him. "Rufus! Come back here! Don't lift your leg—not there! Rufus!"

At first, Angelica and I didn't think Rufus heard very well. Then we thought he might not see us very well. But out of the corner of my eye, I saw him stalking us. I heard him growl and he bolted across the park toward us.

Angelica saw it too and ducked behind me. To try and protect her, I jumped onto her, covering her just as the mangy Rufus leapt aboard, tearing into my rear. With my soft, pliable arms, there wasn't much I could do to fight off a seventy-five-pound dog with a snout full of teeth. He bit into my buttocks and tore off my arm.

"Rufus! Rufus! Dinner!" Rufus ran off away without so much as a sidelong glance at me.

Bleeding red all over my yellow skin, I attended to Angelica first. She was bruised, poor little thing, and asked me what happened to my arm. Oh, dear God! I hadn't felt it tear at all; it was such a clean cut. Angelica and I found it in a hosta plant. The yellow stood out very well against the sea of green, as you can imagine. The blood was ghastly.

Animals like us, indeterminate but plush, do not worry too much about blood. We worry about stuffing. Angelica, as shaken as she was, found a small amount on the gravel path—thank God nothing else was missing. Together, we walked out of the park. I held Angelica's hand and she held my detached arm. My rear end was very sore.

That night and the next, Angelica tended to my wounds. She sewed up my buttocks—the whisky anesthesia did not help at all! More gently, she worked on my arm, sewing me together with two sets of stitches, the ones inside that dissolve and the ones outside that don't. She covered my wound with a blue Band-Aid. I've had it on ever since.

It took the both of us some time to recuperate. Angelica's wounds were deeper, as you might assume, after such a brutal attack. First, I was well enough to walk around our garret. Then we ventured outside. For a few days, Angelica accompanied me, but, fairly quickly, she stopped going out altogether. They call it agoraphobia. She did have the good sense to sew my gray trousers, which totally cover up my scars. In my book, no one needs to see anyone else's naked rear end.

As I grew stronger, Angelica grew weaker. Besieged by some inner demon, she didn't sleep well and kept waking up, struggling to save herself, to save me.

I took great care of myself and my precious little wife. I went back to work as an accountant for Ferguson and Company and often stopped by on my way home for some *jambon, fromage, et pain*—ham, cheese, and bread for my beloved.

The last time I saw my precious Angelica, I was in a happy mood. I'd been promoted and, feeling jaunty, ran all the way home, bounding up our five flights of stairs, my hands full of flowers.

It was not to be.

She lay on the couch, exactly where I'd left her that morning, the homemade coverlet of roses and daisies misaligned on her little body, one leg over the side of the sofa, the other caught in some unpleasant way in the corner of the couch. Her beautiful mouth—as lovely as the rosebuds I held in my hand—was caught in a rictus of the hereafter. My lover, my best friend, my sweetheart, had gone to her reward in the next world.

I hurled myself onto the floor, spraying roses everywhere. I wept uncontrollably and my eyes turned color; they've been red ever since. The landlord, Monsieur Lucas, like many a landlord in France, lives above his pastry shop. He found me a few days later and took care of my needs—and those small needs of my poor, deceased Angelica. He hung me in the window, in front of pastries, in a place of honor. A bold move, especially in Paris.

I stare at the passersby as I hang, limp and inconsolable in the window. Monsieur made me suspenders, so my pants do not fall—but you can still see my permanently sad, red eyes and the Band-Aid where Angelica fixed my arm.

They say Angelica walks by in a new form, along the sidewalk outside, and perhaps they're right. Monsieur Lucas certainly thinks so. If someday you stroll on by and I'm not here in the window, you'll know that Angelica came back, and I left with her to join the angels.

My mother always wore two- to three-inch heels. I can't imagine, not today, the aches in her feet from shoes like those. She paced after my father throughout Europe in those high-heeled shoes, chased after my brothers, stood tall and statuesque at the same level with my father. At five feet ten and in her heels, she often looked down at him as he slouched.

I wonder if she ever wore shoes like the ones I saw in the window in the Marais. Maybe she wanted to feel pretty despite him. Maybe they would have allowed her to fly.

Shoes

In a shop window in the Marais, the mirror image of my mother stares back at me. Beyond the image, a pair of sparkling three-inch tall mules with big pink pom poms are perched on top of an open box. Maybe if my mother had worn these open-toed pink silk shoes, my father would have still loved her.

If you had these three-inch-high bedroom shoes, Mom, I'd say, these pink slip-ons with pink pom poms on the toes, Dad would never take his eyes off you. You could be powerful. Kind of like Tinkerbell. Remember her? She had the same sparkling shoes, and all she had to do was lift her gossamer wings to take to the air. If you had these, you could fly too.

Well, no, you don't have gossamer wings, but you can pretend you do, can't you? Can't you just pretend to fly down the Seine, your little wings beating furiously, the Haussmann buildings spread out below? You could drop in on anyone's courtyard.

Yes, I know you know it's private property. But your feet would sparkle.

Will people think you look pretty if you wear these shoes? Will they notice you're not eighteen anymore? The sparkles will blind them. They won't see that you've filled out some. Even the men walking down the boulevards in Paris, you know the type, in their black-leather jackets, their heads would turn.

Your whole world would change if you bought these shoes. Your dainty feet would dance down the sidewalks. Even little dogs' heads would turn with the sight of your fluffy sparkling toes.

People would offer you jobs—and that's not all. They'd buy you dinners and nights out and cars. Yes, and you'd get a navy-blue Maserati, convertible of course, and if he's very good, you'd let your new boyfriend drive it while you rode along, leaning back with your feet over the door, sparkling shoes blinding everyone as you drove by.

You'd be queen in these shoes. Everyone would do what you asked. Sycophants, all. But you'd be right, see? There'd be no questions. Your authority. No, you wouldn't be a despot, you'd be a gentle leader.

In these shoes, you'd wear a crown. You'd meet the queen of England, who'd let you pet her Corgis. She'd bring you inside Windsor Castle and ask to try them on. And she wouldn't be ninety anymore, she'd be twenty like you.

Oh, the places you'd go if you had these shoes!

NASA would let you into their rockets. For the tour, of course, up high in the tower. But you wouldn't go into orbit on the space station, no, no, no, for they'd make you change your shoes.

These shoes would never hurt your feet. Your toes would have plenty of room and you'd paint your nails fire-engine red. Everyone would follow you with their eyes when you went out. You'd be invited to stroll through magnificent English gardens and have tea in the conservatory, big windows looking out over formal gardens. Little house dogs, Pekingese, would match your shoes, diamond-encrusted collars sparkling like their eyes, and you'd hold court, your ankles crossed, the pom-poms on your shoes as bright as their eyes.

You'd be in the newspaper, above the fold. You'd wear furs. You'd be the talk of the town. You'd be loved, famous, everything. Your eyes would twinkle like your toes.

Oh.

So don't say no, Mom.

Say you'd wear them.

They wouldn't have your size, you say?

They would hurt your feet, you say?

They're too expensive?

Dear me. Pay for it with Dad's American Express traveler's checks.

I should think, if you pooled all your resources, they can't be that expensive.

Your feet can't be that big.

Are you sure you wouldn't be able to fly?

Are you sure the shoes wouldn't make you beautiful?

They will make you beautiful.

Don't tell him.

Don't be sad, Mom. Look at what you can do with these shoes.

Please, take my hand.

We will imagine together. You and me.

You will have lunch with the queen.

Then have lunch with me.

You can wear these shoes. I will buy these shoes for you.

Mom? Please, Mom? Are you there?

No, Mom, please, don't disappear again.

When I was a little kid, I had a stuffed elephant named Hugo. He was gray, of course. His ears were super silky as I used to rub them all the time. I had a lot of stuffed animals, but Hugo always had pride of place; he slept next to my heart, the number-one spot. When I got a little older, my parents gave all my stuffed animals away—to give them to other children, they said, but I knew no one would love my worn-out Hugo the way I loved him. This story is for him.

Placed in the past, a time of horses and carriages, this story is about Bea, a ten-year-old girl who has just lost her mother

HUGO

When the horses pulled through the entry to the courtyard, I tightened up, squeezed my floppy-eared pet elephant Hugo more than he liked, and shut my eyes. Even though Poppa had said that moving to a new place after Momma died would be good for both of us, I didn't want to. Already, I missed Mom's blue-and-white-checked kitchen curtains, Toby next door, and especially Momma. She would not approve of our moving in order to forget her.

"I'm not ready. Hugo isn't either," I said. I peered out the window as we circled the courtyard.

"We've talked about this for weeks, Bea," Poppa said.

"This house is too big." I stroked Hugo where Mom had reattached his ear with her tiny stitches at our kitchen table. If I could go back, just one more day, I wouldn't argue with her, ever.

My father put his arm around me and frowned, crinkling the skin over his eyes. He had a small beard, which I wasn't crazy about, because it was full of gray streaks. "My little Bea, it'll get better, you'll see."

"I don't think so," I mumbled.

The horses snickered as the carriage circled the courtyard and stopped at a door, one of many.

"Our apartment's on the top floor. Aunt Doris is one flat below and across, near the entry arch, is Professor Fourier. Do you remember him from our Christmas dinners? His family lives in Nice now, and he's alone teaching mathematics at the Sorbonne. He said you can visit him anytime."

"And his dog Brandy? You sure? I bet she doesn't remember me."

"Of course she does. And remember, if you wish to walk her, please ask him first."

"Can I do it today?"

"After we unpack, if it's okay with him."

Hugo didn't want to wait and neither did I. Everything about the place seemed unfamiliar, even though we'd visited Aunt Doris, Momma's sister, here many times. Now, I needed a soft muzzle under my hand, even if Brandy wanted to eat Hugo.

Edward, our footman, opened the carriage door. I could see the dark circles under his eyes, just below the rim of his cap. He missed Momma too. I took his hand and stepped down onto the cobblestone in the courtyard.

"You remember that marble staircase, Bea? It goes all the way to our floor, the fifth, at the top," Poppa said. "I'm sure Hugo would like to see the view."

Poppa handed me the key. I tucked Hugo under my arm and told him he was going to be all right. He'd never liked exploring. Maybe this time he'd change his mind.

I ran up the stairs, two at a time. The faster I could get there, the sooner I could tuck in with Hugo and go back to my book about the princess who could fly.

Poppa came up after me, his heavy boots clanging on the stone staircase. I was struggling with the key, as I wasn't about to put Hugo down. Poppa helped me and the large front door creaked open.

The empty rooms looked barren and sad.

But when he opened the shutters, sunlight came pouring through the windows. Hugo perked up too. A little, anyway.

Poppa left me in what would be my room. I looked out at the chimney pots of the Paris rooftops. I stepped outside onto a small balcony and set Hugo to rest on the railing. All gray and white with a round tummy and small warm eyes. Hugo's enormous ears were a little ragged and wonderfully soft. I watched him admire the view, and then I didn't see him anymore. He fell!

I leaned over the railing. It was a long way down. I expected to see him all torn up, missing an ear or something, but he'd landed in a pot of yellow flowers, and I knew he was okay when he waved.

I flew down the stairs, reached the doorway, ran out into the courtyard, and spied a bunch of flowerpots full of pink, white, and yellow flowers.

I saw that my father had returned to the courtyard to help Edward with unpacking the carriage. He saw me running.

"Everything okay, Beatrice?" he called out.

"Right as rain," I answered. I took off behind the carriage where the horses were still snorting and huffing from the cold.

Ten feet, five feet, two feet, I was finally at the flowerpots, the ones full of yellow flowers, but there was no Hugo.

Instead, a girl with long braids was cradling him. I was sure he was cooing under her hands. That Hugo had no shame.

"You could hurt your elephant by throwing him out the window," the girl said. Then I saw that Hugo's head flopped over and his legs swung lifelessly under the girl's hands.

"I didn't throw him. He fell," I said. "Please, give him back."

"You toss all your stuffed animals out the window? Maybe you throw your clothes out too—and I bet your friends too. Hugo's crying. I'm keeping him." She started walking away.

"Wait, no!" I chased her. She was a foot taller. "He's mine!" I reached out for Hugo but only grabbed one soft ear before she pulled him away.

"Finders keepers, losers weepers," the girl said.

"No, no, no!" The delicate threads that Momma had used to repair Hugo's ear broke one, two, three, and I held his ear while the girl raised Hugo high above her head.

"He's mine now!" she shouted, limping across the courtyard. She popped inside a door and slammed it behind her.

I stood there, stunned. The horse and carriage had been taken to the stables. My father, finished with the unpacking, had gone upstairs to put things away. Only a small stack of suitcases and footlockers remained by the main door.

"I'm so sorry, Hugo," I said to his ear, kissing it and tucking it inside my shirt. Then I ran back across the courtyard full speed and went to her door. It was locked.

Even though Poppa had always told me to be polite and not go where I wasn't wanted, I didn't care. I pounded on it.

"You took my elephant, you horrible girl! Give him back!" Tears coursed down my face. Hugo didn't like missing an ear, not one bit.

I shouted, rang the bell over and over, and yelled really loudly until, at last, a second-story window opened. A woman, as old as my grandmother, peered out and screamed, "Stop that infernal racket!"

"But she has my Hugo!" I yelled back.

A man, three stories up, stared out his own window and leaned on the railing. "Be quiet, Madame Bersoulet! Mind your own business for a change!"

Below him, the old woman shut her window with a bang.

The man was the only chance I had. I yelled as loud as I could. "There's a girl who lives in this building. She took my elephant!" I couldn't hold up his ear; it was just too sad. "She's a little taller than I am. Brunette. And mean. Do you know a girl like that? Could you help me, please?"

"Ah, Nadine," the man said with a sigh. "She's on four. Go to the front door and I'll let you in." After the longest time I heard footsteps on the other side, and a man, wearing all black, let me in. Once I got inside, he turned without saying anything and headed up the stairs. I followed him. It was another marble staircase just like in my section of the large building. He disappeared down a hallway, and I was ready to follow him until he turned and waved me away. "Up, up, up!" he said with a frown, slammed his apartment door, and disappeared. Now I wasn't so sure I should be here. Poppa wouldn't like this at all.

At the next landing, I heard footsteps coming down the stairs. Was it the awful Madame Bersoulet? I tucked myself behind a doorway.

A man appeared. He was wearing a black suit and tight jacket, had long hair, and was holding a cane.

"I'm Monsieur Friant. Nadine's upstairs. You say she took your elephant?"

I nodded through my tears.

I followed him, slowly, taking my time. Hugo's ear was in my pocket. I stroked it as I climbed. And prayed, just a little bit.

On the fourth floor, monsieur knocked on the door with the number, 4C.

"Mam'selle Pomfret! Is Nadine home?" the man called. "She's taken something she shouldn't have. I'm sure she made a mistake. Madame?"

Though I stood ten feet back, I could still hear chairs slide across wooden floors inside the apartment.

"Fifty centimes." The door opened a crack, through which a slender hand appeared. "That's all we ask. New girls in town shouldn't throw their things out windows."

The man stared at the hand and shoved his own hand into his pocket.

He cleared his throat. "Madame, two days ago I gave you a croissant and some cheese. Last week, it was some wine. Perhaps you can relent a little and give back what Nadine has taken. It's just a stuffed elephant."

Just a stuffed elephant? I felt bad for Hugo, started to say something, and hesitated. "It's my elephant." Tears pushed at my eyelids. "My best friend."

"Twenty centimes, monsieur. We haven't had anything to eat since yesterday."

I approached and tried to look inside.

"Please, stand back," monsieur ordered. He dug for change, extended a hand. The hand went to grab the money, but monsieur wouldn't let go.

In a flash the door opened wide, and Hugo came flying toward my head. I caught him just as he was about to drop down the stairs.

For a second, I caught a glimpse inside the apartment, a studio. Mattress on the floor. Piles of clothes in a corner. Junk, boxes, and dust everywhere.

"You stand there anymore, monsieur," Madame Pomfrey shouted from the crack in the door, "and I will call the cops!" She slammed the door.

Behind him, I heard more yelling. "Nadine, you can't go 'round stealing things. That's the fourth time this week." Then I heard a slap and someone crying.

I followed monsieur down the stairs, holding Hugo in one hand and his ear in the other, and covered him with kisses. "Thank you, thank you," I said to monsieur.

At the second floor, he turned and looked at me, his face grave. "I'm sure Hugo does not like being thrown out windows, little girl. Don't do it again." He turned to his apartment, entered, and closed the door behind him.

By the time I got back to the courtyard, I was crying. Crying for Nadine, for Hugo, and for me. Moving was hard. I missed my mom. Halfway to our door, I heard Poppa calling my name.

"Beatrice! Beatrice! Where have you been?"

"I'm right here," I said and folded myself into his arms. "There was this horrible girl, and she stole Hugo. I had to get her back."

"You left without telling me or saying anything to anyone. Never do that, Bea. No matter what."

"But she stole my Hugo."

He thought a moment. "Stole Hugo? How could she possible steal Hugo?"

"She . . . she . . ." I couldn't bear to repeat the story. "She just did!"

He smiled at me. "Are you okay? Is Hugo okay?"

"Can you fix his ear?" I asked, holding back sniffles.

"Ask Edward."

That afternoon, I sat on a bale of hay in the tackroom while Edward, squinting hard, poked and prodded at Hugo until his ear was reattached. Not as good as Momma, at all, and Hugo looked a little lopsided, but he was whole. Edward hadn't hurt him one bit.

I told Edward about the girl across the courtyard. He nodded, pulled out some neatsfoot oil and rubbed down his bridles and reins. "You know, Bea, you have lots of things. Sounds like that girl could use a friend."

"Won't be me!" I cried.

Ten minutes later, I was standing in the courtyard, feeling strangely at odds. Hugo was inside my shirt. Part of me wanted to go back up my stairs to find out what happened to the princess in my book, but a nagging feeling kept coming up and bugging me. What if, what if, Bea, what if . . .

I went to Professor Fourier's apartment, where he talked about his childhood in the country, and he allowed me to take Brandy for a walk. Holding her leash, after I'd had all the kisses one kid could handle, I knocked on the door of the apartment next door.

"Can Nadine come out and play?" I asked, holding out a fresh baguette, a part that Brandy hadn't chewed.

Again, a slender hand slid out and took my offering. A moment later, the door opened wider. A bruise was turning blue just above Nadine's eye.

I didn't say anything. But I held out Hugo.

"If you want him, he's yours," I said, holding back tears.

That night, I felt the hollow from Hugo's pillow. I missed the touch of his soft belly.

Passing the pillow, I reached my hand to the foot of the bed and touched Brandy's wire-haired flank. Monsieur Fourier said I could keep Brandy as long as I needed. I loved the sound of her soft snores and the way her paws twitched while she was dreaming. I hoped Hugo was dreaming and thinking about his momma too.

A few days later, Monsieur Fourier headed out of town with Brandy. I was taking out the garbage for Poppa when I thought I saw something gray in the building's trash. I shuddered, held my nose, and reached one hand past a mess of greasy paper, eggshells, and coffee grounds. There was Hugo, much the less for wear, greasy, covered with something black above his nose. I brought him home, cleaned him up, and set him on the bed on top of some of my pillows, so he could recover. I couldn't understand why Nadine had thrown him away. I covered him with kisses.

Two weeks later, when Brandy came home, he went for Hugo. I grabbed Hugo and was about to put him high on a shelf when I heard a noise from the courtyard and turned.

A policewoman was taking Nadine's mother away. I wanted to run down the stairs and make them leave her alone. Father stopped me at the front door. "Not your business, Bea."

"But Nadine, she'll be all alone," I said. Hugo was in my arms, crying.

"Her aunt is taking her in," he said. A beautifully dressed woman came down Nadine's stairs. Nadine followed, kicking at planters in the courtyard. Kicking at the woman's feet.

"I can't go! Not without Hugo!"

"The carriage is waiting, Nadine."

"Mom threw him away! He's right there! I know it. I'll just be a sec— "

"Nadine, NO. We don't dig in the garbage!" She grabbed Nadine's arm.

Nadine shrank inside herself. "I hate you."

"Going to the country will be good for you, Nadine."

"But I can't go without HUGO!"

"I'll be right back, Pop," I said, and shot down the stairs. But I was too late. By the time I got to the door, a carriage was taking Nadine away. I could hear her crying all the way out to the avenue.

All little girls dream of their wedding day. Although my real wedding day was not at all what I had imagined—my father refused to come— my big day was not quite as bad as the one I saw in Paris, where a soaking wet bride and her wedding party ran out of the park past me toward a church in the pouring rain, while I waited, snug, warm, and dry, for a bus.

Twenty minutes earlier, under a cloudless sky, the same group had entered the park, carrying hope and love and coolers and chairs and flowers, the whole party as one, until a girl, dressed in blue jeans and a ratty sweater, dashed across the street behind them, hollering for them to wait.

I imagined myself as that girl, Jean Marie, late to a party to which she had never been invited, the wedding of her ex-best friend.

Parc des Buttes Chaumont

"Hey. Wait for me." I muttered, never intending them to hear me.

Gabrielle, my ex-best friend and her new best friend, Misty, were standing way too close together at the entrance to Parc des Buttes Chaumont across the street from my bus stop. If Gabrielle had heard me across three lanes of traffic, it would be a miracle. Listening had never been her strong suit.

This was my park, not Gabrielle's. I was the one who introduced her to it, who took her to the top of a hill where all of Paris fell away beneath us. Only last month, we'd enjoyed the stunning landscape—buttes, waterfalls, hidden caves—and followed narrow paths through woodlands opening up to sweeping vistas. The sound of birds hadn't been our only music; the dulcet tones of Gabrielle, a friend I'd had since high school, had comforted my bruised heart that day. Fired from a job once again, I turned to her and she told me I'd be all right, and I loved her for it. Now, I watched her hug Misty, and I hated the place.

Oh, Gabrielle looked pretty as a cupcake and all, with fuchsia flowers and pink ribbons cascading down her dress. Flowers clung to her hair, and she fairly dripped with white veils and trains. But deep under that flowery confection, she wore Spanx, lots of Spanx. I should know; we used to work out together every Tuesday.

Now, her friends, her new friends, the bridesmaids, caught up with her. Everyone was all a-flutter. They were wearing garden-party colors, not the party part, the garden part—tangerine, ruby, pink fluffy dresses with hot-pink ribbons and bright-red flowers. A bunch of purple and pink flowers fluttering in the wind. A bunch of weeds.

The sky above was darkening. I hoped it would rain.

As for me, I was wearing my too-tight blue jeans, the ones cropped real low, and I would've had flowers too, but that goddamned Gabrielle had disinvited me to her wedding.

I'd been in a fine old mood when her wedding invitation showed up in my email. I was more than a little taken aback. Gabrielle and I had turned into enemies when she'd taken up with my boyfriend Jacques a month or so before, so I called her, and what did she say? "Oh, I made a mistake. I didn't mean to invite you." Then she laughed and hung up.

That laugh rang in my head as I watched her hug her friends.

A bunch of men joined them, Jacques in the lead. He was chatting with his brother Marty. They were wearing black suits and fuchsia ties and looked like a couple of penguins out for a morning swim. It was a different look for Jacques. I was accustomed to seeing him wearing baggy blue jeans with holes in the knees and muscle shirts, showing off his tats.

He'd been my main squeeze for the last year and a half and had even popped the question, sort of, while he was drunk and lying across my body under the moonlight here in the Eleventh arrondissement in Paris. Light had come through the garret window, and he'd mumbled he'd like to get married.

My eyes had popped open, and I hadn't been able to sleep all night. Dad would be pleased as heck, and as far as Mom went, she'd come to Paris, finally, approve of me, and I could show her around.

But in the morning, when I reminded Jacques, he denied ever saying it. I pressed him. "You're crazy. I'm not the marrying kind," he said.

So imagine my surprise two weeks later when I wandered into my favorite tabac and saw Jacques and Gabrielle chatting over some butter cookies. "We ran into each other. What a treat," they said cheerfully.

How stupid did they think I was?

Jacques stopped calling me after that. I texted him, I followed him on Facebook, I tracked him down to Gabrielle's building near Place Republique, and I watched him follow her through her door at midnight.

Now, I crossed the Boulevard into Parc des Buttes Chaumont, keeping my distance. A hundred yards ahead under a darkening sky, he marched at the head of the line, as happy as I'd ever seen him.

The wedding party seemed to go on forever. Twenty, forty, eighty people? I lost count. Bride and bridesmaids in front, groom and groomsmen following, and behind, a mass of family and friends carrying tables, chairs, bins of food, bunches of flowers, more chairs. None of them looked back at me. I walked freely now, fifty feet behind, crushing fallen rose petals flat as I followed them.

The minister, dressed in black, was at the end of the parade, talking to one of the mothers. He wore a wide black hat and had a distinguished air, even as he hurried, almost running, to keep up, his long skirts hindering his ability. He walked with itty-bitty steps and sweated even though it was kind of a cool day. Gabrielle must've found him at Central Casting.

Behind him came a small brass band—trombonist, trumpet player, and clarinetist. Jacques had never liked jazz. Was this another way Gabrielle had tricked him? How had she gotten him to pop the question when he'd just been with me?

They set up in a circle near a pond.

"Gabrielle!" I waved.

Gabrielle's and Jacques's mothers and fathers heard me and turned. The minister, lost in thought, wandered over to one of the tables and grabbed a tomato.

Gabrielle swept her white train around her back, stood super straight, and stared.

"Jean-Marie, didn't think you could make it," she said, a forced smile cracking her makeup.

"Couldn't miss the wedding of my best friend," I said, leaning back and hooking my fingers into the belt loops of my blue jeans. "Hi, Jacques! How's it hanging?"

He tipped his head toward Marty.

"Yo," I said, stepped forward, and put out my hand.

Marty didn't move.

"I don't have syphilis or anything like that, Marty, so it's okay, you can shake my hand." The groomsmen straightened their ties and moved one step closer to the bride.

"Go on, don't let me slow you down," I said.

The minister, hearing some conversation, turned around, removing a Bible from his pocket. The sun crossed behind another dark cloud.

"And how's with you? Aren't you kinda hot in that black coat?" I asked him.

"Hey, Jean-Marie, don't. Just don't," Jacques mumbled.

"Now, we are gathered together," the minister intoned.

Marty came close to me and whispered, "Go on now, Jean-Marie, you made your point. This is not your day."

"What do you mean, not my day?"

The wedding party stepped back.

"What's not to like about weddings?" I asked. "Good food, great drinks, good weather, huh?"

The clouds overhead gathered together, obscuring all blue. And suddenly I didn't feel so good. I stepped back—hurt, of course, resentful, of course, but I felt so stupid, I wanted to die.

The first crack of thunder brought me to my knees. The second crack caught me crumbling. As the wind roared, rain came lashing down, pelting us like a fever. The third crack brought hail. Lightning flashed across the sky and I fell.

I don't remember much after that.

I came to at the bus stop. People formed a circle around me. They were covered in dripping fuchsia, pink, red, all bleeding from their ribbons as their clothes clung to their skins like shrouds.

"It was too much for her," Jacques said. "Gabrielle, warm up her hands, she's still shivering."

They came into focus, gradually. I didn't know how twenty people, soaking wet, could jam themselves into a bus stop made for five, but I saw all their faces. Streaks of purple, pink, and red swirled before my eyes.

A siren wailed in the distance.

"Do you think she was struck by lightning?" Gabrielle asked, placing one cool hand on my cheek. "She's breathing kind of fast."

"She'd be dead," Jacques said.

"Not necessarily," Gabrielle said. "I'm a nurse. I should know."

"Her sneakers saved her," Jacques said. "The rubber."

The minister stepped forward. "Anything I can do?" he asked. "Last rites?"

Did he really say that? I panicked.

"Give her air, please." A new face, a paramedic in uniform, looking officious, appeared and I placed my faith in him. He took my pulse, blood pressure, even tested my reflexes.

I whispered in his ear. "I'm okay," I said. "I just couldn't stand to hear Gabrielle say yes."

"Did it work?" he wanted to know.

I'd like to say it did, but it didn't. I wanted to say I was sorry, but I wasn't. They got married for real, a week later, and didn't invite anybody.

When I was in high school complaining about how hard math was, my father used to tell me that it was easy. I always felt there was something wrong in my brain where math was concerned, so when I went back to school (in my thirties) to become an engineer, I had to take an arithmetic placement test and I failed. My father had been right. However, guided by a kind teacher, I practiced and practiced. When I got my first A in math, I thought it was a fluke. When I got my fifth, I thought I was onto something. When I graduated six and a half years later, summa cum laude, I stood proud. This story is dedicated to Bart Sarkis, that kind math teacher, who always believed in me.

THE CODE BREAKER

"IF I LOSE THIS PAPER, I'LL never find my Simone again," the older man next to me groaned as he struggled to bend down to reach the floor.

I picked up the orange note he'd dropped and passed it to him. "Thank you," he said.

The Métro train lurched and stopped between stations. The lights flickered out, then went back on, but the train didn't move. I was on my way to Gare D'Austerlitz before heading for the countryside, the Loire Valley. I'd allowed an hour for a ten-minute ride to the station and had plenty of time.

The man had white hair and gnarly hands and tucked the note close to his gray vest. "I'm Bernard," he said. "It's hard for me to move; old age is a bitch, isn't it?"

"I know what that's like," I said.

Arthritic knobs had been growing on my fingers for years and were not going away. I couldn't make a complete fist with my right hand and wondered how long it would take until I lost the ability with my left.

Every year, I tried to push back time. Every year, I failed. There was plenty of gray in my hair and stiffness in my gait in the morning.

"Miss." He cleared his throat. Words came out in a rush. "Please. Help me. My granddaughter didn't come home last night. She left this paper for me. She usually leaves notes to let me know where she is and when she'll be back. But this time is different." The lines on his forehead deepened into canyons.

He held out the note.

All I could see were large black letters. I wondered what they said.

"Make any sense to you?"

The train squealed as it started and went around a corner. Daylight splashed the tunnel walls as we rose to cross the Seine.

"She doesn't have to be so difficult. Who does she think she's fooling? An old man, I guess. I'm pretty sharp, normally. I do the Sunday *Times* crossword, in ink, for Chrissake."

"Can I take a look?" I asked, leaning toward him.

"She thinks she's so clever," Bernard muttered. "This time she went too far."

"How old is she?" I asked. A searcher myself for Une Petite Adventure, I could understand not wanting to go home to my grandfather too.

"Twenty," he said. "My Simone's twenty. I've raised her since her mother went to a cult in Northern California when she was six."

"Simone didn't want to go with her parents?" I asked, incredulous.

"She was in first grade," he said. "Now, about to go to college. And no, no parents, not really. Her father split when she was born and her mother, Louise, she was preoccupied."

I looked out the window, at the rain beating down.

He turned to me and frowned. "Now, are you going to help me or not? It's too early to go to the police. They'll probably just laugh at me or call me a dirty old man or some such shit."

The train pulled into the station and we both walked off. My train to the country was just downstairs and departed at one. It was now noon. "Let me see if I can help you."

We walked over to a bench and sat down not far from the open track door. Outside, rain thundered onto the tracks.

He handed the paper to me. The letters were familiar: K Ca Sc Ti V Cr Mn.

"It's the beginning of the fourth line of the Periodic Table," I said without hesitation. "I took chemistry. It's a mnemonic we had to memorize. Potassium, Calcium, Scandium, Titanium, Vanadium, Manganese. Or Kings Can't Screw 'til Virgins Create Men."

"My granddaughter's missing and you're making fun of me."

"That was not my intention. I'm sorry," I said. His face was full of despair.

"Had Simone taken chemistry too?" I asked.

"Of course. Physics, calculus, dynamics—she loves school. Why would she write that?" he asked. "My Simone is pretty clever, but she wouldn't do anything like this. Staying out all night, forgetting to call. Not like her at all."

"So why would your granddaughter leave that note? She trying to mess with you?"

"Simone's a good girl."

"I'm sure she is," I said, feeling sorry for the guy.

"Has she stayed out before?"

"No, never."

"Does the code mean anything to you?"

"No, nothing."

"Let's try, together. If you can do that crossword, you know all about puzzles. Let's start with K, Kings, Potassium."

"The Sun King," he said.

I checked my cell phone for information. "He had a dozen illegitimate children."

"Simone's not pregnant, if that's what you mean."

"He had Versailles built," I said.

"You think Simone's gone to Versailles? The train leaves just downstairs."

"Hold on, let's keep trying a sec," I said. "How 'bout Ca?"

"Can't? Simone would never say can't."

"Maybe that means she told him she couldn't go to Versailles," I guessed.

Bernard leaned back against the wall of the station.

"Sc. Scandium. Screw," I added.

He frowned. "Now you say she's sleeping around?" he said. "I suppose she might be. Young people have nothing but sex on their minds."

He was so fragile looking.

"What's her favorite place? A park, a café? A bridge? Is there a bridge named after Louis the Fourteenth?"

"No."

"Well, let's keep going with the mnemonic, shall we? 'Til?" I asked. "Was she about to do something? Was she waiting for something?"

"For the king to come, yes, she was waiting for the king to call her, so she'd say yes."

"Now, you're giving *me* a bad time," I said. "I'm only trying to help you."

"I should've stayed home and died. Right there in front of my television, in the middle of a talk show. I wouldn't be bothering anyone, and Simone could do whatever she damn well pleases."

"Mn. Men."

"That's what they all say. Men. Nothing but trouble. And they don't tell the truth, either."

"She have a lover? A boyfriend?"

"No one she told me about," he frowned. "But I wouldn't mind. Why couldn't she tell me? I just want to know she's all right."

He grabbed my arm. "You have children, miss? Do you worry about them?"

"Always, yes," I said, gently extracting his hand from my arm. He had a tight grip, that was for sure. "Two," I said. "And they don't always tell me where they're going, either."

A train came in with a hiss of air brakes, then rolled away again with a squeal.

"If I died in front of the TV, without Julie, it would take a week before anyone would notice I was gone. Mrs. Pouce, the baker at the patisserie downstairs, she'd be the first to notice. 'Where's Bernard? He needs his pain de chocolat.' She'd tell her fat husband and he'd tell her to let it go. 'You worry too much, Françoise,' he'd say, and another day would go by before she wondered again."

"Bernard, I'm sure Simone's fine," I said, noticing his agitated look.

"The lady next door with the little white dog, he'd piss on my door and they'd call the concierge. The concierge would come to my door, clean up the mess, and scold my neighbor. No one would bother with me at all."

"Bernard!"

"They'd find me a week later. 'He died of a broken heart,' the concierge would say, and Madame Pouce, she'd slug her husband and call him names. 'All for a pain de chocolate, Michel, you fat pig. You never care for anyone but yourself.'"

I jolted him out of his sadness. "You're not dying, Monsieur Bernard."

"But my heart is, *ma cherie*. I'm not ready to let Simone go. My heart is breaking."

"It's tough," I said, pressing the paper back into his hands.

Bernard wept. His shoulders shook; he held his cap in his hand.

Another train came into the station, another hiss of brakes, another bunch of people getting off, another whoosh as it left. I had to start thinking about making a move if I was going to make my train downstairs. A young woman came onto the platform, yelling into her cell phone.

"Grandpa!" the girl shouted. "Answer your phone!" Noticing me, she stopped quickly, then looked from me to the old guy sitting on the bench.

"Grandpa! I've been trying to reach you for hours." This time her voice was lower but still held power. She ran to the bench.

Bernard, coming to for a moment, looked up from his hat, from weeping, and stared at the figure coming toward him and smiled. "You left this code. We were trying to figure it out."

"Granddad!" the girl said sharply. "That's just a silly thing from chemistry class. Why in God's name did you wander off this time? Lucky I found you."

"Louise," he asked, "is that you?"

"It's Simone, Grandpa. Louise is . . ." she sputtered.

"Your mother said she'd be here at four," he said, glaring at his watch. "She's late."

We love and hate our parents, at the same time. I could say I always hated my father, but that's not entirely true. He taught me a few things, despite my best intentions. Aside from his love for science, art, travel, and women, he loved poetry. So when I saw a stuffed teddy bear sitting next to a typewriter in a store window in Paris, the name of one of my father's favorite poets, Ezra Pound, popped into my mind.

THE TEDDY BEAR

My name is Ezra Pound. I'm a teddy bear. As you can see by my faithful companion, my typewriter, I'm a literary type. Do not be disappointed; this cardboard box is only a temporary friend. My garret is in the Sixteenth arrondissement. I could tell you that my studio is being painted, but the truth is, it's hard to climb the stairs up to the second floor. Fortunately for me, Monsieur Souvien, the owner of this store, has made me welcome. So my new home is in this window.

Pardon me for avoiding your eyes, Madame Nina, and staring off into the distance, but a beautiful woman is walking down the street—heels, fur coat, of course sunglasses, and a large hat with an enormous red ribbon. I can't take my eyes off her. If I offend you, I am sorry. All the beautiful women come down the street in this direction. Not that you are not beautiful, Nina, but those young ladies, those mademoiselles, they do draw attention, do they not? Sometimes my neck gets stiff. Enough about me. What about you?

You're from America? Tourist or expat?

Oh, I see, tourist. *Merveilleuse.*

You spend your days looking in shop windows and taking photographs. What an odd idea. When I was much younger, the shop windows were quite pretty with snow scenes, miniature people, horses and carts, and sometimes trains. But this shop has been bought and sold two or three times over the generations, so we're left with these dumb cardboard boxes. But I'm here! Pretty? Maybe not, but interesting, *n'est-ce pas?*

Certainly, you've noticed that I'm a bit chubby? You think all teddy bears are chubby? Not true. Once, a long time ago, I was skinny—no reason to imagine it, you'll make me feel bad—but now, more round. Madame, with me, you see what you get and I get tubby. I don't get out much.

I've had a tough life. I do not ask much of you, but please, listen, just for a minute or two. I haven't always lived in a window. I got in with some shady characters years ago—they wanted my soul! Of course, they couldn't find it, so they took out my heart instead. I can be loved, but I can't, shall I be so bold as to say, love back? Shall I show you the scar? No. Never mind, then. Fur covers a multitude of sins. But they broke me when I wanted to leave them. Teddies are a loyal bunch, as you can imagine. All that cuddling!

Anyway, after I relieved myself of command as leader of the bad boys, I went to the States, where they imprisoned me. They called it a hospital. I called it a prison. I couldn't leave, so what else would you call it? I went crazy! I had no choice, mind you. At the hospital, after many years, they finally let me go. For whatever reason, I can't tell you—only that maybe they gave up on trying to make me sane.

Then I came back to France and tried to contact the new leaders of the bad boys, but they turned their back on me. And laughed. And now, I wave at the pretty girls and wish I could be proud of who I was then, but I cannot.

No, I was not a teddy bear then. They say poetry makes the man. I've written a lot of poetry. But I've never looked to help my common man.

God has a weird sense of humor, don't you think? And he loves teddies. Do you think he's a Steiff man? Well, I don't have a clip in *my* ear, as they all do. I have only this scar. Oh no, don't worry, they gave me back my heart. It's just changed, somehow.

Let me tell you a story. It was late, in Paris, the night I left my garret with a sheaf of notices—broadsides—created by the bad boys. My job was to distribute the flyers all over Paris, plaster them to lampposts, fences, stone walls. I had a bottle of paste in one hand and a hundred missives in the left pocket of my great coat. Yes, I needed my coat; it was very cold.

For some reason, I found myself down on the quai by Canal St. Martin, a place I don't recommend for the safety-minded. It was getting dark, but the lights weren't on. Another strike— you've heard of them in Paris, I'm sure. I was pasting these flyers along the wall and nearing the tunnel and locks leading to the Seine. I turned back to return up the stairs whence I'd come, a pair of eyes watching me from the bridge above. He was dressed all in black, like a cat. Coming through the tunnel were several other men, wearing watch caps and coming my way. I headed back up the quai, shoving my hands into my pockets, trying to keep the papers from crinkling and making noise. There were no indentations in the stone wall alongside the quai. No place to hide.

Two men were walking down the stairs. I froze. That made three. And me. A mere poet! A firebrand, but a poet, nonetheless. Two more of them now and I was surrounded. Five against one! They started closing in before I could get it all figured out.

"Pound, Ezra Pound," I said, putting out my hand. I could talk the legs off a gazelle, if they gave me a chance, but they all spoke at once and came in for the kill. One grabbed my great coat, another the glue, and a third found my leaflets.

One of them, the largest, turned me around. "No care for the little man, eh, Pound? Fascist pig," he spat.

They spun me until I was dizzy. Then they splattered the stone with glue and pressed my face, hands, and body onto the cold, sticky wall.

"We fought the war to kill all you fascists, yet here you are. Cover him, boys!"

They painted me all over with glue and covered me with flyers. The largest one even took my shoes and socks and glued my feet to the pavement. Then they all ran.

That was a dark night for me—shall I say, my darkest? The glue hardened quickly. My face froze. My hands and bare feet lost feeling. I grew stiff and the pain from not being able to move was unbearable. I cried out for mercy. I cried out for God. At two in the morning, I fainted from the pain and fear. When I woke up, everything was worse, if that was possible. At four I fell into a fitful sleep.

At five, when it was still dark, soft hands touched my shoulders. Whispers filled my ears. Soft caresses. Hands ran over my back, soothing my muscles, though other hands were exploring my pockets. I waited impatiently for my long-deserved freedom. Only a minute, two at most, I could wait for my prayers to be answered.

Two minutes turned to three. Their voices hushed. Sunlight started to break over the tunnel. They were gone, my wallet and money with them.

God came with the sunlight at least. At least He said he was God. Who was I to disagree?

"I'm not a bad guy," I said. "Just a poet."

"Well-known for treason, Ezra Pound," God said. "Honoring fascists."

"They're friends of my sister's. They said they loved me," I stuttered.

In the approaching light, God didn't look like what I'd imagined. Of course, he had long hair, a long beard, and a robe. But hairy feet? I was surely delusional by then; I imagined his sandals were fur.

He placed his cool hand on my forehead. It was soft, like a baby's, covered with fuzz.

"I'll free you if you relinquish their world of hate," God said, cackling.

That made me feel very peculiar. I didn't know God laughed—at least not like that.

He pressed his palm against my face, softer now. "You'll be all right, Ezra. Just breathe normally. This won't hurt a bit."

To remove me from my sticky prison would hurt a lot, I was sure of it. I'd been there all night and would be there forever if he didn't release me. I winced.

An arm around my waist, a whisper in my ear, and pop. I was free of the wall. My skin stung as feeling returned.

"No more broadsides," God said, looking at me. His eyebrows were so thick. Fur burst from his ears like one of my teachers in grade school.

"How can I thank you, my Lord?" I asked and kneeled.

"You are one of God's chosen, Ezra. You may go free now."

As I stood up, I almost fell over. I'd always been a svelte man, but now I had a big round belly and I had to lean back a little to keep my balance. What had happened to me?

"I always take a little for Myself," He said, walked toward the water, and disappeared.

The sun was casting bright rays down the cobblestone quai. Flyers were stuck to the walls at odd angles, but none were stuck to me. The wind was up, making them flutter. I went to pull one from the wall, but my hands were different now; they didn't move like before. Was it the glue? Fat brown pads had formed where my fingers had been. I could barely grasp the papers, much less pull them free.

I squinted at the sun, looked down the quai and toward the stairs. My legs, once long and lanky, were now stubby and covered with fur; I would never have the strength to climb those stairs.

I ambled down the quai anyway, toward the tunnel, toward the Seine. I remembered the ramp from my walk earlier in the week. I could do a ramp. Halfway into the tunnel, fatigue overcame me, and I sat down, much as I am doing now, and rested. For a day and a half, or two days, maybe three, I sat there. I lost track of time. At some point, monsieur picked me up.

"You poor bear, you poor teddy bear," he muttered and held my hand tight. He picked me up and gave me a squeeze. "Would you like to live in my window?"

I've been here ever since.

The teddy bear in the window wasn't the only one who told me stories.
A block from my hotel on a small side street, just outside the Marais, sandwiched between a pizza place and the back of a bakery, a cobbler's window filled with dusty shoes and leather straps and laces, along with several pairs of enormous bright yellow, green, and red clown shoes, held magic of a different sort. What would it be like, I wondered, to have been a clown?

The Clown

I'm a clown. At least, I was. Does one give up being a clown? I don't think so.

See those big red shoes? Those are mine. Monsieur Catalan is saving them for me for when I'm ready to return to the circus. He's a cobbler and my best friend. He loves the circus. It's just up the street, see? Cirque d'Hiver, a block away at Place de la République, open only in winter.

I used to wear those shoes. And if you think they're easy to walk in, you're sorely mistaken. Look at how long and big they are. Size forty-five. They flop around. You have to be so careful. You might say that for a clown, more falls are better—as long they're planned, mon ami. Unexpected falls are the worst. I broke my arm that way once, at a rehearsal in Winter Park, Florida—the winter home of my former employer, Ringling Bros. and Barnum & Bailey Circus. I needed surgery, but monsieur—the big boss—said we didn't have time for me to see the doc before our next gig, so I went on, face paint covering my pain. It healed crooked. Want to see?

Being a clown is in my blood. I come from a long line. My grandfather, Henri, and my father, Pierre, came before me.

Grandfather started in the small towns in France, where the circus came to town by horse-drawn wagons and everyone came out to watch them set up—the strongmen pounding stakes into the ground, the roustabouts pulling the lines, the horses dragging the heavy poles into place. Village children snuck under the canvas into the shows where they weren't allowed, then had nightmares about two-headed calves for weeks.

My father followed his father's tradition, but he moved it up a notch and went to the big cities, like Nice, Tours, Arles, and Bordeaux, where they set up in semipermanent status and stayed for a month. There he met my mother, a trapeze artist of the first rank. I was born in a circus tent during a long night of torrential rain. The midwives complained about the mud, but my father said that my mother didn't complain at all. I was her second and last. She taught me how to swagger, balance, and laugh under my tears.

We're not Romany, though many people think we are.

As for me, what little talent I had was blood born. I didn't practice nearly enough. I thought I knew everything already. My compatriots, Ben, Jean-Pierre, and Jules, joined the circus as young men, dropping out of school and following the myth of the bright lights. They practiced like hell and were all better than I was. All Jules had to do to get a laugh was raise an eyebrow. You try that in front of a thousand strangers.

We rode bicycles, all four of us, but because I was heavy, I was always the base. And I was clumsy. I couldn't trip gracefully to save my soul and my falls never made anyone laugh. But despite my poor abilities, my parents struggled for me to continue, arguing with the boss until the wee hours and beating circus acts into me until my head hurt.

Mother tried to teach me grace. She was as elegant as a swallow on that trapeze, but I was lazy and too heavy to go aloft. I liked to eat.

On the night of my seventeenth birthday, I was out with the circus boys eating ice cream, drinking beer, and chasing girls. We had scrapped practice and the circus altogether. By the time I got back at midnight, the lights were off in the tent, but there was a small contingent of people by our caravan, everyone holding candles. I thought Father had had an accident, but he came out, found me, and yelled at me, his face full of tears as he told me what had happened. My uncle had been late with the catch fifty feet off the ground and Mother fell in front of a full house. Reeling, I ran back to the village and spent the night under a bridge with a friend named Jim Beam, though he was no friend at all, and another named Southern Comfort, who was no comfort.

Two days later, I came back to the circus, but it was never the same. At first, I tried out of guilt and shame, and later, I just didn't know what else to do. I'd never really been to school. For months, I played Texas Hold 'Em with the circus freaks until the wee hours. Albert was double-jointed and way fatter than I was; Fernand stood a little under four feet in his socks and could bend steel with his bare hands, and Thomas, the contortionist, did weird things with his elbow when he was bluffing. I always won. They cursed and called me names, but the next night, sitting outside under the light of kerosene lanterns, they played me again. Figured I was just a kid, a fluke.

I beat them all the time. I wasn't sure what to do with the money. I felt bad about it but kept playing, figuring the rest of them would stop. But then the contortionist said, "Faith, my boy," and went on losing. Faith never did me any good. I was just a better player, even at seventeen. Eventually, I gave all the money to Monique, my mother's best friend, who took over my mother's role in loving me. How could I ever leave her? She took in strays, like me. Eventually, she fell in love with my father.

But I still am, how do you say, bitter? Sad? I feel despair all the time. For some reason, clowns tend to be one slight step from desperation, so it is a good fit, I think. We are often depressed. Check out some horror movies about clowns if you don't believe me.

As I say, I was far from the best. But I tried. I sure tried. Mother would have wanted me to stay in the circus and do as well as I could.

A hot night in late August turned out to be my last day at the circus. I was feeling pretty good, even though that afternoon, I'd struggled with my costume. First on, white pancake makeup, then lipstick way wider than my mouth, thick eyeliner, and lots of laugh lines. Then the nose.

There are a variety of red noses, and not all are good, *ma cherie*. The cheap ones fall off and when the rest of your face is covered with paint, losing your nose isn't funny in the least. People in the back rows of the big top don't understand and think you've broken your face. And then they cry for you—*pauvre* monsieur!—and the people in the front row disapprove, so now you have two problems. *Non!* You must have the whole audience in the palm of your hand. Buy the expensive red nose. I had six.

I also wore a black hat. The mustache was my own. I strapped on two pillows for my belly, which I didn't really need at the end. My pair of long black pants was made especially for someone with a figure such as mine. A striped shirt under, a plaid shirt over. Suspenders. Shirttails flap in the breeze. Some days I just didn't feel like being funny, but it was my job.

I was working filler, right after the bicycle act and just before the aerials, keeping the audience laughing as the roustabouts adjusted the lines above, when I saw her, a very small girl, in the front row. I winked, gave her a little wave, and approached. I went down on one knee, put my head down, then slowly and carefully brought it up.

"Will you be my queen?"

Her little mouth dropped into a frown. "Mama?" she turned and said in a whisper. Then she grabbed her mother's hand and sank back into her chair.

I took off my hat. "I'm not so bad once you get to know me," I said, dipping my head lower. Now she could see my bald spot.

Overhead, I heard the roustabouts call for slack.

Well, I admit, I'm scary-looking so close. My face is bright white, red paint makes my mouth three times normal size, and I have that large red nose.

"It's all right, Chloe," the little girl's mom said. "It's only a clown."

To call up the greats with that comment would insult them all. Chloe looked only about five. I forgave her—and her ignorant mother.

The music for the trapeze started up. I had just a few moments to make little Chloe laugh. I threw my head back and looked overhead.

Monique was climbing the ladder to the trapeze. She was wearing her candy-apple red sequined costume with feathers. The musicians started a march as she climbed. I put out my palm. "Go on, then, Chloe, touch me on the shoulder," I said. "You will see I'm light as a feather."

Not really. I'm a big man, pushing two hundred pounds. To Chloe, I must've looked enormous. I got down into myself, floppy shoes, flappy pants, enormous jacket, one hand holding my hat, the other out to her like a penitent.

The music rose. Above me, Monique was taking her place on the narrow platform fifty feet over our heads. Down at the audience level, Chloe looked from me to her mom and back at me again. Her eyes were wide. The bottom of her eyelids were wet with tears.

"Bet you can't push me over, Chloe. Bet you're not strong enough," I taunted. I have a mic. My voice echoed through the tent, mixing with the music building to a crescendo. Now was the time for Monique to swing onto the trapeze. The music stopped, momentarily. She stepped out.

The little girl extended one hand, graceful and fearful at the same time, pulling back, pushing out. She checked with her mom, who nodded. Then, with a tentative grin, she pushed one finger against my shoulder, and I fell backward in a heap.

On my back now, I could see the top of the tent. Monique caught the swing and flew across the big top.

Down on the audience floor, Chloe and I had a spotlight on us and the whole audience erupted in cheers. But she didn't laugh. "Go, Chloe, go! Push him down again!" a man shouted. Then the crowd picked up the chant. "Go, Chloe, go!"

I rolled onto my feet and sat on my haunches.

"Go on, Chloe, squeeze my nose," I demanded.

"Go, Chloe, GO!" the crowd roared. And down I went again onto my back.

Chloe squealed. The audience cheered. And above Monique missed my father's hands.

Then nothing. I sat up, panicked, and eyeballed all the trapezes in the high top, all the cables, ladders, and platforms.

The trapeze over my head was empty. I glanced quickly at the other small platform. Empty too. Chloe, feeling bolder by the second, glanced over at her mom. "It's okay, honey," Mom said. "Push him down again."

Where was Monique? The crowd, focused on Chloe and me, hadn't noticed she was no longer on the trapeze.

Chloe went to push me down again, but I held my ground. Her mother frowned. Chloe screamed. And I was sure the rest of the audience was screaming too—screaming for Monique, screaming for my mother, screaming for me.

"Blam!" Chloe yelled. Her puny hand was like a feather on a concrete wall. I stood up, towering over her. She started to cry. Her mother jumped up in front of her. "You're a terrible clown. Go away!"

What did I care? I gathered my hat, scrabbled onto my feet, and ran backstage, then out again to the ropes, to the bottom of the ladder that led aloft. Monique was nowhere to be seen. The roustabouts were standing around, looking at me. Hadn't anyone noticed she'd fallen? If she hadn't fallen, was she tangled somewhere? About to fall?

I threw off my shoes, grabbed the ladder, and climbed, my big feet teetering on the narrow, fragile ladder.

Tom, the spotlight man, eased his big light over onto me as I climbed, desperation filling my heart. I could save her, my Monique. I could do it now.

My stockinged foot slipped on one of the rungs. I steeled my face, ignored the jeers and cheers of the crowd, and rose, my big belly rubbing against the rungs of the ladder.

When I reached the first platform, my father on the opposite platform raised his hand. "What are you doing?" he cried. "I can't catch you!"

I waved him off.

"Where's Monique?" I yelled. The platform under my feet was barely big enough for one of my flipper feet. It wobbled under my weight. I grabbed any cable in sight.

"Get down!" I closed my hands over the trapeze and swung out over the audience.

"Henri!"

I hadn't been aloft since I was a kid. It was fun.

At first.

Then my hands started to hurt. My fingers were slippery on the trapeze tape. It was a lot scarier than I remembered.

It was getting harder to hold onto the swing.

"Let him down!" My father's voice pierced through the oohs and aahs of the audience.

Below me the ringmaster led in the next act, the dancing horses.

Fifty feet off the ground, I felt myself descending. I tightened my fingers around the swing bar, but they were so slippery. I could barely hold on. Who was shouting my name? Where was Monique?

The sound of cantering hooves erupted below me. I was ten feet off their withers. Would I drop in a saddle or be trampled to death? I took a look at the roustabouts. "Hey!" I yelled. "I'm over here!"

But they were standing back, out of the way of the cantering horses.

Below me was the voice, a voice I'd known since forever, calling to me.

Monique? How she'd get down so fast?

"Henri! It's okay! Let go!" Her dulcet voice sang in my ear. She was standing on the side of the ring, holding out her hands.

But if I fell, I'd hurt her. I couldn't hurt her.

The horses went faster. My world spun.

"Stop!" the ringmaster cracked his whip. The horses reared, throwing riders. My father jumped in front of the biggest horse, caught me by the waist, and collapsed under my weight.

"Oof!" The air was knocked out of him.

I hurried backstage. Monique was waiting there, drinking a bottle of water, her face aghast. "What were you thinking, Henri?"

My father hobbled to keep up with me.

"I couldn't see you, I thought you were stuck up there," I gasped.

"Oh, Henri, I was fine all the time. You're making us all crazy. Are you sure you're all right?"

I ran by her, by my father, the roustabouts, the ringmaster, the elephants, the stable boys, and all the way to the train station. I was still in my clown costume at the ticket counter where I booked a ticket.

"One way or round trip?" the agent asked.

"One way," I said, grabbed my ticket, and caught the last train on the last track. I didn't care where it went.

❧

Two months later, I took a train back to Paris and donated my shoes to Monsieur Catalan.

"They will look great in my window," he said. "But how about the nose?"

"That I will keep," I said and strolled out of his shop, down Rue Amelot, to Place Bastille, where I caught a train back to the country. I work as a stable hand now and never put on a show. Alone in Paris, doing whatever I wanted, brought a particular sort of joy. Many places held surprises, but over and over, for reasons dwelling deep in my heart that I thought I'd lost long ago, I kept hearing my mother calling me.

THE CLOCK

MUSÉE D'ORSAY WAS HUGE, A FORMER train station, with soaring glass windows, stairways leading every which way, and a gigantic clock. The day before, I'd visited to see the sculpture of the young dancer, but when I left it was too late to look at the clock more closely. Now was my chance. I charged up three floors so I could stand behind it.

A small crowd milled about at the back side of the enormous timepiece. Then they were gone and I was at the front, alone, and all of Paris, it seemed, spread out behind Roman numeral VI. Haussmann buildings, across the Seine, rose in the distance and a long way off I could see the Basilica of Sacre Coeur.

From my vantage point, the numbers were backward, of course. The clock was meant to be read by people outside, coming to the train station, not by people inside the building looking out.

It was raining. I took my place behind the VI and looked out at the misty Seine below, at the mansard roofs across the river and the swath of green, the Jardin des Tuileries. I imagined walking through the clock and traveling back in time.

What would it have been like?

To be there in 1789 during the revolution when the streets were full of blood? To hear the German jackboots pound the streets as they marched to the Arc de Triomphe in 1940? To wave American flags from open windows on the day the Americans arrived in their tanks, trucks, and jeeps four years later?

I was ten. Maman pressed a small American flag in my hand. Everyone was lining the streets and cheering as the big tanks rolled by. We'd been down so long. I held Maman's hand tight and looked up. Tears ran down her face. She had tried to protect me, but I'd seen the grim lines of hungry people. I'd looked at the soldiers returning from war, leaning on their wooden crutches, desperation and despair filling their eyes. And I remembered our butcher, Abe, and his family disappearing. Maman had prayed every night, and I with her, my knees on a threadbare carpet in front of the windows, listening to Voice of America.

And back further? I could see through the rising mist, through a dark cloud that suddenly dissipated onto a horrifying scene of wagons full of bodies rolling through the streets. When the plague came, we were too poor to move out of the city like so many of our neighbors. Our house was stone, at least, but others who lived in wooden structures had their homes burned down to try to rid the city of rats. Two of my friends in our building had died, and Aunt Renée's baby Ruth was in the worst way and not expected to live. Why I was spared, I'd never know, but as I grew up, we left our memories behind. No one wanted to think about the time when Paris lost a third of its population. It wasn't until I was twenty, a full ten years later, that I stopped having nightmares about seeing wagons piled high with corpses.

The clock in front of me clicked as the hour hand slid to five p.m., while the minute hand, at least ten feet long, marched ahead. I looked through the glass again. I could see myself, a young girl of ten, running in the park across the river.

"Come on, Amy! Play with me!" My cousin Jean-Marie from Lycée Fénelon started running. She held up a red ball as she gestured for me to run back so she could throw it to me, and I ran, as fast as I could, and turned. But Jean-Marie was gone.

"Jean-Marie!" I called.

I ran back to where we'd separated. "Jean-Marie!" I yelled, but no ten-year-old girl with braids was in sight, just an older couple walking arm in arm under some mulberry trees.

Fighting rising panic, I ran around in all directions, hollering her name. There had been news in the papers about bad guys kidnapping girls and chaining them up in crates. Had they already grabbed Jean-Marie? Or would they find *me* out here, all alone in the big park?

The ground beneath my shoes sounded like sandpaper as I ran. I didn't remember running so far away from my mom and my aunt. Had they been standing under this tree? Or that one? In the open or in the shade? I moved fast, covering ground, yelling, "Jean-Marie! Jean-Marie!" until my throat got sore, and I just yelled "Maman! Maman!" and that's when I saw them, my mom and her sister, Françoise, who was pushing a stroller back and forth with her feet. I ran closer, panicked. They would blame me, they'd call the police, and horrible things would happen to Jean-Marie.

"Nina," said my mother, standing up straight, dropping her knitting on the ground. "Come, Nina. Come, she's here."

I ran into my mom, driving my head and shoulders to her belly, and she held me, close, close, as my cries turned into big hacking sobs.

"She's here, dear, right here, don't worry so, my darling," Maman said, and Jean-Marie came over and held me too.

"Where did you go? I ran and ran and you disappeared!"

"I had to stop to tie my shoelace and then I didn't see you anymore," she said with a sob. "That's when I came back."

"That must've been so scary for both of you," Maman said.

I couldn't stop shivering.

"Everything's okay, sweetheart," my mother said and held me for the longest time. My heart was pounding, my hands were clammy and cold, but Jean-Marie was fine. And so was I.

People on benches nearby shook their heads while a group of Parisian teenagers, all girls, gossiped and laughed as they walked in the open, and I held Maman closer until I felt better, if only a little. It took all day, two cups of chamomile tea and cinnamon toast, two slices, before I felt like myself again.

I backed out of the clock. When I'd been in Paris with my own mother, decades before, she'd been wearing her shirtdress as usual. We walked the quai, checked out the books at booksellers along the way, held hands as we crossed streets, and I, so much smaller, had to run to catch up, until she was gone, really gone, when I was fourteen.

The big clock struck six. A guard came up behind me and said, "Madame, *nous fermerons maintenant.* We are closing. Merci, madame."

I followed a few people down the escalator, out the lobby, and into a drizzly rain. I walked around and looked at the giant clock. It was so high up there; I could barely see what time it was. Still, I knew it was time to go. Tomorrow, perhaps, I'd come back, step through the clock, and once again be in my mother's arms.

Even though I sensed my mother beside me everywhere I went in Paris, it was my father's voice that drove me to museums day after day.

THE PICASSO MUSEUM

I'D BEEN LOOKING FOR MUSÉE PICASSO for several days, but I kept getting lost on the narrow cobblestone streets in the Marais and missing it. It was on a side street, Rue de Thorigny. Every day, I headed out, and every day, my feet took me in the same direction, west, until I finally realized I'd keep repeating my steps until I finally paid attention to my father's voice in my head, telling me to quit fooling around and find it.

He'd been an art collector. I'd had Art, with a capital "A," shoved down my throat ever since I'd been a baby—taken to openings, following him around Europe as he sped through museums to see his favorite pieces, my mother and my brothers running after him as I chased along behind. We were going to get an education, no matter what.

So here I was in Paris, finally in front of the massive doors to the Picasso Museum, knowing full well what I was doing here.

As I stepped into the beautiful courtyard, the three-story, seventeeth-century building rising around me, I understood, and I hadn't even gotten inside. It was beautiful.

This building housed over five thousand works of art by Picasso. My father had met him years earlier, the man I knew only because of a famous photo—his big eyes, his striped shirt—and a painting that had been in our living room for over thirty years. An early portrait of one of his lovers.

She'd stared out over her right shoulder at me, with a look of sort of belligerence and haughtiness, yet also a small sense of kindness that I came to love throughout my babyhood, my childhood, Christmases, long nights by the fire, until I left for college and she was sold.

The house felt empty after that.

She wouldn't be here, of course, but maybe I'd find something similar, or maybe I'd come to understand something about Picasso—or about my father. They were both enigmatic difficult men.

Today, walking in, I saw a grand staircase and chandelier and paintings, glorious paintings on the first floor, and mostly blue.

And upstairs, colors. No painting like the woman I'd known, but paintings full of vigor, an explosion of color and eyes and sharp angular lines. Women with both eyes on the same side of their faces. Which made sense to me for the very first time.

I heard a swish and a whisper. A few other tourists were milling about, being quiet. The place was nearly empty.

Someone was standing too close to me. I moved. I'd come here to avoid the crowds, not be squished by some overenthusiastic tourist in Paris.

"This one looks funny," said a small girl in a blue dress, about nine. She was with her family, holding onto her mother's hand.

"She's not 'funny,' Darlene," her father said. "She's supposed to look like that."

"What if I walked around with two eyes on the side of my head?" she asked. "Would you still love me?"

"You'd be a flounder, Darlene, and no one would love you," her brother said.

She elbowed him in the ribs.

"Enough!" her father said. "If you can't behave, we'll have to leave."

"Great idea," the boy said. He looked about eleven.

I kept my peace and didn't move as the family of four made their way to the stairs, the sound of flip-flops, sandals, heels, and men's fashionable leather shoes echoing away, leaving me in peace.

I'd never been obnoxious like that. I'd never been allowed.

"Just step into the painting, Nina." My father's voice in my head. "Believe in it, see what the artist is doing—"

My father's voice—as always—making me angry and frustrated. I shifted my feet. But there was something there, beside me, despite my best intentions. I'd come to Paris to feel something I'd felt at seventeen—confident, brave. But I'd found something different. I'd found my parents.

I knew better than to put out my hand to take my father's. He was not an affectionate man.

"Pay attention, Nina."

He'd hated me the last few decades of his life, for reasons I could never understand. Wouldn't let me see him or even call him and threw out my letters.

"What is Picasso trying to say, Nina?"

"What are you doing here?" I asked, feeling the hurt that rose uncontrolled from my heart. "What did I ever do? You wouldn't answer my calls."

"Study the painting. You might learn something."

"You turned on me. Wouldn't let me even show you your own grandchildren," I said aloud and stopped. Looked around. People would definitely think I was crazy if they thought I was talking to myself.

"What do you think about her eyes?"

"Enticing."

"Exactly. Now, go on, tell me more."

I couldn't. I was twelve, I was sixty-seven, I was no one, I was here, he was not, yet he was, in his suit, bow tie, black glasses, white hair, standing next to me.

"You came back," he said. "Never thought you cared."

"Now, wait a minute." I turned and looked at him, still tall, stooped now. He towered over me.

"You never understood anything about art," he said.

"You tore up my letters. You hung up when I called. And you never told me why."

"You're imagining things, Nina," he said, his thin lips pursed. His thin lips like mine.

"You used to love me," I said, trying to keep myself together. The last years of his life, on the rare occasion he answered the phone, in five minutes I'd feel lousy, like a nobody. It would take me two weeks to get my equilibrium back and feel like myself again.

"You used to be a nice girl, Nina."

Scourge of my life, he'd made me feel useless forever. As soon as I could, I moved three thousand miles away to California to get away from him. I'd been forty when I no longer thought I was stupid, as he'd called me countless times.

And for some strange reason, he was still following me around.

"You didn't have to come to the museum," he said. "You never cared before."

"We were all here the day you made fun of Mom. You made her feel useless," I said.

"She didn't understand me," he said and jiggled the change in his pocket.

"You tried to destroy me the same way you destroyed her," I said. "You killed Mom, you killed Chris. Mark is—"

"You always had a vivid imagination, Nina. I would never do such a thing."

"Exactly what I thought you'd say. You broke her heart."

He moved to another painting, this one full of four women. "Study them. You might learn something."

Frail now, stooped, paper-thin skin, but today, I could still see the fire, the anger in his eyes, his disappointment in me. I'd done everything right in his book, ending up in a marriage to an alcoholic and having no way to make a living, then going back to school. He'd laughed at me for the whole seven years I studied calculus, chemistry, physics. Despite him, I became an engineer and gained my freedom. If only my mother had escaped too.

"Go to some café, Nina. Don't fool yourself. You don't belong here. You'll never understand Picasso."

"No one ever loved you," I said, saying the first thing that popped into my teary eyes.

"You were never very bright."

I stood tall, trembling. "You were a terrible husband and father."

"I made my contribution to society. What about you?"

Stung, I tried to gather my composure. "You're not real."

"But if I'm in your head, I'm real, am I not?" he said. "You hear my voice, don't you?"

"I do my best to ignore you."

"But you can't. You came to Paris to think about me."

"Don't fool yourself. You were cruel to all of us, and you were particularly cruel to Mom."

He turned his back to me, walked to another painting. "This one, Nina, look at this one."

"Look at me," I said.

He jiggled his change, kept his eyes focused on the painting. "Please."

"I gave you everything," he said.

"But not love. You didn't give us love." I felt deranged.

He was quiet a moment. "Picasso kept changing over his life."

"Your family. You're supposed to show love to your family."

"I wanted you to be kids again. Those were the years when I was the happiest," he said, looking out the window at a soft rain.

"And if I was a kid again, what would you say? Would you say I love you?"

"I would say, don't forget to go up the third floor. There's lots to see," he said and disappeared.

Sometimes the Parisian twilight, with its shadows and secrets, the sound of voices coming from open windows, warm yellow light reflecting on the cobblestones, and happy couples strolling arm in arm passing me along the narrow streets made my heart ache. I looked for love. At the time, it didn't seem to matter at all that I was married.

Le Musée de L'Orangerie

I'd been meandering around the chestnut trees of the Tuileries for about fifteen minutes looking for the museum. Finally, there in a corner, a low round dome rose out of the ground. Was that it, Le Musée de L'Orangerie? Hidden in plain sight? When I got closer, I saw a building, not too far away, with columns and a grand door. Why had it been so hard for me to find it? I realized I'd been thinking of home, and Robert, not quite ready to go back to California. Also, I was used to getting lost in Paris, so I didn't mind one bit.

I was there to see the art, of course, but I'd done something different, somewhat daring. I'd hunted around the Internet and found Martin on Meet Up. He was an architect and worked as a part-time guide, giving visitors a local's tour of Paris. I thought, what the hell, live a little—Edna! I reminded myself, it wasn't really me hiring a good-looking guide. Perhaps you could learn a thing or two! Yes, I was definitely getting into it. You could tell Robert all about it, make him listen to me for a change, even though he might not like what he was hearing. What the hell, I signed up.

At the entrance to the museum, I showed the attendant my Pass Musée and followed the signs down a flight of stairs. Most of the museum, it turned out, was underground.

Three people milled about outside the gift shop, one of them a guy looking right at me. "Nina?" he asked. "I'm Martin."

"Hello," I croaked. He was way better looking than his photo.

It was my lucky day. I would follow him anywhere. Thick brown curly hair, lively eyes, blue jeans, a striped shirt, and a killer smile. I shook his hand, held my grin a little too long.

"Shall we?" he asked in his French accent.

"Uh, uh," I replied, tongue-tied. Robert always said I was a chatterbox, but with Martin, I didn't know what to say. After ten seconds, he already held me spellbound. He must've been about forty, way too young for me to act so silly.

"The museum was built in the late 1800s to store orange trees," he explained. "Hence the name."

We meandered through the galleries of impressionist art until we turned a corner. Martin paused, then opened a door.

"In 1921," he said, "the museum's mission was to display the work of current artists, one of whom was Monet. He helped design the galleries for his Water Lilies. Have you seen these before?"

I'd seen them in posters and photographs, of course, but when I came around the corner and found myself in an oval room surrounded by two huge paintings, I was stunned.

Winter. The colors of the lily pads were muted and dark. Diffuse light from skylights created a moody, foggy feeling. I was surrounded by water; it was murky. It was hard to see details in the dim light.

"It does evoke winter, doesn't it?" Martin asked in his perfect, accented English. "I've come here often and, struck with the depth and grandeur, spent the day." His voice was a baritone, his fingers a light tingle on my arm. "So how long are you going to be in Paris, Nina?"

Forever, I wanted to say. I loved the paintings, but I liked Martin more. I felt ashamed as my body was taking over.

"You're blocking the door to the next gallery," he said, and so I was. Embarrassed and feeling awkward, I backed away.

"Just walk in an oval. Try to absorb the water. Let it seep into your skin." His voice, I thought, felt like a tonic to my mixed emotions.

My second thought: Oh, brother.

Still, my temperature rose despite the damp air on my arm. I opened my coat a little wider. At home, no one sees me or wants me. But today, heat came off me like steam.

"This one, of course, shows a dark period in Monet's life," he said.

Hell, I'd take dark if it had Martin in it. Jesus. Had it really been that long since I'd felt this way? How long ago had Robert had ceased to be a thrill? Years.

"And then you walk through the next door—at the far end of the oval. It's a figure eight," Martin went on. "Monet spent months with the architects of this building to get it right. Infinity, yes? The lilies grow, die, and are reborn as you follow the gallery walls, you see."

I was trying to. What had possessed me to request company? I didn't need a guide, I needed a psychiatrist. Good lord. It was only Friday. I had two more days in Paris.

"Let's look at spring," I said, marching into the second gallery. The paintings swooped around the walls. Now the lilies were in bloom and light, Monet's incomparable light, dappled the surface of the water, awakening movement above and below. The lilies were happy, greeting the sun, and I imagined the fish that I couldn't see delightfully swimming in warmer waters. Everything was joyous, including my heart.

"You want a cup of coffee, Nina?" Martin asked as we exited through the gift shop, climbed a ramp, and were once again in the Tuileries. The sun was brilliant. We took a bench under one of the chestnut trees. They looked different now. Bigger, better, more robust.

"How could Monet handle those huge paintings?" I asked.

"Very carefully," Martin answered, taking off his backpack and setting it on the ground. As I hoped he would handle me.

I made some sort of snort, to check myself. Romance be damned. I was old, with a body that I hadn't approved of for decades, and married, and not that much of a fool. But . . . what if? Robert wouldn't be happy, but he was always staring at women when we went out. I could look, couldn't I? I could flirt, couldn't I? No harm in that. Martin and I wandered across Pont de La Concorde and found a café.

"Espresso?" he asked as a waiter came to our table.

Up close, Martin had an effeminate mouth, soft, gentle, and open, and a sense of humor that came easily. He loved buildings and enjoyed showing people around, being a meet-up friend-for-the-day.

"And the money?" I asked him. "Or the company? Which is better?"

"The company's always a lot more interesting than the money," he said with a grin.

I bet he said that to all the middle-aged women, but it still made me laugh.

"I leave day after tomorrow," I said and sipped my espresso. Damn coffee sure had a kick. My hands, my heart, and other places felt jittery. Horrified that my body was trying to embark on its own little journey without me, I tried to cover by asking, "Who are your usual clients?" Clear heads could still prevail.

Martin didn't take the bait. "You're different," he said, pursing those delicate lips. "Clever by half. Self-assured. Full of spunk."

I grinned. I couldn't help myself. I hadn't heard such good pick-up lines in a long time and even though, after only forty-five minutes of me not saying much, Martin was way off base, it was still flattering.

"Let's stroll along the quai. Now, Nina," he placed his arm through mine. "How long has it been?"

My knees suddenly wobbled. "Since what?" I croaked.

"Since you've been to Paris, of course. What did you think I meant?"

I couldn't remember. A week? A month? Since I was thirty? Robert was a cool guy, but after eighteen years of marriage, he was, well, predictable. Robert had paid for my trip. Robert was in the States and I was in Paris. Alone. Robert wouldn't approve. Robert would never know.

Martin and I walked along the Seine as the water glistened in the afternoon light. We paused for salads in Place St. Michel, floated by Shakespeare and Co., admired Notre Dame from afar, and made fun of and also admired the throngs of tourists milling about.

We walked down a cobblestone-covered alleyway, then took a right onto another narrow street, then a second right where we paused at a blue door. He pressed a digicode, and we were inside a lovely courtyard full of flowers. The Haussmann building rose around me.

"Want to see a real Parisian apartment?"

We climbed a set of outside stairs and he led me through a metal door. An orange tabby made my acquaintance as we walked in. Martin kissed me and I fell into his arms.

Light streamed through tall windows, covering the white bedspread that he led me to.

After all the romance movies I'd ever seen and romance novels I'd ever read, I'd thought those would be enough. Hell no! It was so much better to be eager in person. Feeling the strength of a man's back. His lips on mine. Robert always thought those romance novels I always read were a waste of time. Ha!

I'd dreamed about a petite adventure in Paris since I got here. I thought I'd put it out of my mind. But now? Oh God, I could barely slow down. All I'd really wanted. To be wanted. To be listened to. To be caressed. As much as I loved Robert, he was miles away. Martin smelled like the woods, his caresses soft as down on my cheek, his kisses whispers. Robert smelled like Listerine.

I took my cues and started taking off my clothes.

Would Robert ever know? Would I remember everything? I had no schedule to keep, no place to go. And all day with a man who made me so hot I thought about calling the fire department.

Martin put his arms around me, and I melted into him. It had been such a long, long time. I kissed his ear.

He searched my mouth with his tongue, making my whole body tingle. This was better than the sun on my back, better than a long bike ride down by the river, better than . . . Stop it, I said to myself. Uh, no. Keep going.

Martin knew his way around a woman's body.

To Robert, my body was still terra incognita.

Gossamer curtains at the windows blew with a slight breeze and the temperature dropped. Thank God! Despite the sudden chill, I was hotter than I'd been even when I'd had hot flashes. Back when I could set fire to a clock from eight feet away. After twenty years, I still slept with my feet out from the covers. Martin wouldn't need to know about that.

What could I tell this wonderful man? Nothing and everything. I moved under his caresses, returned stroke for stroke.

He was tall, but I was tall enough to reach every part of him. His skin was smooth and just slightly downy. Robert was as hairy as a gorilla.

Martin ran his hands around my breast.

I pulled back.

"Did I hurt you?" he asked.

"I just . . . don't like it."

"Really? You like this better?" He nuzzled my ear.

Ooh boy, I get excited even when my dog nuzzles my ear.

He did it again.

I pulled back. "*Non.*"

"Women never say no to ear kisses," Martin said, kissing my other ear, his hot breath a confusion in my brain.

"Oh God, what am I doing?" I said out loud. Robert would be so hurt.

"*Pardon?*" he asked, his hand on his zipper.

"*Pas pour moi.* Not for me. I shouldn't," I said, backing away.

"You want to say no, Nina? You don't seem like you want to say no." He caressed my face with his soft, velvet fingers.

"*Pas maintenant.* Not now. I have to go." I croaked out the words. The words I didn't want to say. I wanted to touch him, hold him, whisper things in his ear, tell him he was great. "It's not you, it's me."

"Oh, I've heard that line before," he said. "Even in France." He unbuttoned his shirt. Muscles twitching, mouth soft, hair like baby chick down.

Oh, how I wanted him! "Some other time," I said, forcing out the words.

He had such a hurt look on his face. I wanted to kiss away his worry. There was no clock on the wall, no knock on the door, and my pants were down to my knees. I had all afternoon.

I pulled up my pants, tucked in my blouse, ran a hand through my hair. I had to get myself together and fast.

"Nina, you are so beautiful," he said.

I turned to take one last look at him, eager to taste that sweet mouth again, feel his arms around me. Instead, I grabbed my shoes and purse, swung open the door, and ran. I pushed back tears as I crossed the courtyard and, while putting on my shoes, crept through the man door and onto Boulevard Richard Lenoir, cut through a shortcut, and headed to Boulevard Beaumarchais.

Luckily, it wasn't too late to call California. Robert would be so happy to hear from me.

I had composed myself by the time I got to a café and took a table in the back. Dialed Robert. "Hi. Everything good?" I asked, wanting to hear his assurance, his kind voice, imagine his hairy back, smell the Listerine that always lingered on his mouth. I waited for him to tell me he loved me, the way he always did, first off in every phone call.

"Oh, Edna, hi," he said.

"You sound distracted," I said, feeling a little odd.

"Oh, hi, Nina," he said.

"I miss you," I said and caught my breath. "Can't wait to come home. And see you."

"Hold on a sec."

I heard shuffling in the background. Another voice, a woman's voice. A door closing.

"Just got out of the shower," he said.

This was odd. It was nine a.m. in California. He was an early riser and usually popped out of the shower by six. "Slept in then?" I asked. "Feeling sick? Got a fever?" I stopped asking questions real quick. All things were possible, I guess, but not this. Never this. I knew the answer.

"I've been exercising," he said.

"By yourself?" I asked and hung up the phone.

After that adventure, I thought it best to look at more mundane things that could keep me out of trouble. I have always admired the beautiful courtyard doors in the Marais. Often, they're painted bright blue, sometimes bright red, and they're enormous, big enough for a horse and carriage in the old days and a car these days. Usually, they're equipped with a smaller door for people and, of course, a brass digicode panel. As I passed the closed doors, I wondered what secrets lay inside. One day, one of the doors was open and I stepped inside.

THE RED DOOR

I'D BEEN WALKING BY THE SEVENTEENTH-CENTURY red courtyard door on my way to the Marais for three days now, trying to imagine what was inside—a Maserati or Corvette? Or a Tesla? Or a Smart car, tiny enough to tuck into the small and barely visible parking spots in Paris? These double doors (wide enough for a car, but with an inset human-sized door inside them) were the entrances to the Haussmann buildings, five- and six-story structures built around a common courtyard that line the streets of Paris. Concierge and stores below, large apartments on the higher floors, and at the top, rooms for the *bonnes,* the maids, tiny rooms with great views of Paris and, just like my hotel room, barely big enough for me.

The city was filled with these beautiful black or blue or bright-red courtyard doors with filigree along the top and sides. This crimson one pulled at my heart. Every time I passed one of these doors, I imagined life behind: mothers calling their children, a forbidden romance, or people hiding their broken hearts, drowning their loneliness in glasses of wine or bottles of absinthe.

This afternoon, for some reason, the big doors were open. Hesitant about entering private property, I worried at first that the concierge, who usually has a ground-floor apartment with a window in the arched doorway, might be present. But she (mostly women, I've been told) was either not in or busy; her door was closed. I was lucky. I went in. It was cool under the arches. I stepped inside the courtyard. I'd never ventured inside one before. The air was fresh and clean as dampness rose from the freshly washed cobblestones.

Roses in large pots surrounded the courtyard, bringing a fragrance of spring. A fountain tinkled its music in the middle of the parking circle. Higher up, on the third floor behind open shutters, came the sound of drums and, a little in the distance, a flute. And way above, in one of the flats near the top of the building, someone was playing the piccolo. Sparrows fluttered about amid the honeysuckle, bougainvillea, and pots of flowers. I felt like an intruder and hoped, if someone confronted me, that I could pretend I didn't know it was private.

Two small tables were surrounded by several chairs. I'd been walking all day and was tired. Perhaps, for the moment, no one would mind if I took a load off. As soon as I sat down, I heard a shrill call from above and listened again. This wasn't a baby crying or a small child. This was a woman screaming, filling the air with her desperation. Disconcerted, I wasn't sure what to do. Was she being attacked? Had she fallen on a kitchen knife? Got caught behind the dresser? Fighting with her lover? No other voice broke the silence between screams.

I didn't give a thought to who might call me out now. I searched the courtyard for a flight of stairs and, finding it, I sprinted up, following the sound of the screaming. There was no time for a breath at the top of the stairs. I passed by one, two, three landings, then ran along a hallway past closed doors until I reached an open door at the end of a hall on the fourth floor.

By this time a neighbor, a man in his sixties wearing a tweed jacket and trailing a red scarf, had come out to see the ruckus and was running along the hall ahead of me. Right behind him,

I entered a large apartment with shuttered windows and long flowered drapes with rooms heading every which way. I followed the screaming and found a blond woman crawling halfway out an open window, holding onto the drapes with one hand, yelling at someone down in the courtyard and gesturing with her other hand. The neighbor went to grab her legs.

She stopped screaming. "NON! Not me, Claude. It's him! Do you see him?" Her face was red with sweat, her blond hair lay in disarray, and ringlets near her ears were plastered to her temples. "Don't pull." She pushed herself farther out the window.

"You're going to kill yourself, Sylvie! Be careful!"

"He's down there somewhere!" Sylvie yelled at a woman in the courtyard.

"What can I do to help, madame?" I asked and stood on her other side.

"It's my cat, Pickles! He fell! He fell out the window!"

"And where is he now, Sylvie?" Claude asked.

"Somewhere down there! Claude, I don't think you'll ever catch him." She looked from him to me.

Claude was portly, with tufts of hair exploding from just above his ears. He gazed out the window at the courtyard below, back at the blond woman, then at me. He looked tired. He headed for the door and went out.

The woman turned back to the window.

"Flavie!" the blond girl yelled out the window. "Can you see him?"

"I don't see anything!" Flavie cried.

That left me alone with Sylvie. She pulled back inside, frowning at me. "What are you looking at?"

"You were screaming, mam'selle," I said. "May I help you?"

"How did you get in?"

"Nina," I answered. "I'm an American." I put out my right hand. I could pull her back all the way inside if that's what would keep her safe. "Please don't lean so far out of the window."

"Tish tosh. I'm all right. *Non*. My suicide days are over. As for my cat . . ." She reached for the drapes to get a better grip and leaned out the window again.

"Flavie? Keep looking, will you?" And with that she climbed back inside.

Her long blond hair was down to her waist, and she was wearing a Rolling Stones T-shirt and a pair of tight, paisley bell bottoms. Looking better than I would even on my best day.

I wondered why she wasn't moving very fast. Then I recognized the brace, the same one I'd worn two years before when I broke my knee.

"That Pickles." She pulled out a pair of crutches, leaned on them, holding her bad leg in front of her. "What the hell am I supposed to do now? I can barely make it up or down the stairs."

"I'll go help Flavie look for him if you like."

"He hunts birds. He fell out the window. You wouldn't think he could kill them."

"Why not?" I asked. "Cats kill birds all the time in my neighborhood in San Francisco."

"He's blind." She paused, tipping her head toward the balcony just outside. "Flavie!" she called. "See anything?"

No answer from below.

"I'll go to the courtyard, if that's a help," I suggested.

"Pickles took off here—" she gestured to the balcony, and to the one just below. "But I don't think he made it through the trees. Pickles! Pickles!"

I joined her. "Kitty, kitty, here kitty kitty."

A bunch of branches crackled below me.

"Sylvie!" Flavie shouted from below. "He's not anywhere down here!"

"I bet that cat took off to Madame Corizon's place—on the second floor. Chasing that finch of hers. Crazy old bat, she lets the bird fly around her apartment." She searched out the window again.

"Sylvie, Pickles could be . . . anywhere," I said, but I meant lost, hurt, dead.

The branches below moved again and there was a screech and a flash. Something black flew by the window below, then crashed on another set of branches and took off into the bougainvillea.

"Pickles!" Sylvie cheered. "I adopted him a year ago, but he's still like a kitten. You'd think a blind cat would have more sense. Go find him."

"I will," I said.

I sprinted down the corridor, down two flights of stairs, and stopped, out of breath, at the bottom. Doorways and planters, bushes and flowers surrounded the courtyard, while arches led in through smaller courtyards beyond. I'd never find a black cat here, not one who was now scared and possibly hurt. The big courtyard doors were still open.

I found Flavie, a heavyset woman in a flowery dress sitting on one of the chairs, leaning her chin on her elbow, digging in a pocket for another cigarette.

"Seen the cat?" I asked.

"That little bastard's always up to something." Flavie looked at me through a haze of smoke. "He caused Sylvie to break her leg—and she still loves him. For God's sake, that girl has no sense."

I walked around pots and plants, looking for a black ball of fur. I didn't want to disturb the crates and boxes I found in front of one of the doorways. Despite my mission, I didn't belong here.

Something dark behind one of the boxes caught my eye. I bent down slowly, checking for an odor. More times than I'd like to admit, I've put my hands in dog poop.

"Sylvie should've gotten rid of that cat," Flavie said, slouching back in her chair. "I have fish. Fish never run away."

"Easy, easy," I said as I reached for the black thing, about the right size and shape.

"And they don't break things," Flavie chirped.

The cat bolted. He ran to another set of bushes and crouched down. It was a wonder to see a blind cat run and not bump into things. He was across the courtyard from Flavie. I eased over there slowly, not saying anything. Bent down. Grabbed him.

He had long fur and struggled to get away. He scratched me but good. I held his legs away from me for a few minutes and got a better grip. Finally, he relaxed a little and started to purr. For a year-old cat, he was pretty small. His eyes seemed all right, but I could tell he was looking at things with a cocked head, not quite zeroing in, as normal cats do. I tucked him under my arm and, feeling satisfied, climbed, more slowly this time, to the fourth floor and the last unit at the end of the hall.

Sylvie was standing at the door, holding her crutches, favoring her bad leg.

I felt like a hero, having done something useful while I was in Paris. Perhaps Sylvie would invite me in for a drink. She could be someone I could talk to. Perhaps we could become friends.

I held out the small furry kitten. "Safe and sound. Here's your Pickles," I said, rubbing his ear.

"That's not my cat," Sylvie said and slammed the door.

Not only hidden courtyards grabbed my attention while I was in Paris. Every day, I was drawn to cathedrals, where soaring ceilings filled my heart. Even though my parents dragged me into cathedrals when I was a child and I didn't care for them then, now I made a point of it, walking into places where the great spaces made me feel smaller than myself and more loved than I thought possible. Inside, there was a particular, pleasant, and intense odor I smelled nowhere else—musty, and cavernous, and moist, sometimes frankincense, sometimes not, but distinctive, holding stories hundreds of years old.

Hurt and Fire

Summer 2017, before the fire

Despite the swarms of people milling about outside, inside Notre Dame, it was quiet. A few people were whispering in small groups, their faces tipped toward the cavernously tall ceiling soaring overhead. Chairs in rows faced the pulpit; parishioners sat and prayed. Tourists, in hushed tones, walked the transepts, admiring sculptures of saints and the stained-glass windows that exalted the glory of the lord.

I was a tourist, but I was alone, and that was a comfort as I could be here as long as I wanted. I passed by the votive candles and felt the musty air envelop me. It was full of history. I had the time to sit long enough to hear those voices from long ago and far away. I have never been a believer, not in God or spirits, but I knew to step quietly. And something made me wonder. Was it the sculptures of angels and saints? The blue-starred ceiling? The magnificent rose window? Or just the hush over everything that made Notre Dame so grand?

Halfway into the cathedral, I found a collection of chairs in a section away from the masses. I took a seat, third row back, second seat in. My feet were tired.

Then I heard a rustle. Someone sat down right next to me. Were they going to ask me for money like the beggars outside? Should I move? Couldn't I have any peace at all? I gathered my bag, ready to bolt, but when I turned to look, I recognized her.

My mother.

I sat very, very still. My first thought was that it must be someone who looked like her, some Parisian, some stranger, and my mind wanted desperately to make the leap. Maybe I was tired, maybe I was lonely, maybe anything. I'd been imagining her in crowds for years.

I looked again.

In a gray suit, brown-leather three-inch heels, and an alligator purse. Her hair was up, as it had been throughout my childhood, parted on the side and arranged so that it flipped over itself, like the hairstyles of the forties. This was before she cut and curled her hair, before my father started calling her crazy, before she'd killed herself, fifty-five years ago, in the summer of '63.

"Oh," I said, suddenly remembering to breathe.

The last time I thought I had seen her was at horseback-riding camp that summer after she passed, at the pond where we swam in the afternoon to wash the grime off ourselves after riding for hours every day. She walked up like she'd never been gone, and I started to ask her what she was doing visiting me. Parents never just showed up like that. When I looked again, she was gone.

That summer, after I went home for the funeral and returned to camp, her loss was so fresh. She'd been gone a week, maybe two. I woke up every day, forgetting she was gone, and again it would hit me like the first time I'd heard. Now, today, she'd been gone more than half a century and God knows I'd been accustomed to it for a very long time. But here she was, with me, in Paris, where I'd come with her as a child. I wasn't jet-lagged or confused. I could hear her breathing.

"Yes," she said, holding her hands over the clasp of her purse.

"What—church? You never liked . . . What?" I stuttered. My heart was racing a million miles a minute. My head swam. "Mom, what are you doing here?"

"Checking on you."

I'd gotten so used to not having her around. Was there a place in my heart where she could come back? I wanted so desperately to believe.

Oh, how I wished I hadn't just lost my mind, that she was really with me, that she hadn't gone away when I was fourteen. I squeezed my eyes together. I had no time for ghosts, scraps from the past, people I'd lost and longed for; no heart to see shreds of memories disappear, like broken spider webs in the wind. Had I had too much tea? Not enough? Was my stomach going to behave? Oh God. I closed my eyes and hoped no one would accuse me of going crazy talking to an empty chair.

I opened my eyes. She was still there.

"I'm sorry," she said, looking forward, not at me. She smiled ever so slightly, and it was true, I did have her teeth, but not her luscious lips, which my daughter inherited. I had her bust; that was some consolation, I guess.

"You left me," I said, unable to fathom the reality of the situation. She was my mother, she was real, and she was here, sitting with me in a row of chairs in Notre Dame in Paris.

Years ago in college, a fellow student had complained that her mother hovered over her too much when she was recovering from the flu. I told her, in a voice harder than I should've or even meant to, that I would give my right arm to have my mother back. Surprised, the student slunk from the lunchroom and never talked to me again. But now, I had both my arms *and* my mother, apparition or not, and she was sitting next to me. Real as rain.

"Life was hard," I said, "after you left." Those were the words my father used to say when I wanted comfort. "Life is hard." Gee, thanks, Dad. It's your fault, I wanted to tell him. You broke her heart, which broke mine, and now you're telling me to toughen up. I knew life was hard. Jesus.

My mother sat quietly, cleared her throat. "You've been okay? After all this time, I couldn't . . . I tried."

"You're with me now, Mom," I said. Tears filled my eyes.

I began to tell her how I'd hoped, wished, tried to convince myself that she was watching over me every step of the way. But after the first year, I knew I was on my own and had to survive. People used to say I kept them at a distance, and they were right. I had to. And now, now . . .

"You've done okay," she said, "despite—"

"I missed you terribly."

"I know. There's no explanation, really. It's just that, I was so, so unbearably sad."

"I remember," I sobbed. "I remember all of it."

"Yes."

She was here, beside me, like she'd been with me in Paris when I was a little girl, like she'd been with me throughout grade school, showing me her hurt and fire, and her undying love. None of the hurt after that mattered. She'd come back. She loved me. She'd always been with me.

I put out my hand to hold hers.

I felt something cool. Ethereal. Then, nothing.

I closed and opened my eyes. My empty hand was clutching air and whoever, or whatever, had been sitting beside me was gone. I looked up at the soaring ceiling again and felt different.

The whispers of the tourists came through the nave as they made their circumambulation of the church. Parishioners near and far in their hard-back chairs muttered prayers. In the distance, other worshippers lit candles, and in the front of the church, beyond where I could see, a choir began to sing.

There used to be three of us kids in Paris. Three blond-haired children, two boys and a girl, and our parents. Sometimes we had a helper. It was definitely a challenge, getting around Paris, five people in search of entertainment, shops, and interesting sights. My parents were always impatient, yelled a lot, and hit us sometimes. Now, as an adult, I've come to understand them a little more. Still, I think we spent way too much time in museums and churches and not enough time in parks. And not enough time in open markets, like the Marche de Bastille. I stumbled on it by mistake. And then I saw Michael.

MICHAEL

THE MARKET IS SO BIG, I can't see the end of it—blocks and blocks of vendors selling everything, clothes to bread, salads to mussels, sausages to souvenirs.

I'd been there for hours and still wasn't finished checking it out. At first, vendors called out in French and English to passersby. A little later in the morning, Parisians came through with their rolling carts (allowed) and little dogs (not allowed). Parisians pulling carts were serious, intent on their shopping, and bargaining heavily. They squeezed by other shoppers who mindlessly moved out of the way. Many of the shoppers were accompanied by children. The place was packed with people.

There was a commotion to the crowd. I tried to stay out of their way. I leaned against the backs of display booths, low fences, trees. Traffic flowed in two directions, up and down the two aisles of the market, everyone in a hurry, except for me.

I'd never seen such food. Six, seven, eight different types of oysters were all lying in brine in their shells, sparkling and wet in beds of ice. Long tables were covered with clams, scallops, and big pots of paella cooking over small stoves. Mussels sizzling in pans over open flames were juicy, their bellies big and fat as fingers. On the next counter, twenty different species of whole fish were lined up as if they were heading to sea, eyes bright, scales and tails shiny and glistening. Octopus—plump, whitish-purple, and bigger than a café seat—were set on chips of ice, their tentacles spread out below them.

Past the fish were tables full of sausages, at least twenty different kinds from all areas of France. Lettuce, endive, cucumbers, squash, grapes, and breads of every kind were so heavy, the plywood under them sagged from the weight.

Small white bowls of goat and lamb brains, cradled in their white plastic dishes, were whole and delicate as flowers, and I wondered if mine looked anything like them.

I turned to get out of the crowd and almost stepped on a small foot. A child of eight or so was grabbing a tree trunk with one hand and reaching for his mother with the other. The boy was blond, almost white-haired, with a cleft chin and a narrow face. Our eyes met. My breathing ceased. He looked just like my brother years ago, the one I lost when he was twenty-one and I was nineteen. I hadn't thought about him in years and felt guilty.

The boy gave me a familiar glance, and my heart tugged for what could have been.

Looking at him with wide eyes, my heart started pounding a mile a minute. I felt hot all over and a little sick. I knew better, but . . . but . . . my brother. My big brother Chris as a boy. A kid. In Paris. I never imagined I'd see him again, so close I could touch him. Tears pooled in my eyes. Parisian shoppers, haughty and busy, pushed by me while I clung to the bark of a linden tree. No one could shove me now. If I stayed here long enough, my brother, even still a child, would be back.

Or maybe he'd return as an adult, with that same cleft in his chin, eager hazel eyes, and hair curled around his ears and along his collar. Maybe he'd be speaking with his girlfriend

Leslie, chattering in French to the vendors, and buy grapes, *sans pépins*, without seeds, for their apartment in the Marais. Maybe they'd be holding the hands of their little boy—let's call him Michael—raised in both the U.S. and Paris. For sure they'd be happy, shopping here for their weekly groceries and produce. My brother would hoist Michael into the air, and they'd pick out bread and sausages, and Leslie would smile, and she'd recognize me and point me out to Chris.

Maybe my knees would go weak, seeing him again, as they had for weeks after we lost him, thinking that I saw him everywhere.

Maybe nothing. I knew better. We had lost them all. Decades ago.

I was nineteen in 1968 when Chris went missing. In the winters I was away at college, but I was home for the summer, passing time with my boyfriend and working at a job in downtown Boston. A tall man of twenty-one, Chris was stronger and more powerful and way more cool than I was, and he didn't spend a lot of time with his little sister.

One night I woke in a cold sweat, dreaming about him. In the dream, he was in pain and kept calling out to me to come save him, but I couldn't. I didn't know where he was and when I woke, I was trembling all over.

A few days later when my father told me that my brother had died, my first response was "I know." Further details came out: A drug dealer, a meth addict, he'd been thrown off the roof of a building in New York City a block from Max's Kansas City restaurant, and it was a week before anyone found him.

A year before my brother died, his girlfriend, Leslie, had become pregnant at eighteen and had had an abortion. She used to come to me at parties, her hands full of pills. "Take them," she said. "Come on, you'll have fun, Nina." I didn't want to. She laughed at me for being square and I went home, feeling at odds with the world.

Leslie spoke French well. She'd know better than the Americans around me trying to touch the ripe fruit on the tables at the market. The merchants wagged their fingers, frowned, and tried to explain, but people kept moving, a mass, looking for an apple, a mango, a loaf of bread, and just the right chunk of cheese.

That year after my brother died, I left home for good. I got married, moved to California. Convinced I would be next, I couldn't escape the feeling that somehow, somewhere, someone would take a pot shot at me. Everyone knew who I was and where I lived. I fled.

And Leslie disappeared.

Twenty years later, on the same day I was nervously walking toward an appointment to see a lawyer about filing for divorce, I ran into a friend from high school who told me that Leslie—with her eight-year-old son in tow—had had a drug overdose and was dead before she hit the ground on the sidewalk in the middle of Harvard Square. She would have been forty. Trembling from the news and what I was about to do, I marched into 555 Market Street and started what would be my first day of freedom.

I hadn't thought about my brother or Leslie in years. He'd been with us in Paris, at this market, at fourteen, bored as all us kids were, staring at the fish, the oysters, the stacks of bread four feet high.

This little boy tucked in behind his mother's side, and I could see my brother in his clever face, his cleft chin, and I could feel my big brother—gone, Jesus, almost fifty years now—standing next to me at the market, forgiving me for moving on, forgiving me for forgetting him. Then the boy and his mother disappeared into the crowd, his small hand grabbing hers as she headed for the next aisle.

As the crowds jostled and looked for bargains, I moved on toward the middle of the market, a quiet spot where I could sit on the edge of a fountain and look back at the crowd, my memories as fresh as the bread on the tables, my brother a kid sitting next to me.

He would smile and our parents would laugh as if they knew nothing but joy and love and kindness. They'd be beside us too, put their arms around us, give us hugs, cover us with kisses, and ask what we wanted for lunch.

When I was a kid, I used to play with my brothers all the time. They taught me how to play Monopoly and poker, how to cheat and how to climb trees. We messed around with our train set for hours. So when I took Tram 7, a streetcar from Orly Airport to the closest Métro station in Paris, about an hour away, the trolley and the seemingly toy-like business park that we went through reminded me of our train set.

TRAM 7

THE MAN HAD A BODY LIKE a butterball. If it weren't for the suspenders, his pants would be down by his ankles. He held a suitcase in each hand as he strained to get on the tram, but his suspenders caught on something on his way in. I looked away—seeing an obese man in red-polka-dot underwear wasn't my idea of a good time, especially in Paris, in the morning, after flying all night.

In just a minute, the tram started up. A click and a hum and we were off. The butterball man, in a bright-yellow mackintosh, sat in front by the driver, while I sat in the back. Before I left San Francisco, I'd been nervous about my trip; now, on about three hours' sleep, I couldn't be more excited. We were on a streetcar that went from Orly Airport to the Villejuif-Louis Aragon Métro station, the southernmost stop of the Métro Line 7. It was a cheap and easy way to get to Centre Ville, the heart of the city.

Every turn of the articulated white-and-green tram brought a new view as we made our way through a business park of flat two-story buildings, parking lots, and empty two-lane streets. It was Saturday morning and completely deserted. In a light rain, the electric tram went left, right, followed tracks across a parking lot, skimmed around the fronts of buildings, tucked alongside bright-green lollipop-shaped trees, angled across patches of bright lawns, and stopped at tiny stations equipped with narrow benches and bright-red, corrugated-plastic roofs. This wasn't Paris proper but a suburb, south of Rungis, the food distribution center for the whole metropolitan area. The trees, the roofs, the green, and the spotless tram made me feel like I was in a model train, running on a track meandering among buildings, benches, and streets, but there were no people. I was no longer a person, but a toy, G scale. Far above me, giants laughed.

For the giants, the size of King Kong, my toy tram car was about the length of one of their forearms, big enough to run on a railroad track outside. I saw the giant eyelets and laces on a pair of dark-blue tennis shoes, then someone's big brown eye peered into my window. With a jerk, I felt the tram shift and rise, instinctively curled my fingers around the closest pole, and hoped like hell butterball man wouldn't fall on me. He was not only round, but heavy too. I shut my eyes and braced for impact.

"It's my turn," Jeannette said, shifting her blue tennis shoe so she could sit on her feet. "It's not fair. You've been playing with the trains all afternoon."

"So?" Paul grinned.

Jeannette's bigger brother was six inches taller than she was. Two years older had given him an excuse to lord it over her every chance he got. Despite her best intentions to ignore him and play independently, she loved to be with him. He was the cool kid with the red hair, and everyone wanted to be his friend.

Jeannette and Paul were playing with their father's scale-G model-train set. At that scale, the cars and engines were robust and indestructible, but be careful of the tram, he had said, and went out. That left the children, bored and fidgety, inside with their mother on a Saturday morning. Paul would have rather been outside in the rain, exploring the woods with his friends, but wasn't allowed on account of recovering from the flu. Jeannette could've have been doing anything else but chose instead to argue with her brother. That was the best entertainment there was.

She didn't like the way Paul was holding the tram end down like that. Jeannette had placed Helen, her favorite cloth doll, into the tram, but then Paul had shoved a big fat plastic man inside, which had taken a bit of effort, as the man's belly was a little larger than the door, and now poor Helen was on the bottom, getting flattened.

"Put it down! Just put it down. Helen doesn't like to be squished!" Jeannette yelled. She swore she'd heard tiny voices screaming.

Paul was always saying that she was making things up, but that's what kids do, don't they—you know, play? But this wasn't make-believe. Jeannette had told him not to do it, but now poor Helen, wearing a tutu and ballet shoes, was upside down under the butterball man at one end of the car.

"Paul!" she yelled. "Put it down!"

He ignored her and laughed.

"Paul!" she yelled louder.

"Go on, yell as loud as you want," he said. "I don't care."

Jeannette went to grab the car, but that made him jumble up the people inside even more—she swore she could hear poor Helen screaming—and Paul raised his hand out of reach.

The door opened. It was Mama. "What are you doing, Paul?"

Paul was breathing heavily and his face was red, so all he could say was, "Nothing." He placed the tram back down on top of the station. "Jeannette's such a tattle-tale, Mama."

"Don't start, Paul," Mama said and went to close the door. She looked back just as he reached for the tram again. "Play nice or you can come with me to Giselle's salon. You'll spend the afternoon with some lovely ladies who will want to know about how you're doing in school."

Paul dropped his smile. He set the tram down carefully on its tracks, got up from a sitting position, headed to the couch, and pulled out an iPad. "I'll be good, Mama."

"And quit teasing your sister," Mama ordered.

Jeannette blinked her eyes and looked up. The first time Mama had stood up for her! She tossed her braids over her shoulder and braced for the soft words she had waited years to hear.

Mama threw a scarf around her neck. "Don't get any ideas, Jeannette. Listen to your older brother and behave. I'll be back in a few minutes to come check on you."

Jeannette's shoulders slumped. Paul looked at her with a self-satisfied smile. He wasn't the cool kid with the red hair anymore. He was just her annoying big brother. She opened up the tram and removed her doll.

Helen was a little worse for wear. Her hair was mussed and her skirt turned around. Jeannette set the tram on the floor with Mister Butterball. He'd survive.

"Mom's gone out!" Paul roared as he came in and, more quickly than Jeannette could react, stuffed all the people into the car, raised it over his head, and, pretending it was climbing a mountain, dropped it on the floor.

INSIDE THE TRAM AND STILL HANGING onto the pole for dear life, I felt the jolt, heard the crash, and got knocked off my feet.

Mr. Butterball lost his seat and was hurtling toward me. I struggled to stand and jumped up on a seat, grabbed the overhead handle, and screamed.

I couldn't see the red-headed driver. A few other passengers had been jarred off their seats. The back of the tram was smashed.

A little old lady, holding a toy poodle, was bleeding from a cut on her forehead. I heard sirens approach, but I was at her side with the tissues from my bag before the woop-woop-woop wound down as the paramedics stopped just outside the tram. The poodle was whining softly.

"Hey, be careful," Grandma barked when they surrounded her. "I just had my hair done."

The other people who had fallen from their seats onto the floor stood up, brushed themselves off, and headed to the exit doors. Instead of following them, I waited with the dog and took his leash, then went out the door.

It was a sunny day when I stepped down onto the platform. The other people were waiting on a different track, but the tram drivers, distinguished by their white shirts and smart black caps, led us onboard. I handed the leash to the little old lady, who gave me a smile.

"Centre Ville?" I asked one of the drivers.

"*Mais oui,*" he said. Of course.

I picked a seat. My chair had crumbs on it. From what? A baguette? Made sense; I was in Paris. There were just a few stops until the Métro. When a large man came over to stand in front of me, I got off the tram.

I was looking for a pleasant afternoon at Paris's Natural History Museum, Le Muséum d'Histoire Naturelle, when I made an unexpected discovery.

Eloise and Angeline

It was a sultry day in Paris, hot and humid, when I took the Métro to Gare D'Austerlitz and walked next door to the Museum National d'Histoire Naturelle. I felt at home when I saw the dinosaur hiding among the shrubbery. He invited me in.

It was a big building. The roof soared forty feet overhead. As I entered, I saw skeletons of every kind, from baboons and marsupials to monkeys you could hold in the palm of your hand. Also inside was a baleen whale, massive, with the baleen intact. You could step right into the whale's mouth and it would never know. Unlike Jonah, I walked past. I knew it took a lot of krill to feed a whale. But I didn't realize just how big their mouths were.

Sweat was trickling down my back by the time I got to the smaller animals, the specimens—in jars, out of jars, well-preserved all of them. The place smelled like my father's dusty attic, old and full of secrets. And then I saw her. Or, more specifically, them. Two young girls, Siamese twins. Standing free, in a glass box. Standing as if they just stepped off a bus.

Two bodies, wide at the hips, two chests, two pairs of arms, two shoulders, everything normal above the hips on each, necks, faces, full and intact, but attached to one pair of legs. Their skin was pale white, their eyes light blue. Skimpy blond hair, like mine, barely touched their shoulders. I couldn't take my eyes off of them. I couldn't move.

They looked like they'd lived to the age of eight or ten. The girls stared straight ahead, proud and naked.

"What are you staring at?" The question rose in the stultifying air. People were near me coming through the turnstiles at the entrance, but looking over my shoulder, I saw no one behind me, or to my side, in the narrow aisle between glass-covered exhibits. I looked around a partition, expecting a child, a mom shushing a baby, a stroller perhaps. Nothing. I heard the distant sound of footsteps walking away.

"Well?" The voice again.

I turned back to the girls, mesmerized, held by their steely gaze.

"And how would you like to be naked behind glass?"

Their faces hadn't changed expression, nor had their hands. They stood firm, upright, defiant.

Shafts of sunlight full of dust motes crossed in front of my face. There wasn't a hint of breeze. "Not much," I croaked. "Not much at all."

"No, we are not figments of your imagination, if that's what you're thinking. We are, or were, real." The head on the right turned toward me.

"We *are* real, Eloise," the other twin said.

A frown, or was it leftover embalming fluid, made her look like she had a squint.

Perhaps the beer I had for lunch had gone to my head. Only one. I'm such a lightweight, if I'd had two, I wouldn't think twice of conversing with a set of Siamese twins behind glass.

"Eloise, quit pulling on me." The other twin stared at me with an unequivocal gaze.

"Oh, for God's sake, Angeline. She's like all the others. She's not going to talk to us. Give it a rest."

Eloise, the one on the right, raised an eyebrow, or had I? That trick was not in my repertoire. I started sweating overtime. It was way too hot, I hadn't slept well, the beer hadn't been a good idea, and I was still on California time.

"We weren't sick," Eloise said. "It was Angeline's dream—"

"Cut it out, Eloise."

I looked up and down the aisles to see if other people were coming, people who could call the guards if they saw me talking to dead people.

"If you were in a box a hundred years, sister, you'd be pale too," Eloise said.

"Of course," I said, my voice a whisper.

"So! She does talk," Angeline exclaimed and nudged her sister. "Told you so."

The one on the right, Eloise, eyed me with a tight, studious gaze. "You American?"

I nodded.

"French people don't talk to the dead," she said.

That put me back. "Is that so?" I leaned in, curious and feeling very odd. I don't smoke dope and have enough trouble with reality as it is. And I lose things. Maybe I'd lost my reason on the Métro.

"One guy, yeah, years ago," Angeline said. "Eloise, remember? He flirted with you."

"But he was loaded," Eloise answered.

"Aside from that?" I asked.

"Not in a hundred years," Eloise said.

"God, how lonely it must be for you . . . two," I added, bubbling up that "two" with effort.

The girls turned toward each other, then back at me. "Whatever are you thinking, American?"

"Nina, my name's Nina," I croaked, hoping no one would come around the corner, whisper, and point at me the same way I was whispering to the twins.

"When you were born . . ." I asked.

"Oh," said Eloise, "our mother died."

"Must've been a difficult birth," I said.

"It tore her apart," Angeline said.

"We never knew our father. But after that, things were harder. No one wants to adopt freaks," Eloise said.

Standing there, looking at them, I couldn't agree more. It made me feel awkward and uncomfortable like never before.

"People kept abandoning us. We'd be sent from one family to another, and a month or two later, we'd be on our own again. We had no home for years—that is, until we found Monsieur George."

"How did you get by?"

"The clown," Angeline offered.

"He put us in the circus with the other freaks," Eloise said. "Just like today. We felt at home for a while."

I leaned forward, crouched down, pretended to tie my shoe. A family rolled by, two kids, one harried mother, a stroller with a baby. Mom and Dad were scolding the kids, the same way my parents had scolded us when we were children in Paris. In Rome. Everywhere.

"And Monsieur George? Was he the clown?" I asked, now on my knees leaning forward.

Hell, for all my father and mother's screaming and slapping us, I still had a home, a warm bed. What had Eloise and Angeline had?

"Yes. His clown name was Bouffon. He gave us a straw-filled mattress on the floor. No pallet. We had plenty of straw because of the horses," Angeline said, chewing at her nails. She shrugged her shoulders. "I can't help it. They get longer even though we're dead."

"Where did you grow up?" I asked.

"Nantes, Cannes, Lyon, Brittany, Germany, all over. What difference does that make?"

I couldn't tell them what they had never known.

"At first, we had a wagon to ourselves. The grown-ups cooked for us outside over an open fire until we learned how. Among the other freaks, we felt at home, as you can imagine."

"The bearded lady, Madame Bunkus, she treated us like daughters, her own daughters."

My stomach took a turn. Was it the pain au chocolat I ate? I hadn't had much else, other than the beer. The feeling passed.

"Dwarves, midgets, trapeze artists, super tall women, the bearded lady, we were all odd," Eloise said.

"But we were a family, of sorts," Angeline whispered, then fell silent for a long time, staring down the empty corridor behind me. "Until—"

"Monsieur George," Angeline answered. "He discovered that he liked girls."

"Not gay, then?" I asked.

"What a stupid question," Angeline replied. She turned and stroked her sister's hair. "He preferred Eloise."

"But you heard everything," I asked, then realized my mistake.

"It's my body too," Eloise said with a smile.

"He did this for months, watching us, playing games, getting closer. You know the rest."

I did. I knew the sequence all too well. It had happened to me too.

"Monsieur went too far one night, pushing and prodding with his fingers. I started bleeding," Eloise said. "Crying and covering our nakedness, we went to Madame Bunkus's caravan. She cared for us, gave us warm milk—"

"And blankets," Angeline added, with a flourish of her hands. "She let us rest, promised Monsieur George wouldn't bother us again."

"We felt safe," Eloise said.

"About four in the morning, he came in again. Madame Bunkus had left the wagon. A solitary candle flickered against red silken walls. Madame Bunkus had decorated her wagon like a palace in one of our books," Angeline said.

"We felt his step sink the wagon as he climbed up and in—"

"—and onto us," Angeline said quietly, her face forward, without emotion.

"Did his deed—" Eloise whispered.

"And smothered us," Angeline said and withdrew into her stock position, her hands out, imploring me to help her.

I leaned forward, placed my hand on the glass.

A shattering, high-pitched siren exploded in the museum. Lights blasted over my head.

I couldn't see anything for the lights. I stood up, raised my hands, and stayed silent.

Two guards came up to me, one ahead, one behind.

"Didn't you see the sign?!" yelled the larger one. He was burly and had a thin mustache.

Then I noticed. A large sign, to the right of the girls, "Don't Touch!" in four languages. I hadn't seen it before.

The guards duck-walked me toward the exit.

"I don't know why they get so worked up about a dumb exhibit," said the larger guard. "We have two-headed calves in the next building. Nobody makes a big deal out of them."

I tried to glance back at the girls, but the guards wouldn't have it.

Still hot, still sweaty, though this time I was shivering, I walked out the door into bright sunlight, too bright for my eyes. I squinted, stared at my feet, and headed underground.

I came out of the Métro at the station Saint-Germain-des-Prés, needing the touch of something soothing, something beautiful, something that would soothe my troubled mind. I wandered into Église Saint-Sulpice and took a seat.

The voice I heard was not my own.

ÉGLISE SAINT-SULPICE

I sat quietly, hands in my lap, staring ahead and up. Up toward the arches holding up the roof, and between the windows, full of light, white light. The air smelled musty, like my father's attic. Like the whole house now, the one I grew up in, now that they no longer open the windows, nor even the drapes.

Musty like days long ago and far away.

So, is that why I came here, to Saint-Sulpice, to smell the dust?

"You're sitting here quietly. So am I. I won't disturb your peace," a voice near me said.

I didn't turn to look.

"Do you know how to pray?"

"No, not really," I said.

"And sing? Do you know how to sing?"

"Off key, yes. But here, no. I'll just sit, even though the chairs are hard."

"They're supposed to be hard."

"So do you have to put your hands together to pray?" I asked.

Would praying bring my mother back? My brother back? Save those girls, Eloise and Angeline? Save anyone? I didn't know. All

I knew was that I turned my back on the church years ago, and here I was. Again. Sitting in silence.

"No, you don't have to put your hands together."

"Kneel?"

"No."

"Then what do I have to do? Mutter prayers aloud?" I didn't know any prayers, except for "Our Father."

"Not necessary. No. Just sit—and be quiet," the voice said.

My mind didn't want to be quiet.

"That's the point."

Oh.

I was alone in the church.

Would God come in and sit by me? How about his son, or Mary? I would make them all tea. I'd wash their feet. Would they look like the homeless men outside, in their tattered clothes, wishing they were God, but who stepped off the rails years ago headed toward drugs and never looked back?

Maybe God hid Himself among the homeless. How would I know? What if one of the men spoke to me in sonorous tones and told me the end was near? Would I believe him? Would I give him all my euros?

Well, all right then, God wouldn't appear in the world in the body of a homeless man. What about me? Did God reside in me? The priests might say so, but I wasn't sure. Sometimes I'm godless and mean. God knows, doesn't He, about all my transgressions?

But what if I had secrets from Him? What if there was no Him? What if? I used to believe there was a God, a just God, and then my mother committed suicide, and I decided that there couldn't be a God, nor any higher power who could let that happen. If there was a God, He wouldn't have taken my brother away either. I had hated the church for years.

Yet here I was. In the bosom of faith. Feeling comfort in a church. Feeling heard.

It took me decades to start to understand, and I wasn't there yet, just closer.

I looked up at the arches, sweeping far above me. The people who built this church believed. For hours every day, artists and sculptors and builders came here, climbed the scaffolding, and, over years, built this church.

"Pray, girl, just be quiet and pray."

But what about after? Can I go get a pastry?

"Who can say? That's then. This is now."

Can I ask for everything I want?

"It doesn't work that way."

How does it work, then?

"Faith."

Believe in something that's not there?

"That's faith."

But what?

"Just try to listen."

I heard chairs being moved. Low voices. A singular note rose from the organ. The choir.

They were assembling, perhaps.

Do I need to listen?

"You will want to."

And then I heard them. Angelic voices, women, sopranos, altos, then men, basses, and tenors, and then together, soaring, sweeping me up into graciousness, and I was suspended, fifteen feet off the floor. I didn't feel the chair or the floor—I felt angels and wings soaring beneath me, lifting me higher. The song ended with one solid, sustained note, and I floated back toward my chair, my toes hit the floor, my back rested, and I knew, *knew,* that He had been here.

With me. That He listened to me. That it was now time for tea. And pastry, of course.

I passed the first homeless guy by the door and gave him a few centimes. There's no telling, by the way, just who was whom—better safe than sorry. Just in case, I gave the second one a euro, and the third two, and on and on until all my euros were gone. Later, I'd go to the bank. I could do this. I was one of the lucky ones.

Twenty minutes later, I was in Place Bastille, where tourists filled the sidewalks while they waited for tables at a busy sidewalk cafés. Cell phones in hands, they were all chattering, speaking in languages I didn't understand—enjoying the view, enjoying Paris, enjoying the noise and bustle, like thirty million other tourists who came to the City of Love every summer. A few children drifted by, begging, and the tourists looked at each other, pretending they didn't see or care. I crossed the street to find someplace quiet. A moment later, I found myself running down the street at top speed.

History and Pain

"ARRÊT!" I SHOUTED AT THE BOY. "Hey! Kid!"

I chased him down Rue St. Antoine and followed him down Rue des Tournelles, a busy street full of buses and cars, narrow like most in the Marais, both of us dodging pedestrians, bicycles, and cars. He turned right down a much narrower street, then veered again onto Impasse Saint-Claude, a dead end. I chased after him, clutching at an ache in my side that threatened to tear me in two. But I had to catch up. I put on the heat, slapping my Tevas on the cobblestones and trying not to trip. The kid was fast, but I was taller, so I had bigger strides. More than five times his age, though, I ran out of breath first.

It was a hot and sultry afternoon, and I'd been on my way to my hotel for a rest when I felt a strong tug and my bag was ripped from shoulder. By the time I spun around, shocked, the thief was half a block away. Even though my passport and driver's license were in my money belt inside my pants, my bag contained my credit card and three hundred euros.

"Hey! Give it back or I'll call the flics!"

He kept running, pushing on doors—left, right, left, looking for a way out—as he spun down the alley, my feet in hot pursuit.

At the end of the impasse was a stone wall with nibs of rocks sticking out. He was halfway up the wall and sucking for air when I caught him by his foot.

He dumped my bag, paper and pens raining onto my head and cobblestones. I grabbed his pants, found his belt, and yanked him down. His foot came flying by my head. He was the size of my twelve-year-old granddaughter Becky, but I felt like I was fighting with an angry cat, all nails and teeth and spitting with anger. Tight blue eyes full of hatred. I ducked when a fist flew at my head.

He kicked out as I came closer, his hands up to defend whatever blows I might send his way. I took up my best tai chi stance, stood my ground, and when he went for me, I sidestepped, tripped him, and he tumbled to the cobblestones. His blond hair fell away from his face. I recovered my stance and looked closer.

Fiery blue eyes, a swath of blond hair, brown T-shirt, defiant and yelling at me. "*Cochon!*" Twelve? Thirteen? It was hard to tell. This was no boy. This was a girl.

"Me? A pig? I think not," I said back to her in French. As I crouched over her belly, I held down her arms.

"Screw you," she said, trying to kick me. "You've got your goddamn bag. What else do you want?"

"Going around stealing from people. You in a gang? Where's everyone else?"

"I work alone."

"How come you dress like a boy?"

"Ever been beat up? Small, weak, most girls are, you know. But I fool them. Fooled you too, didn't I?"

I let her sit up. "Where's your brother?"

"He didn't feel like working today."

Holding her shoulder with a firm hand, I looked up and down the dead end. I didn't go after my bag; my maps and water could wait. "So you think you can just get away with it, then?"

She turned, wriggled, and I watched her, my right fist cocked. "*Suffissant?*" I asked.

She got the point. She was still panting heavily while my heart was going a mile a minute. What if she had a shiv? What had I been thinking? I hadn't; I'd just reacted. But now I started to tremble, then focused hard to slow my rapid breathing.

"You won. Satisfied?" she demanded, after catching her breath. She puckered her lips as if to spit, and I held my fist up to her face.

If I thought she might burst into tears, that wasn't on her agenda. She was tough, with a tight little mouth, brilliant blue eyes, a piercing gaze, and dirty, disheveled hair.

"You got what you wanted," she said.

I kept my fist in front of her face. "You have that backward."

She looked at me, waiting.

"You didn't get what you wanted."

"Most tourists make good marks," she said.

"So stealing's okay in your book?"

"When I'm hungry, I don't give a shit."

"When was the last time you had a meal?"

"Screw you."

"My heart bleeds."

"Lady, you don't know anything."

"You're right," I said. "But I know a thief when I see one."

"Let me go!"

I backed up about six feet, still seething, as she rose. About five feet two. Just a little taller than Becky. Home with her mom, probably eating Cheerios with strawberries, her favorite, getting ready for school.

But she was too thin, too tough, and those eyes had seen both history and pain. She brushed off her trousers and hands.

"Why aren't you in school? Don't you have anywhere to go? I can't imagine it's very safe out here. You're kind of young."

"Young? I've been on the street since I was ten."

"Don't they have homes, shelters, food pantries?"

She bit her thumbnail, spat onto the ground, looked up. "Yeah. The Ritz has a room. You want to pay for it?"

I had a nice hotel room, with clean sheets and an en suite shower. "Uh, no."

"Ever sleep with rats?"

I shook my head.

"Shitty little beggars run over my toes if I take my shoes off."

At home, I had a service that took care of things like that.

"But I do all right. I don't need anyone's goddamn help. I'd do better if I had a dog. Everyone feels sorry for a puppy—but not for people. Bet it's the same in America."

She was right. I turned, gathered my things, and started walking down the alley. She followed me, too close, still trying to make me into a mark.

"I had a puppy, once. Well, it was Yvette's. But it grew up too fast. People don't like to see children on the street. They keep wanting to adopt me. Then the brothers, or the dads—"

"You *choose* to be on the street—when you could have a home?"

"I'm no one's goddamn pet," she said. "I need another puppy. That clears problems up right away."

I stopped at the busy street. Tourists were everywhere, pecking at their phones, taking photos. No one noticed that I was being accosted by one of Paris's finest little punks, pilferers, bandits?

"I've seen the beggars with their dogs, sitting on cardboard, on the same sidewalks, every day," I said. "Sometimes a bunny. Sometimes a child. I think it's cruel."

"I think it's cruel to go hungry."

"Where do you live? I'll pay for your bus."

She snorted. "What kind of question is that? Everywhere. Nowhere. What do you think?"

"Don't they have homes for children in Paris?"

"Don't make me laugh."

"Want a croissant? I don't know what shape it's in, but I'm sure it's still good to eat. I ordered two for breakfast and shouldn't have. Here."

The girl's face relaxed, but those eyes stayed wary.

"Go, if you want. I'm not keeping you."

She hesitated, turned to leave, turned back, jumpy as a kid in the principal's office.

I dug into the bottom of my bag. The croissant, in its paper, had lodged itself into an inside pocket. "Take it."

She reached out with a scrawny arm, grabbed the croissant, and shoved half of it into her mouth. Two bites and it was gone.

As she chewed, her eyes dashed up and down the street. Her face tensed when she saw someone cross the alley. "Hide me," she said, and I tucked her behind me.

I turned to face the mouth of the alley. Two boys looked down as they walked by. I could hear their muffled voices. About fourteen, all taller than I was, blue jeans, skinny legs, muscles popping out of their shirts. What had I gotten myself into?

Her brothers? Her gypsy family?

They stopped and peered harder, straight at me. I glared back at them, daring them to come near, trying to keep my legs from trembling. They turned and moved away.

"Lisette," the girl said. "My name's Lisette. They'd tell you they're my brothers, but they're not."

"Known them long?" I asked, feeling out of my depth.

"I had a brother who used to watch out for me," she said quietly. "But they got him."

"I'm so sorry."

"Why would you care?"

"I lost a brother also," I said. "Long time ago. Seems like yesterday."

"His name was Billy," she said.

"Mine was Chris. He used to look out for me too."

"Oh."

"What would you prefer, money or food?"

"Both."

At the mouth of the alley, she turned left as I turned right, my homemade bag under my arm, my hand tightened around it.

"I'm sorry," she said, catching up with me. "I shouldn't have made you chase me like that."

"Me too." I paused a moment, checking out the two cafés on the corner up ahead. "Still hungry?"

"Always." She shrugged her shoulders. "I love food. Eggs. Cheeseburgers. Omelets. Croque monsieurs. Sandwiches. Bread. Butter. Jam. Steak frites. Éclairs."

"Billy would be proud of you," I said. "This café work for you?"

She held her breath as she stood beside me.

"And Chris would be happy today, proud of me. Want another croissant?"

"Two," she said, holding the door for me.

Along with the clown shoes, the shoe-repair-shop window was full of puppets. They too had a story to tell.

THE LAST MARIONETTE
IN PARIS

IT WASN'T MY FAULT I WAS put in this window. It was Monsieur Catalan, the owner of this shop. He says it's best for me to retire here so I can watch the action on Rue Amelot if I get lonely. If? I'm always lonely, Monsieur Catalan. There's no action here, just tired people walking home from the market and lost tourists looking for Boulevard Beaumarchais. And mostly the tourists are sad, mon ami. I bet they miss the puppet show. I bet they are a little homesick too.

I said to Monsieur Catalan, take me out, take me to the stage, let me be somebody, but monsieur, now approaching eighty, he says no, he says no one puts on puppet shows anymore. How could this be? We were once heroes! For centuries, puppets were the main entertainment for the world. Our shows were packed! I used to be able to hear cheers from the very back row. Monsieur says children prefer screens now, but let me tell you, mon ami, if you have ever seen an audience of children gasp when a marionette marches across the stage, you know how they light up, giggle, cheer, cry. They support us! And now, no more.

They thought we were alive, not human, but alive. Why else would they cheer us on in our adventures on the little stage, boo when the bad guy, my brother, all in black, came on the stage, and when my parents kissed under a broad red moon as the curtain came down? But now, mon ami, it is only me, and I can't play all the parts, not the part of the boy, not with this dress and pantaloons.

I plead with everyone who comes by. Please, sir, don't walk away. Stop, please, and listen to me! There's not much time left. Don't say no! You say you don't have money? This will cost you not one sou. You say you don't have time? Everyone wants stories, everyone loves to listen to stories. Don't break my heart! Rest a moment, take a load off. There's a bench right there, by the window. Five minutes, please. Then you can have your coffee. It's all I ask.

First, I am still pretty, *n'est-çe pas?* Look at my pantaloons, my big bow, my hat. Madame LaChaise, the owner's wife, made this costume for me.

I am the last marionette in Paris. And no, I was never human, never even close. At twelve inches tall, I would have never survived. I wouldn't have been able to climb aboard a bus, walk down the sidewalk, or attend school. I am a puppet, through and through. My knees bend, as do my wrists and shoulders and arms, but not the rest, *compris?* Wood. And proud of it. When you knock, I answer. Made yourself comfortable? In the shade? Good. My hinges are a little rusty, I know. I need to oil them.

I was born in Nantes—a bit out of Paris, but good for my parents, don't you think? My parents were entertainers at the Chateau, descendants of several generations who lived life, celebrated sensuality, entertained the troops during the Great War. They loved education, which they instilled in me with gusto. Home schooled and proud of it? You bet. We lived above the stables in a dollhouse. We had lots of routines. My parents were full of ideas, and audiences always cheered us on. We loved to dance, to entertain the locals. Tourists would come from Paris for meals, lodging, and us. We were a sensation!

It was years later when my father, while toiling in his wood-shop, was muttering to himself as he carved small figurines, a head there, a hat there, some small hands. He used to tell us that one bundle of kindling became my brother, another my sister, and then another became me.

Mother made all our clothes by hand. Over the years, stacks of fabric rose in her corner in his workshop behind the stable. She saved everything, cast-off clothes, old coats, and socks. She always loved scraps of cloth, all shapes, all sizes, the brighter the color the better. At night, rats and mice scurried between the stones and the foundation and ran along the fabrics and chewed on them, pulling out threads for their nests. Mother, unperturbed, just stripped off the ragged edge and used the middle clean portion for our costumes.

We rented out a small in-holding in the back of one of the chateaus. Father took care of the livestock, pigs, horses, and stuff (from horseback), while Jacques did the lambs (on lambback), my sister Hildy took care of the chickens, and I hung around the kitchen with Mother. How could I do more? I was only five. On the weekends, we entertained the crowds.

Anyway, a year later, when I turned six, Father was in his workshop, designing new legs for his youngest son, Joey, who wasn't ready to be born yet. Joey had bright red circles on his cheeks, active blue eyes, a light waistcoat, and Father was lathing his thighs when the big storm came.

Mother and Father called for Hildy to go out and gather the chickens, but she'd already left. She could fight off German panzers with one hand if she had a mind, and she argued with our parents so much they just gave up. Hildy did whatever she wanted to do. Now she was out, in the storm, chasing chickens. What else was new?

Jacques, my older brother and taller than me by two whole inches, his job was to manage the lambs. Bleating, they had followed him into the barn and settled in the hay while the rain outside came down in torrents. I was hiding in Mother's skirts, standing by the hot stove in the kitchen, while she was listening to the radio, the BBC. Her brow was furrowed as she tested her iron with a wet finger and listened to the weather and war report. She wanted her children near her, as all mothers do, of course, but it was raining hard now, and Hildy had not yet come in.

Mother was short-tempered with me, so I kept out of her way, setting myself down by the stove, which was warming my pantaloons. Life was good, we were all safe, except for Hildy, and no one was worried about her but me. Hildy was argumentative, a difficult sort, but I loved her so. I wanted her home.

Father came in suddenly, banging the wooden door behind him hard. He was followed by Jacques. They were both sopping wet, hair plastered on their foreheads. Jacques had a wound, some branch had hit him, he said, but it was nothing, he said. He waved Mother away, grabbed another jacket, and headed back outside.

Mother was none too pleased when I begged to follow. I was only six. They said later that I had been very brave, but brave had nothing to do with it. I wanted my big brother *and sister* at home.

I struck out while Mother and Father were arguing about me. Like I said, I'm small. I put on my yellow hat and anorak and slipped out the side door. The wind pulled the door out of my hands, then slammed it against the house so bad, I thought the house would cave in. So much for my mysterious and quick escape into the storm to find Hildy. By the time I entered the first soaked field, Mother and Father were yelling at me to return, but my Hildy was out there. It was my job to find her.

I didn't see Jacques until much later. I guess he had been looking on the other side of the house by the creek. I headed to the chicken house. There wasn't anything our Hildy loved more than her little chicks. She used to call to them all the time and every one of them, including Peanut, the smallest, had decorative names.

I found Paris Belle, a Rock Island Red, hiding under the horses' water trough. Sinful Sadie was under one of the cars. Ridiculous Rita was in the truck, curled up by the steering wheel, down in the foot well, squawking. She never liked the rain.

I called out "Hildy! Hildy!" and in between claps of thunder I could hear Jacques calling too. As flashes of light burst above us, I heard another sound, a sound that made me feel faint; it was a high-pitched wail. It couldn't be Hildy. She was twelve, for heaven's sake, and long ago gave up being frightened of thunder or lightning. The sound was faint and strong, in between thunderclaps, a noise called into it. I ran into Jacques, Father, and Mother as I took off for the barn toward the sound. They didn't move. I stopped too, for there she was, our Hildy, between Mother's feet and the door to the barn. Lightning illuminated her. She was splayed on the spot, arms akimbo, her hands clawed, ready for something, anything, feet entwined in a dance of grass, mouth a rictus. Her eyes were full of fear and held an element of surprise.

Father closed her eyes. Then he turned his head up to the trees and cried. Cried for his Hildy, his wife, Jacques, the soul of my sister, and me.

Oh, I felt guilt all right, and shame, for earlier that day I had wanted to tease Hildy, to chase the chickens with aplomb like she did, to gather and wash the eggs. Mom would've been proud that I was being helpful for a change, but I kept getting into Hildy's way, and I swore at her.

Now Hildy was laid out, hard and impenetrable as a stone. We had to call Dr. Nitwell, the weasel, and he came out and measured her and went back to his shop to build a casket. I begged him to put me in it, but he wouldn't, he couldn't, he said. You're not dead yet.

But I felt dead. My Hildy, my favorite person in the whole world. Hildy with the laugh, the soft cry, the hands like velvet, strong and true and vital—but now, her limbs looked like twigs in the dirt. Immovable useless twigs. She looked terrible. Father threw his jacket over her face and led me back to the house. Jacques stayed an hour or so longer, but Mother and Father were not worried about him. He was a big kid even then. I went inside, ran by Mother at the stove, climbed the stairs and went to bed. I stayed there for two whole days.

☙

IT WAS A SUNNY DAY WHEN we buried her. Mother, Father, and I wore black. Jacques stood to the side. Mother had not had time to make him a proper suit.

"Louise," Father said, "stand close to me. You're the only daughter we have now," he whispered and wept. Jacques stood quietly, listening to the minister and not touching anyone. He had his own way of dealing with whatever was going on.

With our house wrecked, our chickens dead, and the countryside full of discarded wood, corrugated tin, broken, fallen trees, there was no reason for us to stay in Nantes. A few weeks later, Father heard from his friend, Henri Holmes, who was a clown in the Cirque d'Hiver in the Marais District in Paris. We always need puppets, he told my father.

We made the long and perilous journey by hiding in a crate in a carriage, and luckily made our way to Paris within a week.

We arrived on a dark night in front of the circular building that housed the circus right across from Place Republique. Henri was supposed to meet us there, but he had no idea that we'd arrive in the middle of the night. We rose from the crate under cover of darkness, curled up behind the back of the building, and waited for dawn.

The circus doors didn't open that day or the next. It was getting chilly and snow fell in the night. Starving, freezing, and thinking that death could be near, Father moved us toward the front of the building where the four of us were leaning in a doorway, under a streetlamp, hoping against hope, too weak to go anywhere.

On the fourth day the cobbler, Monsieur Catalan, found us. "I'm fond of the circus," he said, and, wrapping us in a blanket he had brought from his store down the street, he carried us into his shop and gave us soup by the light of a kerosene lantern. It must've been early dawn, for his shop was filled with the smell of yeast from what turned out to be the bakery next door.

Once we were well enough to stand, Mr. Catalan warmed up to us. Mother stayed inside, working on costumes for us all, for the circus that would start in a month. The cobbler said that would give us plenty of time, then asked if my brother and I would like to sit in the window while Mother sewed, and Father helped the cobbler with his fine stitching.

But that bright future was not to be. The first year, the circus didn't want us. And the next and the next, they said no. Monsieur Catalan stopped asking. For the first five years in the window, my parents were here. We were never allowed out to perform. "Maybe next year," Monsieur Catalan would say every September. Every fall, we'd stare down the street and watch the clowns head off to the circus. Begging Monsieur Catalan only made him mad. He filled up our window with clown shoes, so there wasn't much room.

Being older, Mother and Father's bones started to splinter. Mother's eyes were strained and she stopped sewing. Father could no longer see the controls of the lathe, and, knowing how much the machine could turn his hands into sawdust, he stopped working too.

A year later, their clothes frayed and their paint fading away, Monsieur Catalan took them out of the window, and I never saw them again. A few years later, a passing grandmother, wanting to impress her ten-year-old granddaughter Isabel, bought Father from Monsieur Catalan. Jacques cried when they took him home. He didn't dare kick or scream.

That leaves me. I am alone now. Perhaps, someday, someone will come and take me home. Perhaps, this time, it will be you. You will bring much joy to an old puppet's heart, and I guarantee I will make you laugh. I promise. I still remember how to dance.

Nor could I resist the chocolate shop, Joséphine Vannier, two steps away from Place des Vosges.

THE VEGETABLE NURSES

WELCOME TO MY HOME IN THE chocolate shop Josephine Vannier. Here at 4 Rue du Pas de la Mule in the Third arrondissement, in Paris, we have the best chocolates in the world. Some of our creations are shaped like a violin, oboe, and cello; others a ruler, compass, and erasers for Le Rentrée (the beginning of the school year in September), a clock (Mam'selle Bumpus), and my favorite, my absolute favorite, a chocolate piano. It has black and white keys and I play it, naturally.

Sometimes I play too hard and break the white keys—I've never cared for white chocolate—and even though Monsieur Froissart gets annoyed, he always fixes the keys and wonders what he did to make them break so easily.

At night when the streets are quiet, I descend from my perch above the curtain—where I have a bed, a sink, and a WC. Yes, all people, chocolate included, have needs, you understand. I come down when the steel grates are pulled across the windows, and I play. The others join in, of course. Our music may sound tinny to you, but to us, we're a complete orchestra and the world inside our chocolate shop is filled with music—oboe, cello, four violins, two pianos, and sometimes the boxes of petit fours chime in. They play drums.

One time we were playing, filling the room with notes and arias, a grand sound. Even Hattie Bumpus was chiming in! At that moment, Monsieur Froissart opened the steel grates earlier than we expected and we were exposed. To the world!

Madame Tartine, easing a melody from her cello, was the first to exclaim a swear word that is not found in university texts. Monsieur Concombre—*mais oui*, a cucumber. You think vegetables can't be made of chocolate? Heavens, he made a squeak and hid behind the spinach. All around me were squeals of alarm as we disappeared, too slowly, into the curtains. Monsieur Froissart was not amused.

"Amused" is perhaps the wrong word. We'd always suspected he knew about us, but that turned out to be not quite correct. He saw us, placed one hand on his heart, and shrieked. Then he fell to the floor.

You would think, would you not, that Monsieur Froissart would be a thinnish man, watching his weight around all the chocolates, but that, mon ami, is incorrect. He was—is—a rotund man and quite fastidious. He wears English morning clothes, a gray vest, black jacket, sensible tie, black shoes, gray trousers. All went down, the tea in the cup in his hand and the saucer, his briefcase, his derby hat, bam! Right over there, on the floor.

At first, Mam'sell Courgette thought he was dead.

Had anyone from the outside seen him fall? Could we close the metal shutters? No and no.

The violinists were first. Monsieur Pierrot, the clown, he is married, of course, and his children, Fourchette, Couteau, Cuillère, and Verre (Fork, Knife, Spoon, and Glass), all ran down the curtain pulls and attended to Monsieur Froissart's head. There was no blood, which was a comfort.

Still, the vegetable nurses were concerned that Monsieur Froissart might have had a concussion. They had to keep him awake, but if he were to wake up entirely, he would find out that his chocolate shop was filled with people, no matter how small. The jig would be up. We'd have to find a new home, and none of us wanted to take the Métro, risk everything, and leave all the comforts of home behind.

As for me, I played an aria from Mozart while the ladies whispered into Monsieur Froissart's ears, and the children tugged at his hair.

His mustache twitched, finally. Darcy, the piccolo player and youngest member of the orchestra, whispered sweet things, making Monsieur Froissart dream of romance. We all felt sorry for him not having a wife or girlfriend, so Darcy ventured carefully. She was a thin, small woman, looking exactly, well, like a piccolo.

The rest of us jumped off Monsieur Froissart's ample body and were climbing up the hem of the curtains when monsieur opened his broad mouth and yawned. Darcy almost fell in!

She skittered across the floor in time, finding her way to the drapery by the front door. She climbed faster than I did, hanging onto the fabric, and shot up for the head of the curtain. To my quarters! To my bed! I didn't have time to dissuade her. Not that I wanted to.

"Esmée?" Monsieur Froissart moaned in his deep voice. He sat up, brushed off his hands, a surprised look on his face. "Esmée!" he exclaimed again. She was his bookkeeper and knew him better than anyone.

Darcy and I, by now holding hands, suppressed a giggle. She was in no position to make a lot of noise, a single woman in a gentleman's bedroom, but we shared a look, a quick kiss, and she was gone.

By the time Monsieur Froissart stood up, still groaning a little, we were all tucked away. He brushed dust off his trousers and hands, settled his vest over his ample belly, and straightened his tie.

The bell over the door chimed. It was Madame Bracuse, in for her daily constitutional.

"Bonjour, Monsieur Froissart," madame sang, and he smiled. Our day had begun.

Slowly and furtively, we took up our positions on the shelves and stayed quiet and still for the rest of the day, thankful Monsieur Froissart had not hurt himself. That night, we partied like teenagers. Some of us knew our limits. A thimble full of whisky goes a very long way if you are small.

As for Darcy and me, we continued our courtship until the wee hours—and we have, please excuse my indiscretion, no limits at all.

The chocolate shop was a stone's throw from busy Boulevard Beaumarchais. I hurried across the six-lane avenue, as motorcycles screeched to a stop a moment after I pressed the pedestrian walk button. On the other side, I passed by the motorcycle shops and wandered onto Rue Amelot beyond. This was familiar territory—the peddler's shop with his clown shoes, and down the street, the Paris Opera Bastille where I had gone to see a ballet. Now it was quiet, although pedestrians walked by, sat on the steps, and watched the world go around the rotary Place Bastille. I walked on, past the windows looking down into the Métro Station Bastille, and down the stairs, where the teddy bear had been glued to the stone walls along with his broadsides. At the end of the canal was a boat lock under a steel railroad bridge. I heard the whine of the steel wheels on rails and the squeal of brakes overhead, while a boat engine started to rumble at the entrance to the locks. Then I heard voices.

CANAL ST. MARTIN

"No, Harold, I have the line around my foot. I'll go over. Quit yelling at me!"

Harold, the captain, was in the cockpit handling the wheel and didn't hear her. He was going much too fast and coming straight at me! Their little dog was running around the cockpit barking like crazy. The boat was coming closer and closer, and I stood back, incredulous. No one runs into locks, for heaven's sake! And then they crashed.

The bow hit the side wall where I was standing and almost knocked me over. I know a thing or two about boats, so I worked my way to the lip at the top of the wall and tried to use my legs to fend the boat off. Everyone knows not to use their arms, for Chrissake. I heard the sound of wood rails splintering. The woman dropped everything and screamed. The captain, his face the color of paste, was yelling as well.

That left me, dangling, my feet over the side, pushing the boat away from crashing again, until I couldn't hold the lip of the locks anymore and slipped.

My hands useless and slimy from seaweed on the wall, I found myself falling, convinced I was going to be squished between the boat and the side of the locks. Instead, I dropped onto the deck of the boat. I jumped up, right away, knowing it was a big no-no to go onto anyone's boat without permission, but I figured that since I'd helped them out, that would make it okay.

The big wooden gates to the canal opened up and water poured out of the lock. We started to drop. Water swirled around the hull.

The boat was swinging into the side again, and I pushed her away, took the line from the woman who was screaming in pain due to what I now saw was a broken arm in a cast, and I let out the bow line, imitating the captain as he let out the stern line, and the water in the lock dropped down and down and down, and soon the walkway where I had just been was now topside, twenty feet above me, and we were in some kind of a hole. But at the bottom. A little alarming, I know, but I'd been in locks bunches of times before. No big deal, generally.

The woman came up to me, her face contorted with pain, holding her arm in the cast, and speaking so fast I didn't understand her at first. "I don't know who you are or how you wound up on our boat, but I've got to go help Harold! Name's Evelyn. I'll be back to talk to you in a sec." She took off for the stern.

"In a sec" turned into the longest five minutes of my life. Harold stayed in the cockpit, Evelyn was gone, and I was alone, on the bow of a boat with a couple of people I didn't know, one of them a crazy captain. I started thinking that I'd maybe been a little rash, but then I said to myself, Nina, get a grip, you know better, it's a *code*, you have to help sailors in distress. Then, on the captain's command, I slipped the lines free from the shore above and headed to the cockpit to ask for a lift back to the shore.

It was a narrow deck heading back to the cockpit, but I liked it. I'd been sailing for many years and was content that the boat, along with Harold and Evelyn and the dog and I, were all safe and the boat was handling nicely and even the dog had stopped barking.

The captain would be proud of me. When I reached the cockpit, his face was all red, and I kind of wondered why. Was he ashamed of running into the wall? Evelyn was right next to him, holding her injured arm.

"It's okay," I said to them. "Everyone with a boat runs into something eventually."

"Who the hell are you?" he asked.

"Nina."

"Nina, what are you doing on my boat?"

"Calm your liver, Harold. The bow's okay," Evelyn said. "She helped. A lot."

"For Chrissake, Evelyn, I told you to fend off. But you didn't listen!"

He had a scraggly beard, which I guess he thought was handsome, but he looked kind of bedraggled and tired. And his face was way too red. Was he drunk—like my ex-husband was every time we went sailing?

"You ran into the wall once, were about to do it a second time," I said.

"Evelyn, you're useless."

"Two thousand miles of sailing and you're still an incompetent asshole," Evelyn said, turning her back to him.

"I'm going inside for a drink." He was followed soon by the little dog, which left Evelyn and me in the cockpit, alone.

"I can't wait to get off this boat," she said.

I knew what she was talking about. I'd been married to the same kind of guy. She was my type, older than fifty, wanting to be twenty but didn't have the body for it, hair kind of gray, arms . . . well, all I can say is it had been a long time since she had gone to the gym. Don't ask, I'm planning on going myself.

"I know that feeling," I replied.

"I break my arm four days ago while we're in Le Havre. And he expects me to handle the bowlines with one arm?"

I walked over to the wheel. "Where's your buoy?" I asked.

"Last spot, by the train station."

I knew where that was, like a mile away. I settled in, two hands on the wheel, feet glued to the cockpit sole. The little wheel was nice.

"I couldn't pick up my grandson," Evelyn continued. "He's eighteen months now, heavy and wiggly. I had to sit down to hold him, it hurt so bad."

"I'll hop off as soon as you tie up."

"Thank you. Appreciate your life while you can. Single?"

"It works for me," I lied. My private life was well, private, and I wasn't going to discuss my problems today, with Evelyn, or Harold, or anyone. Me, I had a husband; he just wasn't here. And he was one of the good guys.

As we entered the canal proper, heading to the eventual end near the Bastille Métro station, I remembered the hundreds of times I'd gone sailing, tending the lines, getting yelled at by my ex-husband, navigating in fog with two small children aboard, getting stuck in the mud, fighting the helm for hours in thirty-knot winds, falling exhausted into my berth at midnight. I'd grown to hate it. Now, funny thing, on a power boat in a small body of water, I still hated it. But I liked Evelyn. Go figure. I could just as easily have been her if I'd stuck around long enough with my first husband.

"Good to be back? Or do you wish you were still out there?" I asked.

She gave me a hopeful look. "Maybe he'll let me stay on shore," she smiled weakly. "Take a shower or even a bath, soak in bubbles, see a show, sleep for a week."

"Sounds like heaven to me."

"'It'll be fun, sailing around the world,' Harold said. 'Mid-life crisis,' he said. 'Help me celebrate. After thirty years in the banking business, I can retire early. We'll be together, exploring the world.' I thought it would be good for our marriage," she said with a frown. "To get away from all our obligations, his work schedule, his traveling at a moment's notice, his mistresses in Cannes and Lyon, Bordeaux. 'Spend some quality time with the love of my life,' he offered. And I believed him.

"You know what, Nina?" she added.

I tipped my head.

"I wish I'd never come."

We were halfway up the channel now. I could see the Bastille Métro station hanging out over the canal.

"I prefer staying home," she said. "Then he could have all the girlfriends he wants, and I'd have my life back."

"Evelyn Fenstein! Get on the bow!" Harold's voice echoed sharp and loud across the still air in the canal. He must've come up when I wasn't looking. "Mind the bowline! Don't let the bow hit the dock like you did last time!"

"I got it," I handed the wheel to Evelyn and went forward, grabbed the line, jumped off onto the quai, and made the line fast to a cleat.

I looked back. Their little dog was out in the cockpit again, working on a toy squeaker. Evelyn was looking at me eagerly, one arm cradling the other, waiting for me to invite her ashore? Or maybe not. Either way, she had her life, I had mine. And she looked lonely. She'd probably talk too much or be obnoxious or something. I preferred to be alone.

I waved, turned away, and meandered down the quai, away from the boats that had once held my heart, away from a commanding captain like the one I'd once had at home.

It was raining again. The streetlights had come on, early, but I had my umbrella and raincoat and a café beckoned, warm and dry out on the covered terrace with the heat lamps on as the rain drummed overhead and dripped down from the awning. I thought of Evelyn, on a boat with her husband and dog and broken arm. I had no desire to sail again, ever, no matter what the occasion or whatever romance the idea held. Instead, on my own, on land, I could go wherever I wanted, more or less, whenever I wanted. And I didn't have to answer to anyone.

A soft muzzle rested on my toes. I would've recognized the little dog coming in if I hadn't been studying the menu so hard. A chair shifted beside me. I looked up. It was Harold.

He set his jacket on the back of a chair and sat down. "My wife is driving me crazy. It was her idea—that boat, that dog, traveling the world. Her idea of a good time. Sorry I yelled at you back there. I'd quit if I wasn't so broke. I'm sick and tired of her. Want a drink?"

"She just needs a little time off," I said, sipping my Pernod.

"You seem to know a thing or two about boats."

"I should hope so. I must've sailed a thousand times," I answered. I sipped my drink and patted his little dog.

"Want to come on my next leg, to Barcelona?"

I looked at him, then through him. All of a sudden, I found myself in a triangle with a married couple and one of them was lying to me. Which one? It didn't take long to decide it was Harold. A drinker, mistresses, incompetent captain of a crew of one—it all became clear in the way he sat down, uninvited, and propositioned me. He couldn't have come across more like my ex-husband if I'd conjured him up myself with computer-design software. Now I wished it was Evelyn sitting with me, instead of this wise guy who reminded me of everything I'd tried to forget for a long time.

"You like lesbians?" I asked.

Harold widened his eyes.

I have nothing against anyone's sexual preferences. I just wanted to see his reaction.

I looked at the drippy sky, the mansard roofs across the Seine, felt warm and cozy in my coat, thought about the lull of waves against a hull, the bright light of dawn, the smell of coffee in a galley, the tight quarters, the smell of diesel, rough seas, being sick. Interminable days out on a boat with a guy like Harold.

"You make it sound so enticing," I said, hoping he caught some of the sarcasm. "But not this time."

With a sad look, Harold peered into his drink.

I paid for my Pernod, said goodbye, opened my umbrella, and walked out into a driving rain. Nothing could be better than being alone in Paris, having no particular place to go. I loved walking on the uneven, rain-splattered cobblestones, peering down every narrow street, and wondering where I'd wind up next.

As a teen, I was an eager student at a local ballet school and spent all my time there—two classes on weekdays and one on Saturdays. I not only loved it, it was a way to stay away from the madness at home. But I had neither the body nor ability, and after one excruciating lesson where my teacher yelled at me yet again, I knew it would be the last time. I walked out of the studio, bicycled home, and didn't tell my father for a month. So it was a grand surprise when I discovered that the dancers for the American Ballet Theatre were staying in my hotel.

THE BALLET

WHERE I WAS STAYING ON RUE Amelot was Paris at its best—hidden, with the back doors of shops, a few restaurants, and many secrets. The weather was perfect, and I planned on heading to a park for the day. At ten in the morning, the cafés were full, people taking long drags on their cigarettes, sipping espressos, reading the paper, petting their little dogs. I'd avoided the hotel's breakfast restaurant for a reason; any of these cafés had fresh croissants covering half my plate and showering my shirt with crumbs, orange juice that left a smear of pulp inside the glass and along my lips, and tea, hot with milk and sugar, the way I liked it, and everything for five euros. I lingered as long as I could, delicious as I thought that this was my vacation, and I could do whatever I wanted.

With my mouth full of croissant, I checked my email and almost choked. My first boyfriend, Dieter, had found me on Facebook. Now he was coming to San Francisco and wanted to get together. What would I tell Robert? Hey, sweetheart, I'm going on a date as soon as I get home? This would lead to no end of trouble. Feeling a little guilty, I sent Robert an "I love you" email and turned off my phone. That doggone Dieter—he'd always been hot. I hadn't seen him in twenty years.

But when I got back to the hotel to drop my book off, a posting caught my eye and changed my plans.

It was a schedule and included company class at eleven, rehearsals throughout the afternoon, rooms, and assignments. It was all there. The American Ballet Theatre was performing at Opéra Bastille, a ten-minute walk at the end of Rue Amelot.

I'd been a ballet student for years but never could master turns—I got dizzy as heck and could never keep my balance. I loved it still, even though being on pointe hurt my toes and made them bleed. I knew what it took to be a student; in my teens, I'd been in class eighteen hours a week. But to be in a company took twelve hours a day, with a body I didn't have and stamina and ability I'd never muster.

Still, I could dream, couldn't I? I dropped off my book and magazine and took a ten-minute stroll down Rue Amelot. By the time I got to the theater, I'd forgotten all about Dieter and was the dancer I'd always dreamed I'd become.

AT THE STAGE DOOR, THE GUARD greeted me with a smile as I signed in and shouldered my large duffel bag filled with several pairs of ballet shoes, a few leotards, cropped torn sweaters, leg warmers, short skirts, tights, paper towels, needle and thread, and ribbons. A small lunch was buried deep at the bottom. Today, perhaps, I'd actually get to eat it. I was eighteen, I'd been with the company a year, and now was part of the Corps. And we were on tour in Paris. Life was grand.

A clatter of voices with different accents greeted me as I entered the women's dressing room. Like all ballet companies, ABT was made up of dancers and staff from all over the world. The room was smaller than the one we'd had in New York, but the lights were arranged around the mirrors the same way and counters were covered with our familiar small jars of makeup and brushes. Headpieces and costumes hung from temporary moveable racks. Everything had a name on it: Jolie, Elena, Ruby, Esmeralda, and Nina. Mine.

A door opened and we rushed into a studio carrying our bags with us, as we all did everywhere in the building. The girl dancers leaned against the barres, sewed ribbons on pointe shoes, or stretched their legs over their heads, while the boys pulled up their tights and, turning their backs to us, adjusted their dance belts.

I pulled paper towels from my bag, stuffed them into my pointe shoes, slipped them on, tied the ribbons, and stood on my toes. I'd tried everything—moleskin, cotton, foam pads—and paper towels had turned out to be the best. Still, I had bleeding blisters from time to time. It went with the territory. I lifted a leg onto the barre, leaned forward.

The door opened. "Nina?" a voice called.

It was our instructor. She had a cold handshake and a voice that made my spine hurt. I went over. "Yes, Ms. Jacqueline?"

"Dieter wants to see you. Catch up with class when you come back."

Off went the pointe shoes, on went my pushers. I shouldered my bag, pulled up my warm-up leggings, and headed out. On the way down the hall, I passed studios where principals and soloists were prepping for rehearsal.

Getting a call from Dieter was never good. I tried to think what I might have done. My fouetté turns were coming, though mastering the thirty-two required for *Swan Lake* was still months away. I'd lost weight; my lines and footwork were precise and quick. Sweating now with apprehension, I marched up the last flights of stairs and knocked on his door.

"Come!"

Inside was a spare office, not surprising for visiting companies. Dieter, a man in his early thirties, was wearing a sport jacket and a thin black tie over a black silk shirt. He had a pompadour. On his right was Ms. Térèse, the company owner's daughter and Dieter's right-hand gal, the ballet mistress.

"You asked to see me?" My mouth formed the words, while my heart banged in my hollow chest.

"Ms. Térèse tells me you missed rehearsal yesterday," Dieter said with a frown.

Should I tell him I'd had a migraine and thrown up just as I was about to walk inside the studio? Migraines from the stress of dancing and not eating enough were common, and if I had a dollar for each time a member of the corps threw up, I'd be a millionaire. "My sister called from the States," I said. Better to give some excuse than none. Any girl who had migraines—who had any kind of physical problem—was automatically out.

"Company members don't come late to class, Nina. You know that." Ms. Térèse made a note on her yellow pad.

"She found out she has breast cancer," I said. Oh God, save me. I didn't even have a sister. I prayed quietly for all the women who had it. I'd make a donation when I got a quiet moment.

"I see." Dieter rapped his pencil on his wooden desk. "And her future?"

"We don't know yet," I answered, hoping for God's sake to remember my lie when he asked me about "her" next time. He'd done the same thing to my best friend, Marjorie Charpentier, two months ago, but Marjorie forgot her lie, so she moved back home to Paris and is now kneading dough at three in the morning in her mother's bakery, her pointe shoes hanging from their ribbons in a closet under the stairs.

"How are your fouétte turns?" Ms. Terese asked.

"I'm up to twenty-four," I said.

"In alignment? Precise?"

"Oui, madame." Ms. Térèse was French and, like all ballet classes the world over, her classes were taught in French. We learned by osmosis and repetition and correction.

She made another note on her yellow pad.

"Thin ice, Nina. That's what you're skating on," Dieter said. "As the newest member of the corps . . ."

Twenty-five dancers, many of them better than I was, were clamoring for that spot. I'd been lucky. "Yes sir," I answered.

"Tighten up your schedule. Call your sister on your own time." Dieter closed his notebook.

"Let us know how she is," Ms. Térèse said, and before I was out the door, they were discussing the next dancer on their list, Gael or Esmeralda. I didn't hang around long enough to find out.

The next day, we had the afternoon off, and after company class, I went to see Marjorie at her mother's bakery in Montparnasse, finding my way to her shop with ease. She gave me a big smile when she saw me enter the back room. Her apron, hands, and even face were dusted with flour. Her hair was wrapped up all over her head with fine braids everywhere and bedecked with bright pins and flowers. The ballet studio would never have allowed that.

Returning here hadn't been such a reach for her. Her mother had been and still was a great baker, and Marjorie would've become a baker too, if she hadn't been such a fine dancer and accepted into the company at seventeen, just before me.

We exchanged kisses on the cheek. She was pretty, with long brown hair, a rose-petal mouth, and long neck. Perfect ballet body. Great turnout. I'd always been a bit jealous, but here she was baking, and I was in the company. We dancers all possessed different talents; some had great extensions, others had speed, while some made great character dancers. They hadn't placed me yet. Maybe that meant I could be principal.

I stepped down into a piece of heaven—all around were the smells and sights of baking bread, chocolate tempering, cinnamon, and the sweet smell of yeast. She was rolling triangles, lining up baguettes, her canvas couche at the ready.

"Sit." She gestured one flour-covered hand at a stool. "How's the company? Only in Paris for two weeks. I'm flattered by your visit."

"Dieter was after me—"

"Dieter is after everyone these days." She laughed, pulled a strand of hair from her eyelid. "He's just pissed because Laurent dumped him."

"How do you know?"

"Ballet companies are worse than small towns. Everyone knows your business." She reached for a rolling pin, winked. "By the way, how's your sister?"

That brought me up short.

"You've been talking to Ms. Térèse?"

"No one talks to Ms. Térèse."

I picked up a ball of dough, rolled it in my hands. "And yet?"

"Dieter called."

"You're friends with him? After he threw you out of the company?"

"Bad news travels fast."

My hands started to sweat.

"No. I didn't tell him you only have brothers" Marjorie said, though I could see pain in her eyes.

"But you talk to him?"

"Naturally," Marjorie wiped her forehead, leaving a white smudge on her temple.

"So what do you talk about?"

"You."

"You're kidding, right?" I asked, feeling sick to my stomach.

"Don't worry, Nina," She came over to me and gave me a floury hug. "We talk about everybody. I have to. I take classes every day, just like before. The French teachers here have been trained by dancers from Saint Petersburg. Dieter said there's another chance, if I keep up." She stretched a little. "If I'm not ready, how else could I persuade him to let me back in the company?"

"Ms. Térèse doesn't need to be asked?"

"That old bag. She works for him. Always will be second in command."

"And what do you think your chances are?" There were only so many positions in the corps, and I was the last "add." When Marjorie left, they brought me on board. If I didn't get my turns right, I'd be baking too, or worse, working at my dad's insurance office. Whatever it was, it was equally dreary.

"Help me with this bag of flour, Nina." She gestured to a sack on the floor. I took one end, she the other. Damn thing was heavy.

"I still can't bench press sixty pounds," I said.

She laughed as she poured half of it into a mixer. "Ballet isn't strength training, doesn't do shit for your arms."

"What did he say about Laurent?"

"He said he's always preferred girls."

That was a laugh. More times than I could count, I saw Dieter, face up to the studio windows, watching the men's classes for far too long. Still, I didn't like the looks of this.

I reached around a block of knives for a still-steaming pain au chocolat on a white plate in front of me.

Marjorie slapped my hand. "For the customers, Nina."

Stung, I pulled back my hand. "So what do you think your chances are?" I asked again, though this time a little more tentatively.

"Dieter uses too much cologne," she laughed. "Cedar, pine, smells like a house fire."

"You met with him, then?" I asked.

"He's not so bad," she said.

"He just about threw me out of the company yesterday. What's good about that?"

"What are you complaining about? You're still there!" Marjorie reached for a baking pan. "Twelve years of lessons and I'm stuck making baguettes!"

"Any other companies looking for dancers?"

"Let's see. Le BHV's hiring."

"That's a department store. Come on, let me help you."

"Help? I don't need your help!" Marjorie cried. "I'm doing the best I can, fitting in classes between baking before dawn. You have nothing to complain about."

"Except my feet hurt every day, I have headaches all the time, and today I lied to the boss. Not for the first time, either."

"It's a tight little world, isn't it?"

"Incestuous," I agreed.

"You knew that the first day you walked into class. At what? Five? Six? All the little girls with their hair up and their little underwear lines showing under their tights. And you fell in love with ballet."

I walked over to one of the windows, looked up at the feet of pedestrians walking by. "We're chained to our lives, then."

Marjorie rubbed her eye, leaving a splotch of flour below her eyebrow.

"You're better than half the soloists," I said. Oh God, what if one day I couldn't dance anymore? "But are you happy?"

"Am I happy? Of course I'm happy!" Marjorie threw a pan across the kitchen, making a loud clatter. "And you? Do you think you'll ever get promoted to soloist?"

"They keep asking about my fouetté turns."

"They're always looking for excuses to get rid of dancers," she said and picked up her pan. "We train all our lives for one thing—then, bam, it's finished."

"Marjorie." I didn't want to see her like this. "Go on, tell Dieter you take classes. Go see him."

"I've apologized, I don't know, a hundred times."

"Quit baking. Dance for someone else. Redeem yourself."

"He still says no, Nina."

"I'm so sorry."

She nudged a tray of baguettes into the oven. "I'm only twenty-one. Wendy Whelan danced until she was forty-seven. I don't want to retire from dancing."

"I want to do it forever," I said.

"So do lots of dancers. But longevity, don't count on it. Most dancers get injured. A twisted ankle, a sore hip, a slight hairline fracture, then boom!" She slammed her hand on the counter. "You're finished!"

"What is it that you *do* want?" I asked. I had to change the subject.

"Something different. A family. Pregnant, maybe." She rubbed her belly. "Married to wonderful guy. A little bakery in Provence. With a veggie garden and a swing. My little girl will be seven. My son, six. They'll run through the grass, giggling."

"I'll be principal."

"Get another life, Nina. You never know what can happen."

I had an hour before I had to be back at the studio. A half-hour Métro ride, with a change. I had to leave. We kissed and I ran the last block to the Métro.

Two nights later, standing in the wings with the other cygnets, someone tapped me on the shoulder. Smelling like pine.

A minute before the lights came on.

It was Dieter.

I went to join hands with the other dancers, and he tapped me again. Whispered in my ear.

"Nina, not tonight, my dear. We have a substitute."

I refused to back out of the line. This was my night, my first chance with the corps. I nudged him back.

I started to bourrée, super fast, the step that would take us in a perfect line into the lights. The music rose to a crescendo, the familiar Tchaikovsky filling the hall.

Backstage, the line was taking off without me. I ran to catch up, grabbed the hand of the last dancer. All the dancers looked left, together, then right, and I glimpsed a familiar face next to me. It was Marjorie.

We glided across the stage in a perfect line, except for her. She kept trying to push me off my toes. Feet moving, heads turning, all in unison, pas de bourrée, pas de chat, all perfect, an endless array of precision and beauty. The klieg lights on the stage illuminated my face like the sun. We moved forward, backward, side to side, and when the principals came on, we leapt off.

Catching my breath, I stared at Marjorie, still with those inquisitive eyes, a look of challenge and victory on her face. The other girls congratulated her on her return.

Backstage, the principal dancer, Val Trondant, went to Dieter and complained, saying I'd ruined the performance. Hardly. I went backstage and returned with the knife I'd snatched from the bakery. Hid it in my tutu.

We all knew the rules. The show must go on.

I waited.

I didn't go on with the other cygnets, now that Marjorie had taken my place.

There was a rush while all the girl dancers headed to the other side of the stage, and when they came toward me in a series of fast and powerful piqué turns, I pulled out my knife and held it in place. Marjorie came by and impaled herself. She dropped as the audience, on the other side of the blackout curtains, burst into applause.

At first everyone thought she had fainted.

The police took Dieter to jail.

After that I was allowed back into the corps. And years later, I had my turn to be principal.

ॐ

IF ONLY.

Sunlight glistened on a thousand puddles as I walked the last five minutes down Rue Amelot toward the Opéra de la Bastille. When I got to the theater, it was closed to the public and despite my exhortations with a man at the stage door with mutton-chop sideburns and a haughty air—I would've have kissed him if he would have let me pass, I swear—I still couldn't get in. Feeling a little at odds, I took a turn and wandered away, down to Rue Crémieux to see the pastel houses.

I wasn't paying attention when my cell phone rang, and I practically fell over a child on a tricycle coming up the sidewalk. I melted against one of the walls of a pink house.

"I miss you, Mom. When are you coming home?" My daughter's voice calling from the States was so clear.

"In a few days," I answered. "Soon enough?"

"Daisy had her kittens," she said. "They haven't opened their eyes yet."

"Nice." I suddenly missed her, and my home and my yard and my garden. Bet it was all overgrown now.

"Mom, one more thing," she said. "Some guy named Dieter called. A friend of yours?"

"An old friend, an old boyfriend." Wasn't any use to lie to her; she knew everything anyway.

"He told me he's going to marry Marjorie. Said you'd understand."

My best friend?

"Said he'd call next time he was in the Bay Area."

"Tell Dad I'll be home tomorrow," I said, catching my breath.

In my wanderings in Paris, one afternoon I found myself having lunch on Île St. Louis, across the river from Notre Dame. I'd been there before, twenty years earlier, and if my daughter had been with me now, she'd say, go on, Mom. Despite the tourists, she'd say, go back, climb that tower again. I'm glad I did. Within a year, the grand cathedral would catch on fire.

Notre Dame

Summer 1995

Standing in line on Isle de La Cité, my daughter Alissa knew full well about my phobia, but she still insisted that we climb up to the top of the tower. I moved along beside her reluctantly. The place was busy, crowded with Europeans, Americans, Asians, everyone on the planet, it seemed. Already we had started to sweat from the heat. My body was hotter than most. Like my mother before me, I was afraid of heights. To Alissa, heights were fun.

I was nervous. A week ago, we'd been in Switzerland, caught in a snowstorm in approaching darkness, on a narrow trail on the side of a cliff, thirty minutes from a mountain hut and safety. Snow swirled around us, and a hundred feet below, I could see and hear a tiny creek, crashing over rocks. I had sent her on alone, ahead, for help and had struggled for ten minutes climbing over rocks and gaining higher flat ground, where I had sunk my feet into three-foot-deep snowdrifts. That night, in a platform bed made for ten, I promised myself no more heights, no more scary places, and now here we were.

Alissa understood that I was wary of high places, that I couldn't trust my feet, and my idea of heights was a balcony of a second-story building. She laughed when I told her no, grabbed my arm, and said, "Mom, we're here. Come on. I hear there's a great view." With deep reluctance, I followed her.

A family of four was ahead of us, mom, dad, and two boys who were tired and bickering. I knew exactly how those kids felt. The heat and humidity were getting on everyone's nerves, and we were all eager to move into the cool cathedral.

Suddenly, the line started moving faster and soon we were inside, waiting while guards searched our bags. The musty air of years and decades and centuries clung overhead by the entrance to the narrow spiral stairs to the tower. After another fifteen minutes, we walked up the first flight of corkscrew stairs, worn by innumerable feet, by history, by the family ahead of us, and crowds of tourists behind. Inside I felt safe, but I didn't dare look down.

Alissa laughed as I used the railing. How many hands had touched this black-painted metal before mine? The typical medieval stone spiral stairs were worn in the middle and wide enough for two people at time, maybe, if they were both skinny. To let someone come down, I had to tuck over close to the outer stone wall. Alissa just turned aside. I'd been twenty-one too, once, and was a bit jealous.

I heard footsteps below me, grabbed the railing, and glued my back to the round wall. A small kid, ten maybe, sprinted beside me and was gone, flip-flops slapping stone all the way. He was followed by four others, all giggling and chatting in German.

Occasionally, slotted windows let in light with great views of Paris. We ascended the last stair, walked through a door to a narrow balcony, and all of a sudden were plastered against the front of the cathedral, balanced on a narrow walkway with a railing no higher than my waist. I caught my breath. Alissa laughed. "It's okay, Mom," she said. "Nobody's going anywhere." That was true.

The line that snaked around along the outside of the cathedral had stopped. Below, the Seine poured through the city just below, gathering forces to divide, conquer, then join again on the other side of the Ile De La Cité. On the Plaza, a hundred tiny visitors lined up, eager to get inside the sanctuary.

Inch by inch, we moved forward and were back inside. Another bronze door, another attendant, and another much narrower circular stairway and we were outside again, under a hot bright-blue sky and on the rooftop of Paris. Alissa was radiant, soft brown hair blowing in a breeze. Protected by an aircraft cable mesh, I felt good beside her. I'd made it.

Aircraft cable separated faces, hands, bodies from the abyss. Gargoyles stood hunched over with their tongues out of their mouths as they had for centuries. The roof extended a long way and halfway across, the spire gold and rising toward the sky.

Everyone was chatting excitedly, taking pictures, shutters going off click, click, click. In the distance clouds formed around the Dome of Sacre Coeur in Montmartre, and in another direction, the Eiffel Tower and the Arc de Triomphe stood out. It was all right to be up here, as long as I kept away from the edge. Even encaged by an overhead steel mesh, I still didn't trust my feet.

A gust of wind came up. A woman in front of me grabbed for her floppy straw hat that had flown off, fluttered near a hole in the mesh, and flew through one of the holes. I too could make it through that cable, even though the holes were only eight inches wide. My imagination didn't trust reality. Not with heights, anyway.

A child bumped me, then another and another, and I took a protective stance against a corner tucked inside the ramparts until they passed. Alissa stood at the side of the pathway looking out at the statues below. Across the city, dark clouds advanced quickly, now scouring the Eiffel Tower, obscuring the top. The wind was increasing, while around me everyone reached for their hats—fedoras, straw hats with ribbons, baseball caps worn backward, everything fluttering in the wind. It was both scary and a thrill to be up there in the approaching storm. Alissa always told me to push myself. She was right.

I braced myself for a strong gust that lifted my bag against my shoulder. People were moving fast toward the exit door, hurrying around the top of the tower, eager to get out of a coming sprinkle. I felt a few drops on my forehead.

Now it was just us and an older man, an American. He was oblivious to the weather. He leaned into the cable mesh, his earbuds in, shouting to someone in the States. His words disappeared in the growing breeze. His suit jacket fluttered in the wind; with a gust his tie flipped over his shoulder, then he too headed down.

Still hot and sweaty from the humidity, we welcomed the breeze and the slight rain. The dark clouds swarmed closer, hiding the Seine. I felt a slight tug on my right leg, but with the aircraft cable over my head, I wasn't going anywhere. I love storms.

The guard waved us toward the exit. He was under an overhang at the entrance to the stairs. The wind grew again, to gale force, the rain now hammering us sideways, and just as we decided it was time to descend, the aircraft cable over us flashed in a lightning strike. I ducked. When I looked again, Alissa was airborne.

Her feet were off the ground and rising fast.

The aircraft cable over our heads was open, cut cable flapping in the wind.

Without thinking, I grabbed for her legs and pulled down, but the wind was fierce, spinning over our heads, yanking her upward. She was midway through the wires now, her head above, screaming, "Mom!" Mom!"

My hands were slippery on her sweaty legs. I coiled my hand around one of the cables to pull myself up, to be even with her, to get her down. Her waistband was hooked on a sharp cable, and she was flailing enough to jerk herself free. I tucked my foot in the cable web, screamed back, grabbing for any part of her I could hold—waist, arm, leg, anything—yelling at her to stop moving around, to let me get a grasp. The wind howled at the top of the tower, swirling and churning around us.

Her knees were even with the gap in the mesh. With my feet tangled in the now-weakened aircraft cable, I grabbed one of her ankles and pulled down as hard as I could, tearing her thigh on the sharp edge on her way back down. The wind changed direction, she dropped, and praying to God I wouldn't get caught in a gust, I fell, just outside the cable.

My ankles were twisted in the wire and were the only things holding me from falling onto the steep roof. As the gusts came, they blew me into the mesh, then away. I swung over the plaza. And screamed.

The guard was nowhere. The Seine boiled below. Tiny ant people on the plaza rushed for shelter. I reached back to the mesh, doing my best to hold on, while my fingers slipped on the wet wire. I grabbed again and again while rain pelted me. I couldn't get over the gap. Alissa pulled at me from the inside to no avail. My head swam. I felt like the world was going black as the wind tossed me to and fro. I grabbed a part of the web and, with all the strength I had, gained a little ground. Hand by hand, foot by foot, I worked myself over the gap and fell onto the pathway.

The guard came over, helped Alissa up, and pulled me up sharply.

"What were you doing in the mesh? Didn't you read the signs?"

My arms hurt. Alissa was bleeding from a cut on her leg.

"What were you doing out there?"

I went to speak, but words wouldn't come out. My legs, arms—everything was trembling.

I went to point out the hole in the mesh overhead. It was as wide as I was tall.

He looked from me to her to the clouds overhead. Lightning struck the Eiffel Tower.

"Get inside!" he called. "And hurry!"

The Seine was rolling around the island below. It was raining so hard I could barely see. The guard took our arms and hustled us to the overhang, then guided us down toward the stairs. With wobbly legs, I descended carefully, holding on to the banister the whole way.

When we reached the café, scratched, bleeding, and sweating, gendarmes with their machine guns were patrolling the streets, still watching the crowds. There had been recent bombings. I wasn't sure which was safer, the top of the tower or Rue St. Germain.

Summer 2018

This time, I went back into line, determined to make it on my own. The crowds were the same, but everything else felt new. I had forgotten how narrow the pathway was out on the front of the cathedral. I vowed to stay plastered against the wall, but there is a place there where it is very narrow and you must walk forward and around. No backing up, of course.

As spectacular and beautiful as all of Paris lay before me, her wondrous buildings, her towers, her wide avenues, the Seine below, I was thrilled more than frightened. And no wind today. Just sultry and hot. Time changed nothing for me—except I missed Alissa and her encouragement. As long as I didn't fly out of the mesh, life would be good. At the same time, she wouldn't know if I failed climbing up unless I told her about it.

When I stepped out on the roof, my heart caught. Walking around the tower roof, I couldn't find the spot where she'd gone through.

And then I found it. Yes, this was it, the Eiffel Tower, the view below, the gargoyles crouched as always, and above me, the mesh, repaired with globs of welds, clumsily done but strong enough, connected a gap of about three feet by three feet over my head. This is where I remembered my Alissa, smiling, holding the mesh, glad we were both alive. We hadn't been dreaming. This time my feet were planted on the roof and I wasn't afraid and I still had my daughter, in her forties now, a mother herself, and I thanked the gods, the statues on the roof, the golden spire, and the gargoyles, still looking nasty, protecting my daughter, as I had prayed for a future where we could grow up together. My body felt grounded and safe.

I was in tears on my way down, but it wasn't from sadness, it was from joy. She would be glad to hear I had pushed myself without her. At the cafés on the Rive Gauche, the gendarmes with machine guns were gone, but the tourists were still there, ordering drinks and talking much too loudly. I was worried at first that I wouldn't hear her voice over the din, but when I punched in Alissa's number on my cell phone, she answered on the first ring.

Over a lifetime of visiting Paris, when I returned in my sixties, I didn't expect to run into my own family history. Memories came flooding over me, leading to sensations I hadn't felt in fifty years. I felt my mother's hand in mine on the Quai D'Orsay, heard my father's voice chiding me in the Musée Picasso, spent an afternoon picnic at Places des Vosges remembering my brothers, and my lost brother showed up with the woman who would have been his wife and their son, and thought fondly of my daughter at Notre Dame. Finally, I ran into a stranger I knew well, but who didn't know me.

The Night Train
to Paris

It was eight in the morning and Paris was just waking up. Birds fluttered overhead from chimney top to chimney top. All was silent except for the swish of brooms and the sound of rushing water. Across the street, a young woman, walking with purpose, was following the narrow streets on the Left Bank. Hausman buildings towered over us. Shopkeepers swept the sidewalks in front of their stores while workers hosed off street gutters.

She seemed familiar. Too familiar. Her hair was like mine, just as thin, but blonder, longer. Her figure was thinner, though her jeans and tennis shoes just the same. Her chin was exactly the same as it would always be. Today, at nearly seventy, I disappear everywhere with my wrinkles, middle-aged spread, and graying hair. But she, at seventeen, was illuminated from within. She was both young and purposeful. Maybe she had taken the Orient Express all night from Munich, like I had done years ago, and she was on her way to join her high school class in Paris, then go back home with them to Boston in the morning. I tried to follow without her noticing me. I didn't know yet what to say to her. I was fascinated.

Maybe so. That trip in 1966 had been our father's plan. He said that her high school class trip to France was too expensive, and since her brother already lived in Germany and spoke fluent German, would she like to spend six weeks in Europe with him? She jumped at the chance.

They'd traveled through France (where she spoke French everywhere), and he spoke German. They stayed at youth hostels, on the lobby floors of hotels, out in the fields in the country, taking their time in the Pyrenees, and spent a week with one of their father's friends in Costa Del Sol, Spain. In Cannes, they'd had their suitcases stolen, but not their passports or wallets, and, as planned, had taken the train to Munich to meet their father.

The greatest summer she'd ever had. Now her brother was back in Germany with her father and soon their father would go home, and her brother would go back to school at the Goethe Institute in Munich. And she would meet her class and head home in the morning.

That was why she was walking with purpose; carrying a small suitcase, she was on her way to meet them at their hotel.

I couldn't approach her. I kept a respectable distance.

A guy was following her. I could see him, staying back, but keeping up with her as she twisted and turned down the narrow cobblestoned streets of the Rive Gauche. Just another fool following a pretty girl down a street, I figured, but I was afraid for her anyway, even though I already knew the outcome, of course. I knew everything about her.

He drew closer, then kept pace. I watched them closely now, knowing what she was going to do. Smart girl.

He ran up and stood beside her. She kept her eyes forward—until she stopped, stared at the man, and said something sharp and commanding. He stepped back, let her go, and drifted down a side street. She was okay now.

I know what she said, "Va-t-en. Go away." a phrase we'd practiced in French class.

Watching him disappear, she saw me, stopped, set down her suitcase, and stared.

"Can I do something for you?" she asked.

"The guy. The guy who was pursuing you. You seemed to do all right," I said.

"Guys have been following me for years. What business is it of yours?"

"I was worried, that's all," I said.

She picked up her suitcase.

"Look, it's eight in the morning. I need a croissant and cup of coffee. Would you like to join me?" I asked.

"I'm not hungry."

I couldn't help smiling. I bet she hadn't eaten all night.

"Listen, Nina," I said. "Yes, I know who you are. I know your father, Doctor Solomon. Of Harvard. I've even been to your house."

She straightened her back.

"A lovely house, as I recall. You have a dalmation?"

Her face clouded. "Yes." She gathered her composure.

"My name's Nina, too," I said. "I bet you're starved. Would you like a cup of coffee? A croissant?"

"I don't have much time," she said.

"None of us do," I said, not thinking I was talking to the younger generation, who had nothing but time.

We took opposite sides of a small marble-topped table. It was cold under my sweaty palms.

"What else do you know about me?"

"You were arguing with your father," I said. "Something about politics."

She laughed. "Sounds about right."

Should I tell her more? It seemed bold and crazy enough. At the moment, though, the situation was too delicious for words. Visions of my father, mother, and brother were one thing; why not me too?

She was the reason I'd come here in the first place. She'd never been afraid. But I had been. Once I got here, I felt foolish. Why is it that when we get older, we become frightened of everything?

We were on a narrow street, at a café on a corner, our chairs facing out, our backs against the window. We were the only customers. The sun was breaking through the clouds.

She tucked her suitcase under the table and held her purse on her lap.

"Are you traveling as a tourist, or do you live here?" she asked.

"A tourist," I smiled. A tourist in love with Paris. "It's so uncanny, running into you here, in the Rive Gauche, at eight in the morning. Who would've thought?"

"We ran into some of my father's friends on a pass high in the Italian Alps," she said. "Go figure."

"What brings you to Paris?"

"I'm meeting some friends. And you?"

Three cars came through the intersection super fast, horns blaring. It was such a narrow street, I pulled back my feet from the curb even though they were nowhere close.

"Discovering old friends," I said. "Wandering around. Practicing my French. It's been quite wonderful."

"I've been in Europe for six weeks. Speaking French has gotten easier," she said.

"I study in my own peculiar way," I added. "But I don't speak it at all really. Bet you do."

"Now, yes, way better," she replied. That kept her quiet a moment. She nibbled on her croissant. Looked back at me.

Oh, to be young again.

"Yesterday evening, about seven, my dad took me to the train station in Munich, bought me a ticket on the Orient Express. The Simplon Orient Express. It goes from Istanbul to Paris. Train service on that line started in 1883."

"Wow. I've heard about that train in movies."

"It was great. My dad said, 'Nina, just stay on the train, no transfers. It's the night train to Paris. You'll do fine. Get out at Gare de L'Est. Take the Métro to the hotel to meet the other girls.'" She caught a breath. "'They'll be at the hotel just waking up when you come in. Expecting you. A day or two later, I'll see you in Boston.'"

I nodded, listening. For me, it had been one of my very best summers ever.

"The train was grand," she said. "Red-velvet cushions, ragged at the edges. A stately salon. I had a seat in the economy car." She leaned forward. "A bit worn, but you could tell—such a famous train, like a lady who's seen better days. A man was flirting with me. Nobody at home does that. It was fun," she said. "He had beautiful blue eyes."

I remembered him too.

"I suppose I slept some. But mostly I walked around the train, looking out into the night, at the tiny lights of the villages as we went by, the deeper darkness of the hills, the flat valleys with streetlights here and there, and long patches of nothing. But inside the car," she paused, "there was light, and a sway, and a clickety-clack, and I felt safe and adventurous, and I didn't want the trip to end. I ran into some people, spoke French to them—as I had all summer—and we had a good laugh, and I understood and spoke just fine. That guy didn't believe I was an American, I spoke French so well."

"How wonderful!" I said.

"Then a small light in the sky, somewhere in France. Villages appeared in the mist, a light here, a light there, cows in the fields, thatch in rows, narrow roads, one, two cars, I could see forever. We watched the dawn together. He stood beside me all night, his hand on the small of my back."

"I wish I'd seen it too."

"Then the light spread across the sky, a band of pink and orange and deep red and it became lighter and lighter and then there were more houses, and I had some coffee, and he kissed me. The train slid into the train station. I barely felt it, my feet were so far off the ground. Then I hopped the Métro, and here I am."

"Your first kiss?"

"Not hardly. A guy in seventh grade chased me around the library until he cornered me. But I didn't like him much. I had a big crush on this other guy who was my best friend's boyfriend. But he never paid any attention to me. Not like last night." She sighed.

A few people took outside seats nearby.

"He was just a kid—this guy, a man, I mean. Twenty-seven, he said. Looked like a movie star."

She sighed, looked at her watch. "I gotta go. I have to buy a few things. A few nights ago, our suitcases were stolen in Cannes. Who would want my clothes? Luckily, they missed my purse, with my wallet and passport."

"How'd they miss your purse?"

"I dunno."

"Next time keep it with you, okay?"

The waiter came out and had a smoke.

"When we took the train to meet our father at his hotel in Munich, he was a little peeved we hadn't sent one postcard all summer. He thought we were dead. We'd been having a blast. Anyway," she took a breath, "he recovered. I'll see him again in a week."

I remembered when it seemed like my father had loved me too. Now I knew better. I spent years trying to be the perfect daughter, trying to figure out what I'd done wrong. After he died, my sobbing stepmother admitted that withdrawing from me was one of the biggest regrets of his life. Thirty frigging years lost. She told me he thought I'd sold his grandmother's platinum-and-diamond brooch that's been in my safe deposit box since 1963.

She was digging through her purse.

"Don't worry about it. I invited you, remember?" I said. "I hope you can find something wonderful to wear in Paris."

"I'll get the rest of my things once I'm home."

"How's your brother?"

"I just saw him in Germany," she said, her face clouded.

"Your other one."

"He doesn't spend much time with me."

"Bug him. Ask him to let you do stuff with him," I said, "no matter what he says."

"At nineteen, he has his own friends. His own life. He's not home much."

"Please. Try." I couldn't, just couldn't, tell her that he'd be dead at twenty-one. I picked at my nails instead.

I could see the future unfolding in front of her—the tragedies to come, the marriages, son and daughter, moving to California, all fifty years unspooling in front of her like a long story. If I told her any of it, would it make any difference?

The sun was out, it was a glorious day, and she was starting to fidget. If I was going to tell her anymore, it had better be now. There'd be love, she'd fall in love with a guy in a store. Could I tell her that? But I had to. I had to warn her about that other thing.

"You have a boyfriend?"

She shifted in her seat. "You're sort of in my business," she said. "Do you?"

"I'm married. He doesn't like to travel to foreign countries."

"France isn't foreign. Not to me," she said, and we both laughed.

"I never thought anyone would ever love me," I said. "But they did." My stomach started hurting. Too much coffee. I had to tell her, I had to. "Can I tell you one thing, Nina?"

She was digging in her purse for something. Cocked her head and pulled out a postcard. "Should I send this to my dad now?" she laughed.

"Sure. Why not? But just, you know, be careful. If some older guy—not a guy on a train—takes a liking to you, don't fall for him."

"Right. More advice. Last thing I need," she said. "He was cute."

I couldn't wait anymore. "Lots of guys will take a liking to you."

"Well, they haven't yet. Just creeps on the street and that guy on the train."

"But they will. And when they do—"

"Oh, for God's sake."

"A lot of older guys like girls in high school," I muttered.

"Not hardly."

It was getting on in the morning. She was fidgeting in her chair and our coffees were cold.

"Promise me something," I said, reaching to pat her on the arm. "There'll be this friend of a friend. An older guy, like the one on the train. He'll kiss you."

Her eyes widened. "I wouldn't mind that one bit."

"You'll like him. You'll have a crush on him."

"I have a crush on lots of guys. Except my brothers' friends. They think I'm a 'little sister.'"

Until you get boobs, I wanted to say. I remembered how that came about. All of a sudden, they looked at me different.

"You'll go to see him one afternoon," I pushed ahead.

"Bet he'll have blue eyes."

"Yes, he will."

"How do you know?"

"A wild guess," I said. "Whatever you do, don't go see him in his office. Don't. Just stay away."

"What are you, some kind of wacko or something?"

"Just don't go."

A few pedestrians meandered down the street. Ignoring us, then looking hard at me. Figured I was arguing with my own daughter.

"What are you talking about? You're creeping me out." She pushed back her chair.

"Just listen. Please. Listen to me."

"You sound like my friends' mothers. Don't go to Harvard Square, stay away from boys, be careful of your reputation. Don't drink too much. I'm sick of it."

"Sick of people telling you what to do?"

"I'm seventeen years old, on my own in Paris. You think you know everything about me."

"Because I do."

"I have to go."

"Please. One more minute." I said quietly, "He'll hurt you."

"Why should I listen to you?" Her voice rose.

"He's going to rape you," I said quietly. I remembered the day so well. Warm, sunny spring day. Feeling safe and in the dark in his studio, he surprised me with something different.

"I don't have to listen to you!"

"YES! You do. Promise me! Promise you won't visit him."

"No. There's no way you could know everything about me."

"But I do."

She stood now, cocking one hip, her purse over her shoulder. "Prove it."

"Because I am you, Nina." I reached out for her hand. "I'm you, fifty years on. It's not a coincidence that we have the same name, the same hair, the same chin—the same history, the same everything."

"YOU CRAZY OLD BAT!" she yelled, picked up her stuff, and took off.

She didn't get far before it started.

The ground started to move, slowly, like an earthquake in California. Squeaking and moaning. I wasn't sure what to do, run and save her or save myself. The sidewalk undulated, cracked, and she stopped, looked around. Cobblestones stood at funny angles around her feet.

Other people were screaming. Scattering everywhere. A mother held a six-year-old girl by the hand. The girl was crying.

I stood up, grabbed my purse.

The buildings around us shook and clattered.

She stared at me. A chunk of masonry fell between us.

"Nina, get inside the café!"

I grabbed her and shoved her under a doorway. The waiters crouched, hot cigarettes falling from their fingers.

I heard a boom from below the ground.

"Get down!" the waiters cried.

The floor was cold and dirty. I stood over her, crouching down, taking the splinters on my back. She pushed back a little, then lay flat on the floor under me. I had to keep her safe.

Glass shattered all around us. Just outside, cars ran into each other, smashing into buildings, each other. People ran everywhere, some away from us, others pounded on the café door. We heard shouts and screams, then under us a huge boom, then our little corner exploded.

It was my fault.

I had cracked open the world. I had tried to turn back time.

My last night in Paris, a light rain was falling, and before I knew which way to trace my steps back to my hotel, the city was plunged into darkness.

FULL OF MYSTERY, STILL

Streetlights, house lights, and any illumination disappeared.

In the near-complete darkness, I strode back toward my hotel with determination, but when I turned right on a street that I thought led to Boulevard Beaumarchais, it dead-ended in an alleyway. Cars, in the distance, flicked on their turn signals and flew round corners, brake lights shining unnaturally bright. I backed up and turned left at the last intersection, where darkened shop windows and illegible signs led to a five-star intersection I didn't recognize.

I put out my hand and steadied myself against the wall of a building. A car went by, briefly illuminating the street, leaving me in a haze of exhaust.

Across the street and upstairs, light from flashlights dashed around an apartment. I longed for my own safe haven—or at least that big boulevard I'd been looking for. Listening carefully, I heard voices and, in the distance, traffic. I headed toward the sounds of rubber on the road.

"Ooof. Desolée." A man bumped into me. I smelled cigarette smoke.

I touched his wool coat. *"Moi aussi.* Sorry, I hadn't meant to walk into you."

"Ah, madame. Pardon. Can you find your way?"

I stood back, enough to give a little space between him and me. A gibbous moon cast a pale light in the sky.

"DESOLÉE, NO," I SAID. "I'M LOOKING for Boulevard Beaumarchais."

"Madame, may I guide you?" he asked. "My name is Tomas."

I couldn't see his form in the dark. "Of course," I replied as he slipped his arm through mine. "My name's Nina." We walked side by side as he talked.

"My hand is on the building, Nina. The sidewalks are narrow here. Please be careful of, oof, window boxes. Yes, that's good, step around."

I followed his instructions. He didn't know what I looked like, how old I was, or how clumsy I felt in the dark.

I leaned on him a little. I could've extended my hand, but he wouldn't find it. Along the sidewalk, there were other voices.

"*Zut!*" a person yelled from a little distance away.

"*Merde!*" said another from behind us.

"When will they turn on our power?" shouted a woman from an open window.

"I'm going to miss my movie," said another. All the voices had an edge to them, a fear, their worlds dislodged.

But the one next to me was warm and beautiful. And just then, Tomas found and took my hand. He was kind and solicitous, a little taller than me. He guided me across the narrow streets. We could see the headlights on the boulevard, where I knew he'd head off to find someone young and beautiful.

The traffic was heavy and confused, all the drivers edging forward, but without stoplights, it was a free-for-all. The flash of headlamps across the street illuminated a store I remembered. I knew where I was, at last. "My hotel, it's right there, Tomas. How did you get us here so fast?"

"Let's cross," he said. "The cars have stopped."

But there were so many. Even with car headlights, my dark clothes were hard to see.

"Nina?" Tomas asked.

I stepped forward and we hurried halfway across to the island. A moment later, the lights flashed red. Drivers that were going too fast slammed on their brakes. Women with children and dogs came to a stop, bathed in the too-bright light.

"Ah, it's okay now, Nina," Tomas said, giving my hand a slight hug.

I didn't know which was better, a man with a kind voice or the lights overhead.

"Now!" Tomas said, and we ran the rest of the way across the street, stopping right in front of my hotel.

"Merci beaucoup, Monsieur Tomas!"

"*Rien*, madame."

He looked to be in his forties, had a kind face, soft half-beard, and sad eyes. He didn't glance away but looked at me carefully. "Have you been in Paris before?"

"But of course," I answered. "Merci bien. It's kind of late, *tant pis*."

"A gentleman rescues you in the pitch black of a Marais neighborhood and you won't even let him buy you a drink?"

"Oh, Tomas, of course," I said, taking his arm and heading to a café adjacent to my hotel.

After a while, we drifted upstairs. He looked at me kindly as we stood by my window, light from streetlights falling diagonally against his face as he reached for mine. His hand against my cheek was smooth, his lips on mine were soft, and his arms curled around the small of my back as he lifted me onto the bed.

In the morning, the sunlight hit me in the eyes. I reached over. Tomas was gone, though his pillow was still warm. In the peacefulness of the moment, I knew better than to hunt for any slip of paper with his phone number or email address on it.

When I walked back down to the café for my usual break-fast of croissant, juice, and tea, even the waitress noticed my elevated mood.

"Everything all right, madame?" she asked while she brought me my tea.

"Right as rain."

Now I was finally ready to go home and face the trials of aging and my next later years. My smile lasted until midnight. Seventeen or sixty-seven, Paris was the same, full of beauty, full of soft sweet air, full of mystery, still.

Acknowledgments

This book would not have been possible without the help of the following people to whom I owe a debt of gratitude: James N. Frey, who has been torturing me forever; Melba Beals, JT Morrow, Judie Fouchaux, Jeffrey Phillips, and Cara Black. Other angels include Sydney Murray; Abigail Millikan-States (who knew me way back when); Joan Steidinger; Mark Solomon; J. Macon King, who was an early believer and has published my work in his *Mill Valley Literary Review*; Deke Castleman, editor extraordinaire; Jessica Santina of Lucky Bat Books, who helped me shepherd this project to completion; and to Brooke Warner of She Writes Press for facilitating the cover with artist Tabitha Lahr.

When I went back to Paris in my sixties, I had no idea that I would run into my long-gone parents there. I thank them for the early trips we had together when I was a child that gave me the material for this book.

ABOUT THE AUTHOR

SUSANNA SOLOMON IS THE AUTHOR OF two short story collections, *Point Reyes Sheriff's Calls* and *More Point Reyes Sheriff's Calls*, stories that were inspired by actual sheriff's calls in the West Marin's Pulitzer-Prize-winning newspaper, *The Point Reyes Light*. Solomon is also the author of the novel *Montana Rhapsody*, about a pole dancer, a farmer, and a river, set in the Missouri River in Montana.

Solomon, who was raised back East, has made her home in Northern California for decades. A writer since she was a teen, she found herself, at the age of thirty, in a difficult marriage with two young children to support. With an English degree and a receptionist job where she made $5 an hour, she did something odd for women who were raised in the Fifties: she decided to go back to school and became an engineer. Seven years later, she graduated Summa Cum Laude and hasn't looked back since. She retired in 2022 after thirty-five years of service. "Engineering was the ticket to buying paper for my writing," she says. "And now I have time."

Currently, she is at work on her fifth book, a new collection of short stories inspired by her father's trunk full of family photos and history, which hadn't been opened for seventy-five years.

You can find Susanna Solomon at **www.susannasolomon.com.**